ONE MORE DAY

I am now officially in love with the Alexander family. There was so much about this book that worked for me. First and foremost, I loved the romance between Jackson and Ridley. They had fabulous, explosive chemistry. I loved that Jackson works and lives the music industry. When he sang his song to her, I honestly melted.
--Smitten by Reading (Grade: A-)

Ridley and Jackson explode with passion on the pages of One More Day! While there are some suspense elements this is a pure romance! Ridley and Jackson are a sweet and sensational couple and I can't wait to find out what happens in their future. It was also great getting to spend some more time with Trent and Mara from Teasing Trent.

Malone has a winner with The Alexanders series! Please keep them coming!
--Joyfully Reviewed

This book is STUNNING. Simply irresistible. I absolutely loved this book from beginning to end. Make dinner? Forget it, I ordered a pizza. Laundry? No way, I'll just wear the same thing I had on yesterday....I had to finish this book. I don't generally like stories that include dead wives, because the heroine is constantly being compared. But this book just took my breath away. I adored the heroine. She was beautiful inside and out. And the hero was.....well yummy comes to mind. These two had amazing chemistry. I can't wait for the next book!
--Barnes & Noble Reviewer

continued...

WITHDRAWN

Officially Noted
Edge stained;
moisture damage this
page. 10/ne DS

The book is full of great characters - my favourite had to be Jackson - he is sweet and sexy yet cautious with his heart since he lost his wife in a car accident. The story is well written with plenty of twists to prevent it becoming predictable despite the obligatory fairy tale ending.

I can't wait to read the next installment of the Alexander brothers - The Things I Do For You.
--Fairy Tale Ending Reviews

TEASING TRENT

"I really enjoyed this one...There was a fabulous twist at the end that I didn't see coming, but it was the absolutely PERFECT way to end the book. Just fun and sexy!"
--Smitten By Reading

"Trent and Mara have enough chemistry to fuel a rocket ship. Mara's seduction of Trent is classic and hysterical. I mean this guy is out of his depth with this girl but hey the great thing is that he wants her as bad as she wants him. When they finally give in it's explosive! *Teasing Trent* is hot hot hot!"
--Joyfully Reviewed

This has been one of my favorite erotic short stories so far!

I loved how Mara had this whole elaborate plan to seduce Trent and it turns out the one thing that gets the ball rolling is a drawer that was accidentally left open. The sex between these two is hot! And I must admit I'm thinking about taking up Yoga as a hobby after reading this ;)
--Barnes & Noble Reviewer

Titles by M. Malone

THE ALEXANDERS SERIES

M. MALONE

CRUSHSTAR
★
Romance

Batavia Public Library
Batavia, Illinois

THE THINGS I DO FOR YOU
Copyright © March 2013 M. Malone

Editor: Anne Victory - Victory Editing

CrushStar Romance
An Imprint of CrushStar Multimedia LLC

This book is a work of fiction. The names, characters, places, and incidents are products of the writer's imagination or have been used fictitiously and are not to be construed as real. Any resemblance to persons, living or dead, actual events, locales or organizations is entirely coincidental. All rights reserved.

No part of this book may be reproduced, scanned, or distributed in any manner whatsoever without written permission from the publisher except in the case of brief quotation embodied in critical articles and reviews. For information address CrushStar Romance, 2885 Sanford Ave SW #16301, Grandville, MI 49418

ALL RIGHTS RESERVED

ISBN-10: 1-938789-07-5
ISBN-13: 978-1-938789-07-6

PRINTED IN THE UNITED STATES OF AMERICA

ACKNOWLEDGMENTS

To the readers who've embraced
The Alexanders series:
Thanks for loving my "family" as much as I do.

As always, thank you to my husband,
Andre, for just being you.

for You

Chapter One

~⌒~

RAINA WINTERS OPENED her eyes to the sight of the neon numbers on her alarm clock. She reached out her arm slowly, trying not to raise her heart rate too much.

After she plucked the digital thermometer from the edge of her nightstand, she stuck it under her tongue and waited for the beep to sound. She grabbed the notepad she kept on her nightstand and jotted *98.2* next to the date. Her temperature was still roughly the same as it had been for the past ten days.

It won't be long now, she thought.

She'd just finished her most grueling year since she started modeling, taking on twice as many bookings as usual to earn herself some much-needed time off. In her modeling career, Raina was used to working doggedly when she wanted something, and she had been just as strategic when planning her next goal. She took those awful horse-pill vitamins religiously. She'd cut out alcohol, swordfish, and hot baths. It wasn't even that big of a pain keeping track of her temperature anymore. Nothing was too much if it helped her achieve what she'd been planning for the last six months.

A baby.

If everything went as planned over the next few days, she could be holding her child nine months from now. Everything inside her softened at just the thought of a chubby little bundle with big, brown eyes.

"Rise and shine, sleepyhead."

The door to her room pushed open an inch, then her Chief of Security, Sam Gannon, stuck his head in.

"Sorry to wake you. But you have a doctor's appointment today. I wasn't sure if you remembered."

Not many people knew about her fertility issues. It wasn't something she felt comfortable discussing with anyone other than her twin sister, Ridley, and her doctor. But Sam, as her most trusted advisor and constant companion, had a front row seat to the entire process.

Whether he wanted one or not.

"I definitely didn't forget that," she remarked dryly. The thought of more poking and prodding was enough to make her want to roll over and go back to sleep.

But this is part of what you're signing up for, she thought. If she wanted a baby, regular doctor visits were something she had to get used to. Due to her ongoing fertility issues, it was going to take a minor miracle or some serious medical intervention for her to get pregnant. Once she was lucky enough to be pregnant, there was no way she would risk her or the baby's health by skipping prenatal visits.

Sam crossed to the window and pulled the drapes open, his muscular shoulders rolling beneath the tight black shirt he wore. With his deep summer tan and his dark hair razored off in a short brush cut, he looked like a model himself. She could definitely see him gracing the cover of some magazine for bodybuilders or something.

"What? Do these jeans make my ass look big?" Sam teased.

Raina laughed, not even embarrassed to be caught staring. "Just admiring the view. Why couldn't I be smart enough to fall in love with you, Sam?"

Sam grinned. "You couldn't handle me." He walked over to her handbag sitting on a chair next to the bed and pulled out her cell phone.

"You have a missed call from Silvestre. Do you need to call him back and let him know you're running behind?"

Oh boy. Raina pushed back her comforter, figuring if they were going to fight she might as well get up. Sam had made no secret of his disapproval of her fiancé. Or rather, the fact that they rarely saw each other and their relationship was more like a business deal.

"He's not coming with me. He's still in New York." She didn't meet his eyes. She was going to get up in just a minute. It just felt so heavenly to lie amongst the jumble of pillows. The world could wait for a little bit.

Sam shook his head. "I really don't get you sometimes."

She huffed and sat up. It felt like it took a herculean effort but finally she was upright. "What, Sam? *What?* I already know you don't like him. You've made that abundantly clear."

He knelt next to the bed. In this position it was impossible to avoid looking at him.

"This isn't about him. It's about you. I don't get *you*. You can have any man you want. You've turned tons of other men, better men, down. But you hook up with Silvestre? Why? That guy would sell his own mother to make a buck."

"Sam, come on. You don't think that's a little harsh? I've been accused of being mercenary myself."

"He's a weasel."

"Oh, is that your professional assessment?" Sam had been her bodyguard since her early days of modeling. Now he was her Chief of Security and her best friend.

Possibly her only friend.

"No, that's my man-to-man assessment. You can do better than him."

"Steven is educated, sophisticated, and successful. By anyone's standards, he's a real catch."

"He doesn't love you." Sam stilled. Neither of them spoke for a moment.

"I don't love him, either. I don't need love. I'm probably not even capable of it."

Sam tipped up her chin until their eyes met. "I think you and I both know that's not true."

Raina closed her eyes and after a moment, Sam cleared his throat.

"You still don't want to talk about Alexander? Fine. I'll leave you alone so you can call Lover Boy back."

"Stop calling him that."

Once he was gone, she punched her pillow a few times. It was funny that Sam thought she could have any man she wanted. If she were just looking for guys who wanted to hang out and have a good time, it would be a different story. But when you were asking a man to get you pregnant, the pool of interested candidates shrank considerably.

Raina closed her eyes, remembering the last time she'd been engaged. It didn't hurt as much to think about Brian these days, more of an ache instead of a true pain. They'd met at an audition and he'd teased her about being nervous. He'd made her laugh.

They'd been so young and it seemed so ridiculous now but oh, how he'd made her feel. She'd planned to travel the world, modeling, and then retire so he could do photography while she stayed at home with the three kids they wanted. He'd understood her drive and her desire for more. At least until she'd found out his attraction to her lasted only as long as she was popular. When she'd struggled to find work, he'd left her behind like an out-of-season accessory.

She knew better than anyone that people could turn on you at any time. But at least if you didn't love them, it wouldn't tear your heart out.

Raina pulled out her phone and hit the first speed dial. She'd been trying to reach Steven since yesterday so she could tell him her good news. He knew how important it was for her to branch out into different areas of entertainment, so he'd be happy for her when he found out the network had picked up her reality show. When she got voicemail, she hung up. It would be better to give him the news in person when he got back in town.

"Are you calling Lover Boy or can I come back now?" Sam called from the living room.

"Give me a minute!" she yelled. "And stop calling him that," she muttered under her breath.

Steven might not love her, but that didn't mean he'd be a bad husband. People got divorced every day who'd been oh-so-in-love just months prior. Steven and his first wife had, in fact, divorced because she hadn't wanted children and Steven did. Wanting a family was one of the things that had drawn them to each other.

What she shared with Steven was common goals and determination to succeed. The reality show she'd just sold to a major cable network would give them both exactly what they wanted. The world would get to watch the carefully constructed fantasy they would put on for the cameras leading up to their uber-expensive, fairy-tale wedding. Steven would get promotion for his new line of nightclubs in New York and she would gain a whole new audience to help her break in to show business.

Sam was wrong. Steven wasn't a boy like certain other people who were photographed every day with a new girl on each arm.

He was a man.

Most importantly, he was the man who'd agreed to marry her and father her child.

*   *   *   *   *

"KAY? DID YOU already bring the latest reports for the foundation youth project?"

Nicholas Alexander flinched as a loud beep followed by the sound of static came through his desk phone's speaker.

"*Oops...*" There was another few seconds of fumbling and another loud beep. "Where is that stupid button? Oh, *there it is*. I have the reports, sir. I'll bring them now."

Nick smothered a laugh when the door to his office flew open and Kaylee Wilhelm, his new assistant, stumbled in carrying a stack of files.

"I have it right here!"

Kaylee was a singer in a girl group that his younger brother, a music producer, was trying to launch. She'd lost her prior job as a waitress because she couldn't work the night shift anymore. Jackson needed her available to record and to attend industry parties in the evening. He was also worried about her being on her feet so much since she was pregnant. Nick had hired her as a favor to his brother when his usual assistant had moved away.

"I want to thank you again for hiring me full time, Mr. Alexander. I know I'm not fully up to speed yet, but I really appreciate you giving me a chance."

She handed him the files and swiped her hands over her hair. When they'd first met she'd been wearing no makeup and her thick hair had been bound back in a messy ponytail. Today, her smooth brown skin looked perfectly clear and her eyes looked brighter, no doubt due to some sort of mystical female makeup voodoo. Her thick dark hair had been braided back into several neat twists. Jackson's image consultants had obviously gotten their hands on her and given her a makeover.

It was too bad they hadn't been able to give her confidence a makeover as well.

"I've told you a million times to call me Nick. You don't need to thank me again, Kay. I should be thanking *you*. Most of the assistants I got from the temp agency didn't fit well. I guess I was a little... unorthodox."

Nick thought back to the days prior to hiring Kaylee. Assistants who spent the majority of their workday bringing him files he didn't need, standing entirely too close, and finding every excuse to lean over his desk and flash their cleavage.

Things that he might have found amusing at one point, but not any longer.

Kaylee had been honest about her work experience and confessed that she had no prior experience in office administration. Something he would have known even if she hadn't told him. She'd had no idea how to work a multiline phone system, seemed slightly afraid of the copy machine, and still looked terrified when she had to greet visitors who came to his office for meetings.

But despite all that, she had adapted quickly. Nick was used to keeping crazy hours and had never expected his assistants to get in as early as he did. But once Kaylee found out that his day started at seven a.m., she'd started showing up then, too.

He'd fallen asleep at his desk after a really late night and asked Kaylee to go pick up his dry cleaning when she got in that morning. He could shower at the gym downstairs and change into one of the suits he'd just had cleaned. Not only had Kay done it without any hysterics or unnecessary questions, but at the end of the day, she'd pointed to his lower desk drawer and said "just in case." He'd pulled the drawer open to find a stack of neatly folded shirts, slacks, and ties. The remainder of his cleaning she'd left on the hook behind his office door.

That had been the day he'd decided he was keeping her.

"Even though I hired you as a favor to Jackson, I kept you on because you're doing a hell of a job. You've earned the right to be here."

Kay looked down at her shoes, clearly embarrassed by the praise. "Thanks. I've been enjoying it. This is certainly the most *unusual* job I've ever had."

"Good. I'm a lot of things, but I hope I'm never boring. So, did we get word yet about our bid for the Alexander Foundation youth project?"

Kay was suddenly very interested in the pattern of the carpet. "Yes, sir. Unfortunately, we were outbid."

"We were outbid? *Damn* it." Nick pounded his desk in frustration. He'd started the Alexander Foundation to help kids who hadn't been lucky enough to grow up with parents like his. He'd been searching for months for the perfect piece of land to build his retreat for troubled youth.

Not that he hadn't always wanted to help others, but watching his little brother fall head over ass in love had made him start thinking about the future. Being a bachelor had always suited him. His brothers, Bennett and Elliott, seemed to feel the same way. They had the freedom to do what they wanted and when they needed a fix of family time, they had a blast playing uncle to Jackson's two boys, Chris and Jase.

Marriage and parenthood were things he'd considered to be on a distant horizon. He knew he'd want them one day, but that day had never seemed particularly close.

Lately though, as he spent more time with Jackson and Ridley, he wondered if that time was finally here. Actually, if he was honest, it was spending time with his future sister-in-law, Raina Winters, that had him thinking differently.

Their one-night stand earlier in the year had rocked him down to the core. He hadn't been able to get her out of his mind since. But she obviously hadn't felt the same way—she'd avoided his calls and emails afterward. They'd been forced to spend more and more time together lately as Jackson and Ridley planned their wedding. He'd hoped their forced interaction would cure him of his obsession, especially since they seemed to annoy each other at every opportunity.

Unfortunately, as time went on, he fell deeper in love and she became more and more indifferent.

"I've already starting working on the bid for the next site on our list," Kaylee assured him. "I know we'll find something soon."

"Great. I was really hoping to get this project off the ground before winter, but I guess that was too good to be true."

"It's an amazing project. It's going to help a lot of

kids. You might want to be careful, Mr. Alexander. You'll tarnish your image as a happy-go-lucky playboy. People might actually start taking you seriously."

Nick tried and failed to crack a smile. "We can't have that, can we?"

Normally it wouldn't bother him to joke about his playboy status. He'd always done whatever he wanted and hadn't cared if other people liked it or not. It was only in recent months that his lack of relationship experience had been a problem and his reputation had stood in the way of him getting something he wanted.

Someone he wanted.

All he could do was hope she'd finally thaw toward him a little. She didn't have his cell phone number, but she knew she could always reach him at his office.

He could only hope, anyway.

"Any messages?" he asked. Most of his family called him on his cell phone, so he doubted there were.

"Oh yes, just one." Kay raced back out to her desk and then reappeared a few moments later. "Your brother wanted to remind you that you were supposed to come over and look at his investment portfolio today."

"Which brother?"

Kay looked up from the paper. "Huh?"

Nick smiled. "Which one of my brothers? I have three."

"Oh. Right! Sorry, it was Jackson. Actually, it was Ridley who called but she told me to say the message was from your brother," Kay said sheepishly.

"No worries. I know firsthand how hard it is to say no to my future sister-in-law."

"Yeah. Ridley is awesome. Anyway, I'll bring in that new bid when I'm done with it." She nodded at him and then turned to leave.

Just before she reached the door, Nick called out,

"Kaylee? Just out of curiosity, did you happen to hear who won the bid?"

She stopped in her tracks but didn't turn. "Yes, sir. It was Steven Silvestre. Again." She rushed out and pulled the door closed behind her.

*   *   *   *   *

RAINA PARKED BEHIND Jackson's car and sat staring at the house for a moment. Her phone let out a chirp. Recognizing Steven's ringtone, she immediately answered.

"Hey, there you are! I've been trying to get in touch with you since yesterday."

"I know, I'm so sorry about that. Negotiations aren't going well here. I meant to call you last night and then just passed out when I got back to my hotel."

She'd always loved Steven's voice, perfectly smooth and well-modulated. At thirty-four, he was just so much more mature than the other guys she'd dated.

"I'm sure you were exhausted. I know you're working really hard on this deal. I just missed hearing your voice, that's all."

There was an awkward pause as if he didn't know how to respond.

"Well, I've missed you, too. I'm flying back in tomorrow. Let me have the honor of taking you to dinner. You pick the place. We haven't had time to really talk in a while. There's been a lot going on."

Raina smiled. Typical Steven. Even when they were just talking on the phone, he was always so formal. "Of course we can have dinner. I have a lot to tell you, too. I think you're going to be excited when you hear my news."

He knew she was trying to work out a deal for her

own reality show and had already agreed to allow himself to be filmed for a certain number of episodes after they were married. He'd even given her pointers on negotiating with the network.

Steven was truly her perfect complement. Someone calm and steady to keep her focused on what was really important. He never raised his voice or lost his temper.

She thought of her last conversation with Nick. Calm and steady were not the adjectives that came to mind. She'd probably used every four-letter word in the English language during that conversation.

She looked up and saw her sister standing in the doorway of Jackson's house. "Oh, I have to go. I'm meeting Ridley for lunch."

"That's fine. I'll see you tomorrow. Just text me the time and place and I'll meet you at the restaurant." He paused for a moment and then said, "I'm glad things seem to be going well for you, Raina. I want you to be happy."

She frowned as the call disconnected. She enjoyed spending time with Steven, but she couldn't help wishing he wasn't always so... stuffy. He'd been so busy working on his latest acquisition deal that she'd barely seen him over the last month. He was flying back and forth to New York several times a week and holed up in his office the rest of the time.

Raina considered herself a completely modern, enlightened woman and wasn't even slightly ashamed of her healthy sex drive. Which was why it was a shame that she didn't really miss the sex when Steven was traveling. They'd never been overly demonstrative with each other and to be honest, their sex life was much like the rest of their interaction. Calm, steady, and mature.

Boring.

Steven was simply too cultured to get worked up about

much of anything other than business.

It probably didn't help that she'd met him right after the most intense sexual experience of her life. *No, don't think about Nick.* She refused to believe that one night with Nicholas Alexander had ruined her for all other men.

Besides, sex isn't everything, she thought, feeling slightly disloyal. Steven wasn't the most exciting man, perhaps, but he knew what was important. He'd never hurt or embarrass her, at least. He'd be a steady father figure for the three children they planned to have.

She pushed open the car door just as Ridley noticed her.

"Raina! You're here." Ridley stepped onto the porch and set the oversized pot of flowers she was carrying down on the step. "Come on, I've just finished cooking."

When Ridley had invited her over for lunch the prior day, she'd agreed before she remembered her doctor's appointment scheduled for ten o'clock. If she'd been thinking clearly, she would have rescheduled lunch. The last thing she needed after hearing that her chances of having a baby were getting worse every day was to watch her sister and Jackson coo at each other.

Chapter Two

RAINA LOCKED THE car and watched her sister stroke the blooms on the potted plant like she was petting a dog. For as long as she could remember, her sister had loved flowers. Personally, she could barely tell a daisy from a sunflower, but Ri had an exhaustive memory for the different types and how to care for them. Since she'd moved into Jackson's house, his yard had been completely redone, the walk leading to the front steps taking each visitor through an array of colors and scents.

Raina took a deep breath of the fragrant air as she passed the clusters of flowers lining the walkway. Ridley pulled her into a quick hug. "I hope pasta is okay. I didn't feel up to much else."

Instantly, Raina was on alert. "Are you feeling okay? Is your scar giving you trouble?"

Just a month ago, Ridley had been held at gunpoint and shot by a stalker. Every time she thought about it, Raina experienced a surge of helplessness. Nothing would ever erase the raw fear she'd felt when she'd gotten the call that her sister was in the hospital. Especially since the call had come from Nick. What if she hadn't answered? It had been a sober reminder that their feud affected more than just the two of them.

"I'm doing my physical therapy and of course, Jackson won't let me do anything. I'm still pretty tired. Once I'm able to move around more, I think I'll feel better."

Raina followed Ridley into the house, noting all the changes her sister had made in recent weeks. Under different circumstances she'd probably tease her about playing house with a guy she'd just met. But even someone as cynical as she was could appreciate that Jackson was truly in love with her sister. You could practically see the hearts and flowers circling the guy's head when he looked at her.

If it wasn't so damn sweet it would be nauseating.

"So, what have you been up to? Besides being waited on hand and foot by your hot fiancé," Raina teased.

Ridley looked uncomfortable and then said, "I met our father."

Raina's mood immediately soured. "Oh. So, what are we having for lunch? I'm starving."

"That's all you have to say? 'What's for lunch?' Don't you want to know what happened?"

"Not really. I understand that you're curious about

him, but I don't particularly need to hear excuses from some guy about why he abandoned his wife and two kids."

"There are two sides to every story, Raina. I just want the chance to get to know him. He was really worried when he heard I was injured."

Struggling to keep her voice even, Raina replied, "I'm sure it's easier to worry now that we're all grown up and don't require any actual care. Now, I don't want to talk about this. I want to enjoy the afternoon with my sister." She smiled to hopefully take the sting out of her words.

"Fine. I made spaghetti. I hope that's okay." Ridley led her out to the back patio. The food was in a pretty white warming dish and there were colorful plates and cups already laid out. Raina dropped her purse next to one of the chairs and sat down.

"That sounds delicious. If I was at home, it would be a microwave dinner, so I'm hardly going to complain."

Despite how successful she'd become in recent years, Raina was wary of hiring help. She had enough people making up stories about her as it was. The last thing she needed was a tabloid tell-all from a chef or driver. Jackson had recommended a trustworthy maid service but other than that, she did things herself. And by doing things herself, she meant ordering takeout.

It was just one more thing she'd have to get used to changing in her life. Once filming started for the remaining episodes of her show, her well-guarded private time would be a thing of the past.

Ridley bustled around the table, filling her drinking glass with iced tea and spooning the pasta into their bowls. As she passed Raina's chair, her foot accidentally bumped against the handbag sitting on the floor, knocking it over. Several colorful brochures spilled out of the top along with Raina's cell phone and keys.

"What are these?"

Before Raina could react, Ridley picked up one of the pamphlets and flipped it open. Her forehead furrowed as she started reading. "Raina, what is this?"

"It's just some stuff the doctor gave me." Raina scooped them up and dropped them back in her handbag. Awkward silence descended on the table. Raina glanced at Ridley and was shocked to see tears in her eyes.

"Ri, what is it? Are you in pain?" She pushed away from the table and knelt next to her sister. It was an old habit, but she'd always thought of herself as Ri's protector. Not because she was a scant three minutes older, but because her sister had always seemed so fragile. Easily hurt. She believed the best of people and Raina wanted her to be free to keep thinking that way. Even though she knew it was crap.

Ridley shook her head. "You're thinking about having in vitro and you didn't even tell me?"

"No, no. Ri, the doctor just gave me that stuff today. I was going to tell you all about it."

Ridley sniffled. "Really?"

"Yeah, I wasn't hiding it. I promise."

She got up and sat in her seat. She twirled her fork in her spaghetti absently. "Remember how I told you a few years ago that I was diagnosed with endometriosis?"

Ridley nodded. "Yeah, I remember. The doctors thought you might have trouble conceiving one day." She looked up sharply.

"Apparently I'm already running out of time." Raina looked down at the swirl of noodles on her plate. "The doctor said things have gotten worse. We'll be twenty-five soon, so I don't have the luxury of taking my time. That's why he gave me the brochures about egg harvesting and about surrogacy. He just wants me to be informed."

"Does Steven… I mean, does he have issues?" Ridley blushed and looked down at her food. "Sorry. That was really nosy. Don't answer that."

"It's okay," Raina replied. "You can ask me anything. We've never had secrets. Plus, I'm not really sure. We haven't talked about it."

Ridley dropped her fork and glared at her. "How can you not have talked about it? How can you marry someone that you don't even talk to?"

"Shhhh! Not so loud." Raina glanced around, satisfied when she saw that the yard was empty. Jackson's two sons were usually nearby and she knew that tiny ears heard everything. "I didn't say we don't talk, just that we haven't talked about *that* yet. He'll be back from New York tomorrow and he already agreed to start trying early if things got worse, instead of waiting until after the wedding."

"The wedding is only two months away," Ridley groused.

"Exactly. Close enough that it won't matter if I'm pregnant since I won't be showing yet. This isn't the 1950s, so it's not like I'll be shunned because I'm not a virgin on my wedding night." She snorted at the thought.

Even Ridley laughed at that. "It's about a decade too late to worry about your virtue, huh?"

"Not a decade," she cried. She swatted at Ridley with her napkin. "Anyway, I have no reason to believe that Steven can't father children. I refuse to believe the universe is cruel enough to give *both* of us fertility issues and I don't want him to undergo a lot of poking and prodding if he doesn't have to."

Ridley was smiling now, but she still didn't look mollified. "I'm not worried about Steven being uncomfortable. I'm worried about *you*."

Raina reached across the table and grabbed her sister's hand. "I know you don't approve, but I really need your support on this. Steven and I get each other. We may not have the typical relationship, but we want the same things. Financial security, stability, and a family. Plenty of people have gotten married with less in common than that."

"I still don't like it. He hasn't even had time in his *oh-so-busy* schedule to come over and meet me. You deserve a man who loves you. Every guy isn't like Brian."

Raina pulled her hand back. "I know that."

"Do you? I want so much more for you. I want you to find what I have with Jackson."

Raina ignored the disapproving look on her sister's face. "Don't give me that look. Everyone isn't lucky enough to be in twu-wuv like you two lovebirds."

Ridley took another bite of spaghetti. "Um hmm. Well, I hope you know that you don't need a surrogate or an egg donor, anyway. You know I'd do it if you needed me to."

"I have a feeling that you'll be busy having your own babies in the very near future. If you aren't pregnant already."

"What? I am not pregnant," she whispered. "Why are you saying that? Do I look like I've gained weight?" Tears immediately sprang to her eyes.

"For starters, you're usually a watering pot but even you aren't this weepy." Raina reached across the table and brushed Ridley's tears away. "Plus, your boobs are huge. I'm so jealous."

Ridley's eyes widened before she burst out laughing.

"It looks like we're missing the fun."

Raina froze and then turned slowly. Jackson and Nick stood in the doorway, watching them. As usual, Nick looked *GQ*-fine in a suit and tie with his dark, curly hair slicked back. His golden-brown skin tone was slightly lighter, as if he'd been holed up in his office instead of outside in the sun. He was quite a contrast to Jackson, who looked like an advertisement for some kind of Caribbean drink in a casual Hawaiian shirt and cargo shorts, his skin gleaming a deep bronze.

Jackson, as usual, made a beeline for Ridley. He picked her up and then sat down in her chair with her in his lap.

"What are you girls out here talking about?"

Ridley giggled and settled back into his embrace. "Just girl talk." She looked up at Nick. "I didn't realize you were here already, Nick. Are you hungry? I made plenty."

He smiled indulgently at her and shook his head. "I already ate, but thanks."

His eyes came to rest on Raina and she suppressed a shiver. "Hi, Raina."

"Hi." When she couldn't think of anything else to say, she turned back to Ridley. "I'll get started cleaning up before I go." She jumped up and pushed her chair under the table. Nick moved back so she could walk past him.

"You don't have to do that. It's not much," Ridley protested.

"No, I want to," she assured her. *Boy, did she want to.* "I'll see you guys later." She deliberately didn't look at anyone in particular when she said it.

Anything was better than sitting here awkwardly with the man who made her wish for impossible things.

*　*　*　*　*

NICK WATCHED RAINA until the back of her brightly patterned T-shirt disappeared behind the sliding glass door.

20

You would think that months of forced interaction would have made it easier to be around her. But instead, it seemed even harder to breathe. Mainly because being around Jackson and Ridley made him more aware of everything he didn't have.

He sat in the chair Raina had vacated and stretched out his legs. When his foot hit something, he pushed back to see what it was and spied a paper pamphlet under the table near Ridley's chair. He reached down to pick it up.

Sperm donation?

When he saw the title, he immediately shoved the brochure in the inner pocket of his suit jacket.

He turned back to Jackson and Ridley and found them deep in whispered conversation. Although they were still high on the lovey-dovey scale, Jackson and Ridley seemed tenser than usual today. Could this be the reason? Were they having fertility problems? It made him sad to think that his brother hadn't confided in him, but he could understand not wanting to talk about this kind of thing.

He crossed his arms, feeling the sharp edge of the pamphlet beneath his jacket. "Can I talk to you for a minute?"

Ridley patted Jackson on the chest. "I'll just go help Raina. She always insists on cleaning up when I cook, which is really sweet but she puts everything back in the wrong places."

"No, Ridley, I actually wanted you to stay."

Her mouth fell open into a little "oh" of surprise. He tensed under her scrutiny. It wasn't like he'd never talked to Ridley before. But, he supposed, it was rare for him to have an extended conversation with her. It was a little awkward after everything that happened when he'd thought she was Raina and kissed her. He hadn't held anything back in that wild exchange. His jaw ached at the memory.

His brother hadn't held anything back when he'd punched him afterward, either.

"Of course I'll stay," Ridley finally said. "What did you want to talk to us about?"

Nick couldn't look her in the eye. It felt invasive, like he'd violated their privacy by seeing the brochure. But he couldn't *unsee* it and what they needed to talk about was more important that any feelings of embarrassment this conversation was sure to bring.

"Well, it's pretty well-known that the Alexander men have... you know... no issues fathering kids." Nick wouldn't have thought it possible, but he blushed for the first time in two decades.

"Um, I guess so," Jackson replied. "I mean, there's four of us and then, well I guess Auntie Maria's kids don't count in this case, but Uncle Stewart has six kids, right? Or he could have more by now and we wouldn't even know. I wish he and Dad would let their feud go. It's ridiculous that they're still at odds for something that happened years ago. In fact—"

"Jackson, focus." Nick clapped his hands. "I'm trying to talk to you about something serious."

Jackson frowned. "Okay. Let's take a little walk. You know you can talk to me about anything."

They stepped down off the patio into the yard. Nick pushed one of Jase's tricycles to the side with his foot.

"Well, I know that. But I want to make sure that you know you can talk to *me* about anything. Ridley, you're family now and I'd do anything to help you, too. Even if it's weird to ask or awkward to talk about. I know reproductive stuff is not exactly dinner conversation, but if you guys are thinking about having more kids and are having trouble, I hope you know that you can ask me for help. I'd literally give the shirt off my back for any of my brothers, so what's a little DNA on the side, right?" He laughed weakly at his own joke.

"Nick, what are you saying?" Ridley asked gently.

Nick's heart stuttered to a stop. He supposed he wasn't being too clear but hell, did he have to spell it out? Dammit, what if they thought he was trying to hit on Ridley in a weird way? He had kissed her once and even though it was a case of mistaken identity, he knew his brother hadn't forgotten. He didn't want to just flat-out offer to impregnate his brother's future wife, but what was the alternative? It wasn't like there was a proper way to offer stud services.

Jackson wasn't trying to bail him out, either. He looked like he was on the point of bursting into laughter.

"Jackson, this is serious." Exasperated, he finally pulled the brochure he'd found from his suit pocket. "I found this and I was trying to find a discreet way to let you know that if you guys were having *issues*, I'd be willing to help out."

At that point, Jackson did laugh. "I was wondering what the hell you were getting at. Nick, are you offering to be our sperm donor?"

Nick flushed again. He was trying to do what was right for his family and his brother was just making him feel like an idiot. "Yes, dammit. But you don't have to put it like that. I'm just saying, you know, if you're shooting blanks or something, you don't have to buy it from a sperm bank. I'm your brother. I'd do anything for you."

He broke off then because it suddenly looked like both Ridley and Jackson were struggling to hide smiles.

"*What?* Okay, never mind. I was trying to do the right thing and you two are not taking me seriously at all."

Ridley finally recovered and came over to him. She

stood silently and watched him for a moment before enfolding him in a warm hug. Nick wasn't sure what to do so he looked up to Jackson for help. His brother just shrugged.

"Um, Ridley. Is everything okay? Maybe I shouldn't have brought it up but I just wanted—"

Ridley shook her head. "No, that's not it. I'm just amazed that you would do that for us. Really amazed and really happy." She glanced back at Jackson with a soft smile. "I am truly the luckiest girl in the world. I've gone from having almost no family at all to being a part of the most supportive family ever."

Nick relaxed. As long as she wasn't going to cry, he was okay. "We're the lucky ones. Just seeing how happy you've made my brother is a miracle in itself."

A smile broke out on Ridley's face and when Jackson held his arms open to her she raced into them. Nick watched them, not even surprised by the small pang of envy he felt. There was a time when he couldn't think of anything worse than chaining himself to one woman at his age. But observing how close his brother was to Ridley, how supportive they were of each other's dreams, he found himself wondering what it would be like to have that for himself.

What would it be like to have someone miss him when he worked late? Someone there to hold him when he was stressed or worried about things? Someone to confide in when the burdens he carried seemed too great? Something made him look back at the house. Even from this distance, he could see the bright color of Raina's shirt as she moved around the kitchen. As if she could feel his gaze on her, she turned and their eyes met through the glass.

What would it be like to know she loved me?

He turned around, shocked to see Ridley grinning at

him openly. "Should I assume that you aren't offended by my offer then?"

Ridley nodded. "I'm not offended at all. I almost hate to ruin this warm, squishy moment by telling you we don't need your, um, *services*. That brochure wasn't for us."

Nick pulled the brochure out and looked at it. The title read *The Tidewater Sperm Bank: Is Artificial Insemination Right for You?*

"But it was next to your chair? If it's not yours, then…"

Ridley just watched him, her large, dark eyes holding his until he thought back to earlier. Earlier when she'd been sitting on the patio, eating lunch with her sister.

Ridley crossed her arms. "I can't talk about this with you. I shouldn't have even said this much. But Nick, please keep whatever you're thinking or think you know about it to yourself. I know you guys don't get along, but this cannot be ammunition in your battle. You need to forget about ever seeing that brochure. Please. For me."

He nodded, but he knew he wouldn't be forgetting about it any time soon.

Why the hell would Raina need a sperm bank?

Chapter Three

~

PAPARAZZI WERE A part of life in the modeling industry. Raina had quickly learned that having a few photographers on your side was not a bad idea. Since she lived off the beaten path now, most of the major paparazzi left her alone. They had more opportunities to get random celeb shots in New York or Los Angeles. It wasn't worth it to them to follow her out to a small, semi-rural Virginia town, which was one of the main reasons she loved living in New Haven so much.

However, there were some local photographers who

had started making their living getting exclusive shots of her just because they were there. After a few weeks of pretending she didn't notice they were around, she'd finally just turned around and introduced herself. It turned out that her main stalkerazzi, Dagger Kincaid, was an art student using the photos he sold of her to pay his way through college. They'd come to a friendly agreement. She'd allow him to take several shots of her every day and he'd make sure he only sold good shots of her to the press.

Which came in really handy on mornings like this one where she wasn't feeling her best.

"Good morning, Dagger. I'm on my way to get coffee. You want to get a shot now or after?"

Dagger shook back his mane of stringy black hair. "I'll take a few of you walking to the car. Move your stuff to the other side. Great."

She leaned against the car door, swinging her handbag over her arm nonchalantly. "Look good?"

"Looks amazing. As always." He shot her a lopsided grin before stowing his camera back in his shoulder bag.

"How's school going? You're almost done, right?"

"Yeah. Finally. I only have one more semester left."

"That's great. You should be really proud. I always kind of wished I'd gone to college first. Before everything got so crazy." He was looking at her like she was crazy, so she shrugged. "I always wanted to go to a frat party," she joked.

He nodded, as if *that* he could understand. "I hear that. Oh, hey. Not sure if it's true, but someone said your boy was seen in New York with some chick who's on a soap opera. Did y'all break up or something?"

Raina's heart skipped a beat. She made a show of looking in her bag for her cell phone. "You know I never comment on my personal life."

It probably didn't mean anything. She'd just talked to Steven yesterday. If he was photographed with a woman it could be anyone. It could be someone he knew casually or one of the attorneys negotiating the buyout deal for him. She knew better than anyone how easy it was for a picture to be misinterpreted.

Although, hadn't Steven's ex-wife been on a soap opera at some point?

She looked up to find Dagger watching her closely. Pasting a bright smile on her face, she pulled open her car door and threw her handbag on the seat. "Well, I have to go. I have so much to do. If you want a photo that will earn enough to pay for that final semester, make sure you're at Sweetie's at eight o'clock tonight."

His eyes lit up. "Is this the big announcement you keep hinting about?"

"Uh huh. After tonight it won't be a secret anymore." She got in her car and pulled a pair of oversized shades from her bag.

Sam got in the passenger side. Just as she was about to put her key in the ignition, he covered her hand with his. He was always on the serious side, a side effect of his profession, but she'd never seen him look so grave before.

"Sam, what is it?"

"I know you said you don't want me spying on Silvestre, but asking a few questions isn't the same as spying."

Raina sighed and turned the key in the ignition. "Leave it alone, Sam."

"You really want me to believe that none of this bothers you? You aren't even a *little* interested to know who this soap opera chick is? I don't believe there's that much love in the world," he muttered.

"This isn't about being *so in love*. Sam, you know I

don't believe in all that gooey, romantic crap. Half of all marriages end in divorce. Most people my age getting married are doing it at a drive-through chapel in Vegas when they're too drunk to even remember it. This is about trust. I trust Steven and I don't want you checking up on him."

"I just don't get why you're so cynical. Especially when your sister is the poster child for true love. That's what love is supposed to look like."

Raina closed her eyes and was immediately assaulted with images. Dark, thickly lashed bedroom eyes. Smooth, golden-brown skin. Those curls she couldn't keep her hands out of. She knew what love looked like.

It looked like Nicholas Alexander.

Raina ducked her head, hoping Sam wouldn't notice how she'd tensed up. It was sweet of him to worry about her. He'd always had her best interest at heart. But if he was trying to shield her from heartbreak, he was several months too late.

It had all started with Jackson asking her for a favor. Raina had never had anything more than a mild flirtation with Jackson and his two boys were adorable, so it hadn't been a big deal when he'd asked her to accompany his brother to an event. She got plenty of exposure at fashion events, but showing up on the arm of a respected businessman at a charity dinner was something she didn't get to do that often. It had been as much to her benefit as Nick's.

When she'd opened her door that night and seen Nick waiting for her, as soon as their eyes met, she'd known. Electricity sparked between them from the first time he took her hand. It had been pure carnal torture to sit next to him in the limo, their thighs brushing. The shocking heat between them had probably been why she'd been so off-kilter when they arrived. Despite years of posing in front of a camera, Raina still wasn't comfortable with public speaking. She could strike a pose and stalk a runway, but when someone shoved a microphone in front of her face as soon as they'd exited the limo, she'd just frozen up.

Nick had seen and somehow he'd realized she was terrified. She'd never forget how he'd made a joke and pulled her to his side. He'd taken control of the situation and sent the reporter away with a juicy sound bite instead of whatever foolish garbled mess would have come out of her mouth.

He'd looked at her and said, "I thought all models loved the spotlight. But you really don't like all this, do you?"

With one look, he'd seen a part of her she didn't show to anyone else.

She'd known exactly what she was risking when she invited him in that night. Men like Nicholas Alexander didn't change their ways, but she'd believed that she could have one night with him to treasure always. One night to look back on with no regrets.

Only it hadn't worked out that way because that one night hadn't been nearly enough to satisfy her. As much as she'd tried to play it cool and hold back, he'd seen straight through her carefully constructed image to the real woman beneath. He'd seen her *feelings* and that more than anything had terrified her. If he left her, it wouldn't be just the playboy leaving another one of his one-night stands.

It would be Nick leaving Raina because he didn't feel as deeply for her as she did for him.

So the next morning, she'd done the only thing she could to take back some control. She'd left. She'd left him behind and refused to take any of his calls or respond to any of his emails in the days after. It had taken a few weeks, but he'd eventually gotten the message.

"Have you ever considered what it will be like if you marry him and then you meet the love of your life afterward?" Sam asked.

She turned to Sam and gave him what she hoped was a convincing smile. "No, not at all." She didn't have to worry about meeting the love of her life after she married Steven.

She'd already met him and lost him in the same day.

*   *   *   *   *

"DON'T SHOOT THE messenger."

Nick looked up blearily from the spreadsheet he was working on. He'd been staring at the numbers so long they were starting to blend together. Matt stood in the doorway to his office with his hands held up in front of him.

"What now? I don't care what Mara threatened you with, I am not going to see any more chick flicks."

Ever since Matt's twin sister had hooked up with their friend Trent, she'd tried to include Nick on their outings to keep her brother from feeling like a third wheel.

Matt shook his head. "Come on, it wasn't that bad."

"There was a dude behind me *crying* last time." Nick shook his head in mock disgust.

Matt snickered. "You might like that better than what I have to tell you. Ridley sent me here to pick you up."

Nick hung his head in defeat. He'd gotten used to accommodating random requests from Matt's twin sister over the past few years. Mainly he didn't mind. He didn't have any sisters, but he imagined he'd feel this same sort of affectionate exasperation for them if he did. Mara was difficult to say no to, but she was nowhere near as good at laying a guilt trip as his little brother's future wife.

"Say no more. I might as well just give up now."

Matt shook his head. "It was like I literally couldn't say no to her. How does she do that?"

"She turns those big, brown eyes on full power and gives you a look like you alone have the power to solve all the world's problems. I no longer tease Jackson about being whipped. She's not even my woman and she has me whipped, too. It's easier just to do what she wants. Otherwise, you end up feeling like you've kicked a puppy."

Matt crossed his arms. "You say that now but I have a feeling there's a reason she sent me here to pick you up instead of coming herself. Apparently Raina is having some sort of event tonight and Ridley really wants us all to be there to support her. She wouldn't say what it is, but it's supposed to be a pretty huge deal."

"No. Wait, let me rephrase. Hell-to-the-no. I'm sure Ridley means well, but if Raina is having an event I'm sure I'm the last person she wants there. That woman makes me... *ragey*. Is that even a word?"

"I don't think so, but let's go with it."

Nick pointed at him. "You think this is funny because you don't know what she's really like. Oh, she looks just as sweet and innocent as Ridley but behind those big, brown eyes lays the heart of a cobra."

"Whatever, man. I'm just here to make sure you show up. I really don't want to have to tell Ridley that you aren't coming."

Nick sighed and pushed back from his desk. "Okay, okay. Man, would you look at us. Terrified of a woman who'd probably blow away in a stiff breeze."

He saved the document he'd been working on and logged off his computer. There wasn't much point to him staring at the screen longer, anyway. The numbers didn't lie and what they were saying wasn't pretty. He'd injected a lot of his personal capital into the Alexander Foundation youth project and if he didn't find more investors soon, he'd be in trouble. Several of his peers and all of his brothers had invested as well, but they needed deeper pockets if they were to have any chance of getting the camp open this year.

He'd hesitated about asking Jackson to start working the celebrity angle, but it was probably time to put his pride on the back burner. If his little brother could bring some much-needed attention to the foundation, it might be just the financial life support they needed. Perhaps he could even convince Kaylee to perform at a benefit or something.

Not for the first time he wished he'd been born with some sort of talent besides just an affinity for numbers. If he'd gotten even half of his little brother's musical talent, he wouldn't hesitate to use it to his advantage. Financial acumen was a great thing but people didn't revere intelligence these days. They wanted excitement. Entertainment. They wanted people who were larger than life.

People like Raina.

He stopped in his tracks. As much as she hated him, Raina had a huge soft spot for her sister. If he could convince Ridley to intercede on his behalf, there was a very good chance that Raina would help. All it would take on her part would be a few print ads and a couple of mentions on Twitter or Facebook and they'd be in business. Not only would he have big-name investors lining up to contribute, but her legions of fans would probably want to donate, too.

He hung his head. How ironic that the solution to his problem lay with the only woman he couldn't charm.

"You're not having second thoughts, are you?" Matt

held the door to his office open. He could see Kaylee sitting behind her desk, typing away.

"No. I'm definitely not having second thoughts."

Matt exhaled. "Good, because I have no problem ratting you out to your future sister-in-law. Come on. We'd better go or we'll be late."

He followed Matt to the elevator and they rode down to the parking level in silence. Once they stepped out into the garage, Nick loosened his tie. July in Virginia always felt like you were at a barbecue in hell. It wasn't just that it was hot. It was that it was hot *and* humid, so humid it felt like you were breathing water.

"We're supposed to meet everybody at Sweetie's, that fancy restaurant in Newport News."

Nick took off his jacket and threw it over his arm. "I know it very well, believe me. And so does my American Express card."

"Well, excuse me. Who would have thought the king of beer pong would be a suited-up tight ass now."

Nick chuckled. "I may be a suit now, but I can still beat your ass at beer pong. Believe it."

Matt got into his truck and pulled out. Nick fired up his Mercedes and followed him onto the main road leading to the highway. Sweetie's was in Harper's Creek, an upscale suburb in the neighboring city of Newport News. The area was part of an ongoing gentrification so the restaurants and shops were an eclectic mix. You might find a Dominican restaurant a few steps away from an old-school jazz speakeasy. Sweetie's itself was on a corner next to an old-fashioned haberdashery. It was a popular spot for locals and tourists alike. He'd dated an amateur chef once who'd raved about the food.

They left their cars with the valet and walked past the line of people waiting to get in. Once Matt gave their names to the man at the door, they were allowed to enter.

"You're going to introduce me to her, right?" Matt asked.

Nick forced down a growl. He had no right to be jealous. It wasn't like he was her man or anything. She'd made her views on him taking that position perfectly clear.

"I'll introduce you, but I take no responsibility for what happens after that."

"I just need to meet the woman who has the number-one player so off-balance." Matt elbowed him. "She must really be something."

Nick ignored his friend's pointed look. "First of all, I am not a player. That insinuates that this is a game. It's not. I just do what I want and refuse to apologize for it. Second, she does not have me off-balance. We just don't get along. End of story."

"Uh huh. Whatever you say. I still want to meet her." Matt raised a hand in greeting when they spotted Ridley and Jackson on the other side of the restaurant near the bar. Nick heaved a great sigh of relief.

If he was going to be forced into close proximity to Raina, a drink was the least of what he'd need to get through the night.

*   *   *   *   *

RAINA GRIPPED HER wineglass tighter, trying not to let her agitation show. She'd been at the restaurant for over an hour and Steven still hadn't shown up.

Dagger's words from earlier in the day were ringing through her head. *Someone said your boy was seen in New York with some chick who's on a soap opera...*

Words she'd so easily dismissed until she saw the tabloid Sam had brought home. The same tabloid that felt like it was calling out to her from her handbag.

She checked her cell phone again.

"He still hasn't called?" Sam murmured. He'd been unusually quiet all afternoon. After he'd handed her that tabloid with the tacky picture of Steven and his ex-wife kissing on it, she'd expected to hear any number of things ranging from "I told you so" to "do you want me to take care of him?" But Sam hadn't uttered a word, just handed her the paper and then retreated to his study. He hadn't emerged until it was time for them to leave.

"No. And he's not answering his office phone or his cell."

"At least no one knows he was supposed to be here. You can always just make your announcement and no one will be the wiser."

She looked around the crowded restaurant. Dagger had apparently spread the word far and wide because it looked like most of the Tidewater area had come out. The maître d' had been forced to set up a queue outside for all the people waiting to get in who didn't have reservations. If she hadn't already planned this informal press conference to announce her new reality show, she would have just stayed in bed with the covers over her head. It was hard enough feeling like she'd just had the bottom of her life yanked out from under her, but having to smile and act normal in front of an audience was cruel and unusual punishment.

Not that she was ready to give up just yet. There was a tiny part of her still hoping it wasn't true. Maybe it was an old picture taken back when he'd still been married. Or maybe it was Photoshopped. That could have been anyone's body with Steven's head pasted on there.

"You're right. Maybe I—" She broke off when Sam gestured behind her. She turned to see Ridley and Jackson making their way through the crowd.

"Ri! You made it." To her horror, she felt tears start to build. She pressed the heels of her hands against her eyes. Hard. "I didn't think you were going to come!" She allowed her sister to pull her into a hug.

"When you said you were meeting Steven here, I made time. I'm sorry I wasn't more supportive earlier." She looked around at all the people crowded in the restaurant. "So, where is he?"

"That's the question of the hour. He isn't here." Her phone beeped and she held it up to read the text message.

- - - *I'm sure you've seen the papers by now. I'm so sorry. I never meant for you to find out this way. -S*

The noise of the restaurant fell away. Raina closed her eyes, afraid that the little bit of food she'd managed to choke down was going to come back up. She opened her eyes, looking around frantically. Even though no one else could see the message, she felt like she had a neon sign on her forehead letting everyone know what a fool she'd been. A blind fool.

"Raina? *Raina*!"

She looked up into Ridley's concerned eyes. She must have looked pretty bad because Ridley grabbed her arm and pulled her into the corner. Sam and Jackson followed, then stood in front of them, blocking them from the crowd.

"Okay, what is going on?"

Raina pulled the tabloid from her bag and held it out. Ridley looked at the picture and then looked up at Raina. "Tell me this isn't true."

"It's true. He didn't even have the decency to tell me himself. He just sent me a text that he was sorry I found out this way. Sam tried to warn me that he was a weasel. I should have listened."

Ridley folded the paper in half and handed it back. "What are you going to do about..." She glanced behind her. "You know?"

"I guess I'll need those brochures after all." Raina ignored the pitying look on her sister's face and straightened her spine. There were too many people here for her to allow herself to break down. She would make her announcement about the show and then get the hell out of there. The show was still the biggest accomplishment of her professional life.

She wasn't going to let anyone or anything take that joy away from her.

"I guess I should just go ahead and make a statement about the show. I'm really sorry I asked you to come out for nothing."

Ridley put a hand on her arm. "Of course we don't mind. I'm just pissed on your behalf."

"Wait, what are we pissed about?" Jackson asked. He leaned closer to hear over the noise of the crowd.

"Steven's not coming," Ridley hissed.

"Well, let's not indict the guy yet. Maybe he got stuck in traffic and that's why he couldn't make it. Or maybe he was in a car accident." Jackson pursed his lips and then whistled softly when they both turned to glare at him. "Or maybe I won't say anything else until I get the whole story."

"Whatever, it doesn't even matter. Let me just do this so we can get out of here," Raina muttered.

She walked over to the small stage in the corner. The bandmaster saw her coming and the music stopped abruptly. "Ladies and gentlemen, it's Raina Winters!"

Chapter Four

⁓

RAINA MADE HER way carefully up the steps
leading to the stage. *All I need right now is to face plant
in front of all these people*, she thought. She thanked the
bandmaster before taking the microphone. Once she
faced the crowd, everyone quieted a little.

At the sight of all those faces staring up at her, Raina
felt the familiar tightening in her throat. God, it was so
much easier to be photographed than to have to stand up
in front of people and talk. She gulped. At least she knew
she looked good. The red Marchesa cocktail dress she

wore fit like a second skin, showcasing every curve she had. It was short enough to show off her long legs but long enough not to be completely scandalous.

Well, almost.

"Thank you all for coming out today." She paused and took a breath, blinking against the sudden flurry of flashing lights as the photographers in the crowd took pictures.

"I'm so excited to announce that the Ntertainment Network has picked up my new reality show about life behind the scenes in the cutthroat world of modeling!"

Cheers and applause broke out. She looked to her left and grinned when she saw Ridley, Jackson, and Sam jumping up and down and hooting.

"Raina, is it true that your fiancé will star with you in your new reality show?"

Raina squinted into the crowd, trying to see where the question came from. "What? Who said that?"

"Is it true, Raina?"

"Who's the lucky guy?"

"Is there any truth to the rumor that you're dating a married man? Is that why you won't discuss your personal life?"

The sound level in the room seemed to have risen several decibels. There was a rash of excited whispers before the room went crazy with everyone shouting questions at once and holding their microphones over the crowd.

"Can everyone please stay calm?"

There was a loud squeal in the crowd as a scuffle broke out as people pushed and shoved to get closer to the stage. Probably so they could get better shots of her expression. Pictures to accompany the horrible stories that were no doubt going to be written as soon as this disaster of a press conference was over.

Panicked, Raina turned to Sam. He motioned for several of the security guards he'd employed for the night to move forward and hold the crowd back.

Her eyes met a familiar face in the crowd. *Nick.* Even as her heart leaped, she tamped down the excitement. Just one more person to witness her humiliation. Except he didn't look as though he was enjoying this at all. He looked upset. When their eyes met, she saw something she hadn't expected to see.

Sympathy.

Being the center of attention was the key to her success. It had given her security, the chance to travel, and enough money to make sure that Ridley could go to college and study whatever she wanted. She would never complain about her life. But the truth was she hated every second of being in the spotlight. In one night, Nick had seen the truth that she took great pains to hide from everyone in her life. He'd seen it and understood. He'd saved her then and even though she hated being indebted to him, she couldn't help wishing he was up there with her now.

"There is no truth to any of these rumors. My fiancé is not married and he is not part of the reality show. The show will be a behind-the-scenes look at my life as a model."

"You've been photographed with Steven Silvestre several times in recent months. Were you surprised to find out that he is reconciling with his ex-wife?"

Raina gripped the microphone tighter and looked to Sam for help. He looked just as panicked as she felt.

How had things gotten so out of control?

*   *   *   *   *

"I REALLY HOPE she's okay."

41

Nick looked over at Ridley. She was staring up at the stage where Raina was talking to the band leader. She looked like pure seduction in a tight, clingy dress that made his blood boil. Her legs looked like they went on for miles and when she turned to face the crowd, her pert bottom was showcased by the tight material.

"Okay? She looks like she's in her element up there."

Ridley looked over at him as if just realizing he was there. "Nothing. I shouldn't have said anything."

They both turned up front and listened as Raina made her announcement and the crowd went wild. Nick looked behind him at Matt, who shrugged.

"Raina, is it true that your fiancé will star with you in your new reality show?" someone yelled.

Nick tensed. He knew she was engaged, of course, but usually avoided thinking about it. He had his suspicions that Silvestre had approached her after seeing her on Nick's arm. Even Murphy's Law wasn't foul enough to randomly hook up the only woman he wanted with his number-one rival.

"Hey, watch it!" Ridley cried. The crowd was getting more aggressive, with several people pushing to the front trying to get pictures on their cell phones.

"I wish she'd just called this whole thing off. The last thing she needs right now is questions about that jerk."

Nick stepped to Ridley's side, helping to shield her from the jostling crowd.

"Ridley, is something going on? I just want to help. Raina and I have had our issues," Nick said, ignoring the sarcastic face Jackson made, "but I hope you know that I'd never want to see her hurt. And this crowd is starting to look more and more like a group of sharks that has just scented fresh blood."

"No, I don't think you'd ever want to see her hurt," Ridley whispered, a strangely tender look in her eyes. "I think you feel a lot more for my sister than you want anyone to know." She narrowed her eyes, then leaned forward and spoke in a hushed tone.

"Her engagement is over. He's going back to his ex-wife. Which is devastating to her for more than just the obvious reasons."

Nick leaned closer so that no one else around them could hear. "Does this have anything to do with that brochure?"

"Remember what you offered us when you found it? Well, we're not the ones that need the offer."

Nick's head spun as the implication of what she was saying hit him. *Raina needs a sperm donor?* He opened his mouth to say something else but Ridley put her hand over his mouth.

"I can't tell you anything else, Nick. She'll kill me if she finds out I said this much. But I will say that after all this time of chasing Raina, it looks like you finally have something my sister wants."

She turned around and was immediately enfolded in Jackson's arms. His thoughts were spinning in a million different directions. It was almost unbelievable, but it seemed that Ridley was on his side if she was telling him that Raina's desire to have a baby might be his key to getting through to her. He snorted under his breath. He finally had something she wanted, indeed.

"Is it true, Raina?"

"Who's the lucky guy?"

"Is there any truth to the rumor that you're dating a married man? Is that why you won't discuss your personal life?"

Nick looked up sharply at the question. Raina looked like she was on the verge of running off the stage. He'd only seen her look like that once before. Nick looked back at Ridley.

She nodded at him. He wasn't sure what she was telling him, but he suddenly knew what he wanted to do. He pushed through the crowd until he got to the stage. The big, beefy guy standing there narrowed his eyes at him.

"Sam, right?" Nick held out his hand. The other guy stared at it before shaking it, reluctantly. "I'm Nick Alexander—"

"I know who you are," the big guy said, interrupting him. "I hope you have a plan. Because this is getting ugly."

Nick sighed. "I have a plan, but Raina probably isn't going to like it."

Sam moved aside. "Anything is better than this."

Nick walked across the stage until he stood next to Raina. "Okay, folks. Sorry I'm late."

He was glad he'd come straight from work. If he was going to be photographed, at least he knew he looked good.

Armani didn't have a bad side.

The crowd quieted for a moment, then flashbulbs started popping again. Nick wasn't famous like Jackson, but he was well-known in Virginia as both a businessman and a philanthropist. He'd been named as one of the *Virginia Chronicle*'s most eligible bachelors for the past three years in a row.

"Mr. Alexander! Mr. Alexander! Is your family going to be involved in the reality show now that your siblings are engaged?"

"Nick. What are you doing up here?" Raina whispered. Her voice came out husky. Nick couldn't help comparing it to the last time it had sounded like that. The night they'd spent together was as fresh in his mind as if it had happened yesterday instead of months ago. She'd cried out his name so many times she'd gone hoarse. Her voice had sounded much as it did now.

He straightened his tie and flashed the crowd a grin. "Whatever I say in the next few minutes, just go with it," he whispered back.

Raina tensed when he slid his arm around her waist and pulled her to his side. He turned to the photographer who'd yelled the question.

"Actually, I'm just here to support Raina. You kept asking her about her fiancé, so I figured we might as well not try to hide it any longer. Right, baby?"

As flashbulbs exploded around them, Nick could hear people calling out questions but it was all a blur. All he could see was Raina's confused expression as he dipped his head to whisper in her ear.

"We might as well give them something to talk about."

Then he yanked her against him and covered her lips with his.

* * * * *

"WHAT THE HELL was that?"

As soon as they were in his car, Raina whipped around in her seat to face him. Nick didn't even look disturbed, just put the car in gear and pulled away from the restaurant.

"*Thank you, Nick, for saving my pretty ass back there. That was such a selfless and kind thing for you to do,*" Nick parroted in a high, feminine voice.

"Thank you? You want me to thank you for lying to everyone that we're engaged?"

"Ridley told me what happened. That crowd wanted a story and they were going to keep digging until they got one. I figured if we just gave them what they wanted, maybe they wouldn't keep pushing. Although I'm not entirely sure it worked."

"Ridley told you what happened?"

"Well, she only told me that you were having a rough time. And that your engagement is off."

"I can't believe she did that. I told her that in confidence." Incensed, Raina couldn't even think of anything else to say. She'd never held anything back from her sister. It wouldn't even occur to her not to tell Ridley something. But she'd never had to worry about her sister blabbing her business before.

It felt like she'd been slugged in the stomach.

"Don't look like that. She didn't mean to. I found one of those brochures for the sperm bank and I thought it was hers and Jackson's. After an incredibly awkward conversation in which I offered to be their sperm donor, she might have let a few things slip. Although, you can't really blame her. She was probably just flustered. I think I'm permanently scarred by that conversation, too."

Raina tried not to smile. She was still pissed at him and was determined not to let him joke his way out of it. "Oh, well. Good. I mean, it's really none of your business."

"You're right. It isn't. But that doesn't mean I don't still want to know if you're okay."

Raina didn't answer, just looked out the window as they raced along the streets and then pulled out onto the highway.

"Wait, where are you going? Town is the other way."

"I'm not taking you back to town. I'm taking you to my place in Virginia Beach. Just hang tight—we'll be there in about thirty minutes."

"Are you crazy? First you take over my press conference. Now you're kidnapping me?"

"You want to go back to your house right now with all those vultures watching?"

"I have to at least let Sam know where I am."

Nick frowned. "Oh yes, you can't make a move without letting your loyal watchdog know where you are. Will he be jealous?"

"Don't be an ass. It isn't like that with us. I'm his boss."

"Hey, I'll let you be on top if that's the way you like it."

"Ugh, you are such a pig." She turned her back to him and typed out a text to Sam. He immediately replied.

- - - *Where the hell are you? Tell Alexander I'm going to kick his ass.*

Raina rolled her eyes. She was surrounded by machismo. Although, she figured Sam did have a point. His livelihood was keeping her safe and she paid him very well to make sure that nothing happened to her. Jumping in a car with a guy she wasn't even sure she liked probably wasn't the best move.

"Nick, you really have to take me back. This isn't cool."

"Tell your watchdog that he can meet you at my place tomorrow morning. My building has twenty-four-hour security on site. You're going to be the headline in tomorrow's gossip rags no matter what you do, Raina. But you can control whether it's good press or bad press. Which would you rather be, the scorned ex-girlfriend or the happy, future bride?"

"Okay, fine. But Sam is coming to get me first thing."

They raced over the darkened highways until they reached the Hampton Roads Bridge Tunnel. The radio signal shut out as soon as they entered and the car filled with the sounds of static. She reached for the knob to turn the sound down. Her fingers collided with Nick's and she yanked her hand back. "Sorry."

She could feel his eyes on her as they drove, but he didn't say anything else. After about fifteen minutes they

47

pulled off the highway. Raina sat up as they turned off the main strip. The casual vibe of the tourist area changed into a more modern look with rows of white stucco buildings. They drove up to a gate and Nick leaned out the window and handed his key tag to the man in the security booth.

"I've never been to this part of Virginia Beach before. I had no idea you lived here." Raina bit her lip. She hadn't actually meant to speak the thought aloud.

"I've lived here for almost two years now. I like the privacy and it has a great view. I'll show you."

He turned onto the next street and eased his car into one of the numbered spaces in front of his building. She got out of the car and followed him hesitantly.

The last time they'd been alone together, she'd ended up pinned beneath him on her couch. Goose bumps rose on her skin and she rubbed her arms briskly.

I am not going to sleep with him. I am not going to sleep with him.

She could spend time behind closed doors with Nick without anything happening. Especially now that she knew how dangerous he really was. She'd escaped with her heart intact last time, barely.

But if she let him back into her bed or her heart, she wasn't so sure she'd be able to do it again.

*   *   *   *   *

THEY RODE THE elevator with another couple that Nick didn't recognize. When the car stopped on the fourth floor, Nick motioned for her to precede him. Raina stepped out into the plushly carpeted hallway.

"This is a really nice building."

He led her to the second door on the left. She followed him into the quiet, dark interior. He'd left the light on in the kitchen but the rest of the place was dark. He moved around the room, switching on lamps and kicking the pair of gym sneakers he'd left in the middle of the floor to the side. He wasn't a neat freak by any means but the things that normally didn't bother him suddenly looked really sloppy.

He finally realized that he was moving around at hyperspeed while Raina stood uncertainly in the middle of the room. Damn, he hadn't even offered her a seat.

Being nervous was a completely alien feeling.

"Please, sit. Can I offer you a drink?" He gestured to the kitchen. "I have iced tea, some type of white wine, and beer."

"You know, it doesn't matter. Surprise me."

As he moved around his kitchen pulling down glasses and pouring their drinks, he thought of the incredibly well-stocked bar he'd seen at her house on their long-ago disaster of a date. She was probably used to colorful mixed drinks and parties every weekend. Ever since he'd started the foundation's youth project, he hadn't had much time for partying. Or friends.

Which suddenly seemed really lonely and pathetic.

"No, I actually haven't done this in ages." When she spoke, he realized he'd spoken his thoughts aloud.

She sat down in one of the plush armchairs by the window. "I did more bookings than ever this year so I could take time off after the wedding. I haven't taken the time to sit and relax with a drink in a really long time. Not since before my mom's death."

He sat in the chair across from her and set their drinks carefully on the glass coffee table. He leaned over and took one of her hands. Her skin was warm and smooth. "I'm sorry you lost her so young. You must miss her."

Raina didn't answer for a moment. When she did, her eyes were sad. "You're going to think I'm awful, but I really don't. It's hard to miss what you never had. My mother never had much use for me. Ridley was her favorite. That really isn't saying a lot, though. She never had a kind word to say to either of us, really." She laughed, the sound harsh. "I think I miss the *idea* of her. Which is worse."

"I'm really sorry, Raina. I can't even imagine."

"Of course you can't. Your family is like an episode of *The Cosby Show*. I'm sure your mom helped you with your homework and had cookies and milk ready when you got home from school."

She took her hand back and tucked it in her lap. Nick had to resist the urge to reach out for her again. Touching her was becoming too easy, a habit he couldn't afford to adopt just yet. He had a feeling that if he approached her with too much emotion at once she would do what she did best. Leave him behind. If he had any chance at getting to her, he had to do it slow. Easy.

No sudden movements.

"That wouldn't be far off the mark," he admitted. "We were heathens growing up, I'm sure, but my parents managed to corral us somehow. I'm sure there were days they wondered what the hell they'd gotten themselves into."

"I can't imagine what that must have been like." She glanced at him and then snickered. "I can't believe there are four of you."

She took another sip of her iced tea and sat back. Nick took it as a cue to keep talking.

"I was the second to youngest, so I had to learn to talk fast. There was always a lot of chaos in our house. I don't really remember the years before Jackson came along. We're only two years apart, so it feels like he's always been a part of my life."

"I always kind of wished we'd had more siblings. But

50

I'm lucky I had at least Ri. If it had been just me..."

Nick leaned forward. "Is that why having a baby is so important to you?"

She immediately tensed up and set her drink down on the table. "You are relentless!"

"That's why you should just tell me. The faster you tell me, the faster we can move on to finding a solution."

"Not everything has a solution, Nick. This isn't a business deal." She pushed her hair back and rubbed her hands over her face. It killed him to see her looking so tired. So defeated.

"If you don't tell me, then I'm just going to work with the facts I have. Let's see..." He pretended to think. "I find a brochure for a sperm bank that *does not* belong to my brother and Ridley. Since you were the only other person on the patio that day, it must have been yours. But that doesn't make sense since last I knew you were engaged. What am I missing?"

Raina glared at him. "Fine. Since you apparently aren't going to stop until I tell you everything, consider yourself warned. I hope you're not the type to get squeamish when talking about girl stuff."

Nick leaned over and took her hand again and held it fast when she tried to pull back. "Raina, this is not high school. Despite our past, I want to know that you're okay. If that involves talking about feminine stuff, then so be it. So, why would you need a sperm donor when you had a fiancé?"

Raina stood and he let her. She didn't look at him as she walked over to the window. She stood there so long that he wondered if she was reconsidering her decision to talk. She finally turned to face him.

"I have a condition called endometriosis. I won't bore you with the details."

"Nothing about you bores me, Raina."

"Anyway, bottom line is that I'm a ticking time bomb. Every month that passes where I'm not pregnant means it's less likely I'll get to be a mother. A baby is all I want."

"Did Steven not want children?"

"No, he said he did. We weren't in love but we both wanted the same things. Partnership. Family. Children. Marriages built on common goals have higher success rates. It made sense to get married and start trying right away. My doctor gave me a bunch of brochures about in vitro fertilization, egg donation, and surrogacy just so that I could be informed. Turns out I'll actually need them now."

She turned away and he realized she was wiping away tears. The sight of her crying sent a paralyzing wave of fear through Nick.

"Oh, sweetheart. Please don't cry." The endearment slipped out before he could catch himself.

"Sorry. Ugh, I hate crying. As awful as it sounds, I'm less upset about Steven and more heartbroken over losing my dream."

"What if you could still have it?"

"I don't think Steven is going to change his mind." Raina laughed bitterly. "Not that I'd want him to. We were supposed to have a relationship based on mutual respect and trust. If I wanted someone who'd cheat and lie I could just have a normal relationship."

It was all he could do not to growl. "I'm not talking about Steven. And we'll have to talk about your shitty relationship expectations later. But I'm saying what if someone else offered to help you out?"

He debated the best way to present his idea to her. He could do what he really wanted to do, which was fall to one knee and tell her he adored her. But their interactions had proven time and time again that Raina didn't respond well to romantic gestures from him. If he told her he loved her, she'd probably just assume he was trying to get in her panties and just saying what he thought she wanted to hear.

There was only one thing he hadn't tried. She freely admitted that she hadn't loved her fiancé and was just marrying him because it "made sense." Well, Nick would be damned if she considered Silvestre a better bet than him. It was going to kill him to play it cool, but if pretending their interaction was just a business deal got him what he wanted, then he wasn't above a little deception.

"Help me out? How likely is that? It's not like I'm asking to borrow a cup of sugar, Nick! How many men would offer to father my child?"

Nick stood and thrust his hands in his pockets, aware that his next words would change his life forever.

"You're looking at one."

Chapter Five

FOR A MOMENT, Raina wondered if it was possible to be dreaming while standing up. Because she was pretty sure Nick Alexander had just offered to get her pregnant.

And he wasn't laughing.

"Are you crazy? Why would you say that? You and I don't even get along."

Not to mention that she'd been shutting him down for months. Why would he want to do her a favor now?

"Well, as you just pointed out, it's not about being in love. It's about shared goals. I'm a businessman, Raina. I can appreciate the logic of what you've described. A stable mother for my children and someone who has the kind of DNA that money can't buy."

Nick stood and joined her at the window. If it was possible, he was even more handsome with his clothes all rumpled and his tie askew. He looked like he'd just been rolling around in bed. Which made her think about what he'd just offered to do.

Focus, Raina!

"You want to do this because you like my DNA?" she asked skeptically.

"You are without a doubt one of the most beautiful women I've ever seen," he stated. "Clearly you're smart, your career trajectory proves that, and you seem healthy, fertility issues notwithstanding. I want children and I want them to have the best mother possible. Why shouldn't it be you?"

He said it so matter-of-factly, as if he picked out the mother of his children every day.

"Nick, are you serious? Please don't toy with me about something like this."

At that, his face softened. "With all that you know about me, have I ever been cruel? A little too persistent, perhaps, but never mean." He looked tense despite his relaxed pose, the lines around his eyes and mouth more prominent.

"No, you haven't. That label probably applies more to me than you."

"Well, I'm guessing you had your reasons." Nick regarded her from beneath lowered lashes. "I bet you never expected this. Contemplating carrying the child of a man you hate."

She squirmed. Was there any tactful way to respond? Even though he drove her crazy and she didn't really want to get emotionally attached to him, it didn't mean she wanted to hurt him. She was just trying to keep her own emotions in check so she wouldn't grow to depend on him.

"I don't hate you, Nick. I could never hate you."

"Well, then, what is it? Tell me what it is that's keeping you from saying yes."

"I'm trying to understand why you want to do this."

"Raina, men are wired differently than women. I think we only have three levers. Food, money, and sex. Most men don't have a biological clock. We have children when we feel it's time to settle down. This is a little earlier than I'd planned, but if I wait I might not find anyone as well-suited to me as you are. Especially sexually."

"That makes sense but, Nick, let's be real. You're used to having a lot of women. Getting pregnant can be a lengthy process. It's going to screw up your game if you're spending so much time with me."

He curled his hand around her neck, tangling his fingers in her long curls. His thumb stroked her bottom lip. "You've already screwed up my game because I can't get the night we spent together out of my mind. I can't sleep without reliving it. I can't focus on anything without screwing it up. I can't *breathe* because all I want is the one thing I can't have."

"That doesn't mean you have to father my child."

"It does if I don't want you with anyone else." His fingers tightened against her skin. The little bite of pain was unbelievably arousing.

"You're jealous," she breathed.

"Hell yes, I'm jealous. Just the thought of you with someone else…"

It was startling to realize he wanted her so much that he was willing to go this far to keep her from turning to another man. Part of her was alarmed. This level of intensity was exactly the kind of thing she avoided. Emotions ran too high when jealousy was involved. But she was honest enough to admit that what he was offering was too good to turn down.

"Well, I guess we could have a lawyer draw up one of those contracts. So you'll know I'm not after your money and visitation is clearly spelled out."

"We won't need that." Nick's hand trailed down her back, drawing slow circles on the small of her back.

She bit her lip to hold in a moan. His hand felt so good it should be illegal. "Aren't you worried about me trying to keep the baby from you later?"

He looked her deeply in the eyes. "No, I'm not. I don't think you'd want to keep a loving father away."

Raina looked away. "Well, what about finances? You're a little older, so I'm sure you've accumulated more wealth than I have."

He shrugged. "Money is my business, so yeah. Probably."

"Aren't you worried that I'll try to get my hands on your money?"

"Nope. I'm actually expecting that you will." He smirked and tapped her on the end of the nose. "Which means I'll just have to work harder and earn more."

Raina gaped at him. "You're being awfully cavalier about this. You really don't care if I take the baby anywhere and spend all your money?"

"That's what wives do, isn't it? At least according to most of my married friends."

"Married?" Her mouth fell open.

"Oh, hell. I'm making a mess of this, aren't I? Raina, I'm not just giving you my DNA and then walking away. I have conditions. If you want my baby, then this isn't going to be a turkey-baster job. You'll get it the good old-fashioned way. And I promise you, we'll both enjoy it." He leaned down until their eyes met. She shivered when he held her gaze. "But you also have to give me something I want just as much."

He leaned down even farther until their lips were just a breath apart and then said, "You."

* * * * *

NICK KNEW HE was walking a fine line. Raina looked like she was shell-shocked, her brown eyes slightly unfocused as she swayed against him. It probably wasn't fair to expect her to make a decision about something this monumental right away, but a huge part of him wanted to pressure her for an immediate response.

The caveman in him wanted to get her answer, marry her, and get her pregnant before she had a chance to reconsider.

"So you're blackmailing me?" Raina said. She didn't sound angry as much as confused. As if she couldn't understand why he'd want to do it.

"No. I'm not holding anything over your head. I'm not going to go running to the press with this story if you say no. I would never hurt you like that. I'm just telling you my conditions for helping you. You want something from me. Something huge. But you have to give me something I want just as much."

"Me," she whispered. "That's really all you want?"

"Yes." Talk about the understatement of the century. His obsession with her was on the verge of taking over his life. He had to have her. It didn't even matter if she didn't love him. *If you only knew, pretty girl. I'll take you any way I can get you.*

"What happens when you wake up and realize the infatuation is over? Aren't you going to feel trapped?"

"What was it you said earlier? Oh yes, marriages built on commonalities have a higher success rate than ones based on emotions. Let's look at our common traits. We're both intelligent, hardworking, driven, and value family. If you know nothing else about me, you know how much family means to me. I had the best possible role models for a successful marriage. My parents have always been a team. I think we could have that kind of partnership, too. Like I said, this is a little earlier than I'd planned, but I knew I'd want kids eventually. If we start now, our kids won't be too much younger than their cousins."

He pulled her to the chair he'd been sitting in and knelt at her feet, his eyes holding hers. Her hand covered her mouth.

"This is all just crazy. I don't know what to say."

"At the core of all this, what do you want most? A baby?"

"Yeah."

"Then let me make that happen for you."

Raina looked into his eyes and he let her, hoping she could see his certainty, his absolute determination to give her what she wanted. It wasn't just that he wanted her more than his next breath. It wasn't just that this was the only woman he'd ever wanted to give his last name to.

It was the fact that he could give her the thing she wanted most.

"Come on." He tugged her up and before she could protest, picked her up, and cradled her against his chest.

"Where are we going?" Raina squirmed in his arms.

He didn't answer, just walked down the hallway leading toward his bedroom. He set Raina carefully on her feet and turned on the small lamp on his bedside table.

She stood still, looking as vulnerable as a child as he

stripped her tiny excuse for a dress from her body. He gritted his teeth as every inch of her honey-colored skin was revealed. Finally she stood before him in nothing more than a heart-attack-inducing black lace bra and panty set. He didn't even want to contemplate if the panties had a thong back.

"*Jesus.* We have to find something for you to wear." His goal was for her to rest, which wouldn't be happening if he had to look at her in those scraps of black lace much longer. He turned blindly to his closet and yanked the first shirt his fingers touched off the hanger.

"Here, put your arms in this." He helped her slide her arms into the sleeves of one of his dress shirts. Once she was mainly covered up, he picked her up again and carried her into the bathroom.

"Nick, I can walk," she complained.

"Humor me, please. I'm very much enjoying the opportunity to carry you." He set her on the counter and took a clean washcloth from beneath the sink. He wet it and dabbed at the mascara trails on her cheeks.

"Pervert," she replied, but she was smiling as she said it.

"I have never pretended to be anything else."

After her face was clean, he left the bathroom briefly to go get her a new toothbrush. When he returned, he stopped at the sight of Raina with her hair loose around her shoulders and her skin shiny and clean. A bunch of black pins sat on the counter in a neat pile.

He couldn't say why the sight pleased him so much.

"Thanks," she said as he handed over the new toothbrush. He couldn't stop staring at her as she wet the brush, squeezed on a glob of toothpaste, and leaned closer to the mirror to inspect her teeth as she brushed.

"What," she mumbled around her mouthful of soap.

"Why are you staring?"

Nick chuckled. "Sorry. It's just not every day that I get to see you like this."

She spit in the sink and cupped her hand under the faucet to rinse her mouth. "Like what? A hot mess?"

He shook his head. "Normal. Human. You look adorable."

She wiped her face on his towel and then flicked the light off. "Now I know you're lying. There's nothing adorable about this."

He pulled back the comforter and she slid beneath it, covering her mouth with the back of her hand as she yawned. When he turned the light off, she sat up straight.

"Wait? Where are you going? You aren't going to…"

Nick turned the light back on. "Raina Winters," he said mockingly. "Did you think I was going to get you half-naked in my bed and then take advantage of you while you're too weak to resist me?"

Raina stared at him for a minute before saying, "Well, yes."

Nick leaned down and took her lips in a soft kiss. He swallowed her soft moan, teasing her lips with his until she opened for the first stroke of his tongue. Her hands tangled in the front of his shirt, pulling him closer as she kissed him back.

Just before he lost his mind, he pulled back and nipped her bottom lip gently.

"One of the things a husband does is put your needs ahead of his. You need to sleep on this decision."

Raina cupped his cheek. "I've already decided. Let's get married."

Nick was quiet for a moment, then he nodded. "Okay. I'll wake you early tomorrow and we'll fly to Vegas. I'll go book our seats now."

Then he turned the lights out and left her alone in his

bed.

*　*　*　*　*

LATER THAT NIGHT, Ridley got into bed and pulled the covers up to her neck. Jackson was still in the shower, so she had a few minutes to brood before he came back.

What was I thinking telling Nick all that?

As much as she loved her future brother-in-law, she was well aware of his faults. He was so used to women throwing themselves at him that a woman like Raina, who was genuinely hard to get, had to present an unusual challenge.

One he couldn't resist trying to conquer.

But what if it was more than that? Ridley couldn't pinpoint exactly why, but there was something about the way Nick looked at her sister. Something that made her think his continued attempts to romance Raina were about more than just sex. He watched her when he thought no one else was looking and his eyes revealed more than the words coming out of his mouth.

"Okay, I was going to just let you stew in peace, but I can't take it anymore. What's wrong with you?"

Ridley turned to see Jackson standing in the doorway that connected to the en suite bathroom, rubbing the water from his arms with a towel. Her mouth went dry as she followed the path of a single drop down his muscular chest, below his belly button...

"As much as I appreciate your distraction, I actually want an answer to this question," Jackson remarked dryly.

Ridley reluctantly pulled her gaze up to meet his eyes. Good grief, the man was fine. Too fine for his own good. It was scary at times to think what her life would be like if she'd turned left instead of right, or done anything that would have prevented her from coming to Virginia last month. She would have missed out on the best thing that had ever happened to her. She was just trying to make sure that Nick and Raina didn't miss their chance. Which made a little bit of meddling okay, didn't it?

"Nothing. I'm just thinking about everything that happened tonight. The tabloid picture and then that awful press conference. And then Nick going on stage. I'm just worried."

Jackson threw the towel over his shoulder and walked across the room stark-naked to rummage through his dresser. "I know she's your sister and worry comes with the territory, but Nick would never hurt her. Plus, I think we might need to be more worried about Nick."

Ridley sat up. "I did something tonight. Something I probably shouldn't have."

Jackson finally selected a pair of sweatpants and pulled them on. He padded over to the other side of the bed and slid beneath the covers. "Does this have anything to do with Nick's insane behavior tonight?"

Ridley bit her lip. "Um, it might. I sort of told him about Raina's fertility issues and how she wants to have a baby. I may have suggested that he make her the same offer he made us."

Jackson sat straight up in bed, dragging the covers off her. "You did what? Why would you do that? I thought you wanted Nick to stay away from her?"

Ridley drew her knees up to her chest. "I know, I know! That's what I thought was best, but you didn't see the way he was looking at her. I think he really loves her, Jackson."

Jackson made a noncommittal sound. "You may be right. I've actually never seen Nick like this over a woman. Any woman. But still, that doesn't mean I think he should offer to be her sperm donor."

"If he offers to father her child, I very much doubt if he'll be donating in a cup."

Jackson smirked. "Well, yeah. This is my brother we're talking about."

"I'm worried she'll regret this. Raina pretends to be so modern and unaffected, but she's not. I think inside she wants the same things I do. Family. And not by some guy who's a random number in a database."

"Is this about your dad?"

"What? No! This is about Raina."

"I know you love your sister, but I think you're also worried about the baby. Growing up without a father. Without even knowing who he is..."

"Okay. It's a little about that. I just don't want her to do something she'll regret because she feels like she's running out of time. I'd rather she gets pregnant by someone who cares about her than some guy she doesn't even know. No matter what else happens, I know Nick would love his child."

"That is, without a doubt, true. And she would have a big, rambling, loving family to help her out if she needed it. No matter what, Alexanders stick together."

Ridley clapped her hands over her face and fell back against her pillows. "I really hope this doesn't end up being a disaster."

"Come on, let's go to sleep. There's nothing more we can do about it tonight. I doubt Nick is going to kidnap your sister and steal her away somewhere. You can always go check on her in the morning."

"Okay," Ridley agreed. But even after they were snuggled under the covers and Jackson had her spooned right up against his chest, it was a long time before she was able to fall asleep.

Chapter Six

THE BUSTLING TERMINAL did nothing to soothe Raina's nerves as they waited for their flight to board. Nick had woken her at the ungodly hour of four a.m. so they could catch the first flight to Vegas leaving from Norfolk International.

The past two hours had been a flurry of excitement. He'd loaned her a small suitcase and they'd stopped at the store so she could buy a few weekend outfits. He'd been able to get tickets in first class so at least she would have enough room on the flight to stretch out a little and rest her head. She typed out a text to Sam and then sent it before switching off her phone.

She could already feel the beginning of a migraine swimming around the back of her skull.

She glanced over at Nick, surprised to find he looked almost as nervous as she felt. She couldn't help wondering if he was having second thoughts about this whole crazy plan. After all, the majority of the benefits to this alliance were on her side. She was going to get the baby she'd always wanted, an extended family and support system, and a doting father to help her care for the child.

What was he getting? A wife who acted like she could barely tolerate him.

"I'm sorry."

He looked up from the magazine he was reading, some kind of business journal with a picture of a stack of coins on the front.

"Sorry? For what?"

Raina shrugged. "I've been nothing but bitchy to you this whole time. What you're doing is really sweet. I can't pretend I understand all this yet, but I do appreciate it. A lot."

He smiled at her, his eyes crinkling slightly at the edges. Her stomach did that weird drop-and-roll thing again. She coughed and sat up straighter, hoping to get her equilibrium back.

"I told you. I'm getting something pretty huge out of this deal, too. I get to be married to the most beautiful woman I've ever seen. There are tons of men who'd pay good money to be in my shoes right now, believe me."

She smiled at his joke because she knew he'd been trying to amuse her. But inside, she couldn't help wondering about the women in Nick's past. Had he ever wanted to marry any of them? Surely his family was used to seeing a different woman on his arm every year. They probably wouldn't even try to get to know her since she was more than likely just the flavor of the month, anyway.

But then why would he want to make this permanent? Nothing about this proposal made any sense to her.

Pushing these negative thoughts to the back of her mind, she hurriedly gathered her belongings when the voice on the PA system announced that their flight was boarding. Nick reached over and picked up her small carry-on suitcase.

"Oh, you don't have to do that."

He gave her a look like she was crazy. "Raina, it's not a problem. Chivalry may be considered dead to most people, but not in my family. I can't stand back and watch a woman lugging a bag. If that's antifeminist, then so be it."

"No, I think it's nice." Raina stepped back and allowed him to carry her bag up to the gate. They showed their tickets to the agent and then walked down a long hallway to board the plane.

Once on board, she stretched out her legs and gratefully accepted the orange juice the flight attendants were handing out. She waved away the offer of champagne, knowing the frothy drink would only make her headache worse. Settling back, she closed her eyes, hoping that when she opened them again they would have reached their destination.

When Raina woke up, she found she wasn't in Sin City but instead still on the plane. Her right hand was encased in Nick's large grip and she could feel the slight calluses on his palm. Turning her head, she found him staring right at her.

"We're almost there." He lifted her hand and kissed her fingers. Unsure of how to respond to the tenderness in his gaze, she nodded mutely and turned to face the front.

Thirty minutes later, the captain announced that they were approaching McCarran International Airport. As the flight attendants walked down the rows checking seatbelts, Raina noticed for the first time that Nick had a death grip on the armrest.

"You're scared of flying?"

He glanced at her from the corner of his eye. "I'm not scared of flying. I just don't *enjoy* flying. There is a difference."

Despite how conflicted she still felt, Raina couldn't help smiling. "Right. I've noticed you're big on rephrasing things. But it still comes down to the same thing."

"Actually, I think words do matter. Words have power. That's why I say *exactly* what I mean." He turned to look at her, their faces so close she could feel the soft puff of his breath against her lips. "For example, some men think it's okay to promise marriage to a woman and then back out without any warning. But I would never do that. When I say I'm going to do something, I do it. When I make a promise, I keep it. And when I tell a woman I want her to be my wife, I mean forever."

Raina sucked in a breath. They stayed like that, staring at each other, until a flight attendant stopped next to their row.

"Sir, we need your seat in a full upright position."

Nick looked away, breaking the spell. "Of course," he replied.

They touched down without incident and then the next half hour was filled with the hustle of deplaning. Once they finally cleared the secure area, they stood in the middle of the airport, their bags at their feet.

Nick turned to her. "Did you want to go to the hotel first? You could rest a little. Put your feet up."

Raina glanced around the bustling terminal. She'd been to Vegas for a shoot before, but she'd never been just for fun.

You're not here for fun now, either. This is not about fun. This is about getting pregnant.

Her face heated and she looked up into Nick's concerned gaze. As sweet as it was that he was worried about her welfare, she wasn't here to rest or relax. They were here to get married so he would get her pregnant. Anything else was veering dangerously close to the kind of emotional territory that she was determined to avoid.

"Actually, no. I just want to find the closest Elvis impersonator who can marry us. Then I want you to take me back to the hotel and make love to me."

Nick's mouth fell open. Raina leaned up and kissed him softly on the cheek, strangely satisfied with his reaction.

"Sound good, baby?"

Then she turned and walked outside to see about getting a cab.

*   *   *   *   *

"OKAY, WHAT HAVE we got? There are three chapels near us. The Wedding Bell, Little Love Chapel and Chapel O' Love."

They'd decided to stop by the hotel first after all when Nick pointed out they'd have to lug their bags up and down the Strip and she'd have to do it in heels. Nick had booked a suite at the Aria, which was gorgeous and large enough to house a small family.

After checking in and dumping their bags, Raina had changed from her strappy high-heeled sandals into the pair of rainbow-colored flip-flops she'd purchased just for the weekend. Now they were standing on the sidewalk in front of the hotel, searching for the nearest wedding chapel.

Raina shrugged. "Let's just pick whichever is closest."

"Chapel O' Love it is." Nick grabbed her hand and they made their way down the Strip. Raina was surprised at how busy it was. It was a Thursday afternoon and the Strip was packed already.

"Wow. This is so great. Ooh, look, a mime!" Raina stopped to watch a man dressed in all black with the traditional face paint of a mime as he went through the standard repertoire.

"Not that I don't appreciate the talent it takes to do this, but his routine is pretty weak," Nick whispered. "I'm pretty sure Jackson did the exact same thing in summer camp when he was eight."

"Sshhh, be quiet. I want to see the rest." Raina swatted Nick on the arm and turned back to the performance. She watched for a few more minutes until she became suddenly aware that some of the things he was acting out were a little… suggestive. Just when he was starting to mimic stroking himself, Nick took her arm and pulled her away.

"Damn pervert," Nick grumbled.

Raina giggled. "Don't be such a prude. He probably heard your comment that his performance was boring and was trying to liven things up a bit."

They walked farther down the Strip, passing the famous Bellagio hotel. "Ooh, Nick I want to watch the water show later. Can we come back?"

"Of course. That'll be part of our honeymoon."

Raina instantly sobered. How could she have forgotten so quickly why they were here? She was about to sign her freedom away and she was planning her sightseeing like she was on vacation.

"Hey, I didn't say that to make you sad. It's all going to work out, you'll see." Nick pulled her closer.

"Hey, pretty mama. Here you go." A man passing by pressed a small square of paper in her hand.

"What's this?" She held it up to read what it said.

"Oh, you might not want to read that." Nick took the paper from her hand but not before she saw the half-naked girl on it.

"I'm not an idiot, Nick. I know there are hooker services in Vegas. I watch TV. Hell, I probably know some of them. I heard a few of the girls I used to model with ended up as escorts. I'm hardly going to swoon because I see a dirty flyer."

"Well, good, because I'm sure that's not the worst thing you'll see before we get back to our hotel." He consulted his phone and then stopped. "Here we are. This is the closest wedding chapel."

He held open the door for her and she walked into the cool interior of the shop. It was incredibly quiet compared to the bustle and chaos of the Strip. Too quiet, actually. Was it even open? She was just about to hit the silver bell on the counter when a man stumbled through the dangling beads separating the entryway from the rest of the building.

"Well, hellooooo. Welcome to Chapel O' Love. That's O as in 'One Night,' by the way. That was a great song. *Great* song." The man who spoke was dressed as Elvis in a sequined white jumpsuit, except his pompadour was dyed electric blue.

Nick shot Raina an amused grin. "Or O as in Of could work, too."

The blue-haired Elvis stopped and scratched his head, knocking his wig slightly askew. "That is a very fine point, young man."

Raina watched as he became absorbed in one of the long blue strands of his wig, seeming to forget they were even there.

"Is he drunk?"

Nick heaved a sigh. "I hope so. Because I would hate to think he was acting like this sober."

Elvis staggered behind the counter in the reception area and flipped open the large book on the counter.

"Names," he barked.

"Nicholas Alexander and Raina Winters," Nick replied.

Elvis leaned on the counter and whispered conspiratorially, "Come on, boyo, you can give your real names. Because between you and me, there is no way you could pull a babe like Raina Winters."

Raina giggled and even when Nick turned around and glared at her, she couldn't stop. "I'm sorry."

Elvis finally noticed her behind Nick and leered. "Hey, now. That's no Raina Winters, but she's a close second." He looked back at Nick. "How'd you pull that one off?"

Raina buried her face against Nick's shoulder to muffle her laughter. "Yeah, Nick. Do you want to tell him how you pulled it off?"

The edges of Nick's lips twitched but he managed to keep a straight face. "I think we'll save that for another time."

He turned back to Elvis and picked up the pen that was on the counter. "Where do we sign?" He filled out everything on the form and scrawled his name at the bottom. When he was done, he handed the pen to Raina.

She filled out her name on the opposite side of the form next to Nick's and then glanced up at him innocently. "Your middle name is *Eugene*?"

"If you tell anyone that I cannot be held responsible for the consequences."

She just smiled and filled out the rest of the form. When she was done, she looked up to give the paperwork to the Elvis impersonator, only to realize they were alone.

"Where did he go?"

Nicholas grasped his head between his hands. "I swear, if he passed out somewhere..."

Raina followed the sound of music to the inner sanctum, if you could even call it that. It felt sacrilegious to even call this place a chapel. The interior was just as gaudy as the entryway with large plastic cupids hanging from the ceiling.

There was a table below the altar with a bouquet of flowers and a rhinestone tiara on it. As she approached the front of the room, a canned rendition of "Love Me Tender" started playing.

"Wow. Raina, we can go somewhere else. I know we're sacrificing a lot by having a quickie wedding, but I think we can do better than this."

"There is nowhere better! You won't find a better chapel on the Strip than the Chapel O' Love."

Nick jumped when the blue-haired Elvis popped up from behind the podium at the altar. "*Jesus!* Has he been back there the whole time?"

Raina felt a bubble of completely inappropriate laughter rising in her belly. She clamped her lips together, trying to hold it in, but the whole situation was so ridiculous. She was standing in a chapel decorated with plastic babies about to be married to the only man with the power to break her heart.

By a drunk Elvis impersonator with a bad wig.

"It's okay. We can stay here." She finally lost the battle and dissolved into giggles. The longer she laughed the more confused Nick looked until he finally cracked a smile.

"I'm glad you can find the humor in all this. Because this is not what I imagined my wedding would be like."

Raina wiped the tears from her cheeks and marched up to the podium. She picked up the plastic bouquet and jammed the rhinestone-encrusted tiara with the attached bridal veil on her head. It was strange, but the tackiness of this wedding was only going to help her stick to her determination to keep this union businesslike.

She wasn't sure if she could stick to her guns and not fall in love if she had to take vows with Nick in a real church. But being married by a drunken Elvis while holding plastic flowers shouldn't be too hard. She was doing this for one reason and one reason only. Because Nick's old-fashioned sense of honor wouldn't let him impregnate her unless they were married.

But once she was moody and eating everything in sight and had cankles, he'd realize she'd been right all along. He'd leave and she'd be ready. As long as she didn't fall in love with him, she could let him go and focus on what she had left.

Her baby.

"Raina, are you sure about this? I meant what I said. We can find another chapel. One that's not so cheesy." Nick peered at her, seemingly not convinced by her enthusiastic embrace of the Chapel O' Love.

"I'm ready," she repeated. She was beyond ready to get this farce of a wedding over with so they could get down to why they were really here. So she could drag his sexy ass back to the hotel room and get him naked.

She held up the plastic roses. "Let's do this."

* * * * *

NICK KNEW HE'D always had it easy. Up until now, he'd made his way using a mixture of brains, charm and bravado. In business it had served him well. He'd achieved everything he'd ever dreamed of and more.

But for the first time in his adult life, he found himself wondering if he would be able to measure up. Because as much as he loved his career, nothing he'd accomplished there was anywhere near as important as convincing his new wife that she hadn't made a mistake. He wanted her to realize their connection was deeper than just sex.

But it was hard to remember that when she was looking at him like she wanted to devour him whole.

"That was the longest wedding ceremony ever." Raina kicked the door to the suite closed behind them and grabbed him by the collar of his shirt.

Before he could respond, she pulled him down and her tongue was in his mouth. Nick groaned as her hands slid into his hair, grabbing and holding the strands tight. All thought fled as everything within him responded.

He pulled her into his arms and stumbled through the main living area until he reached the bedroom. She clung to him with her legs wrapped around his waist and her arms around his neck. She kissed his throat and he shuddered when she bit him on the throat.

"Christ, Raina. You're killing me."

Her small breasts pressed against his chest and he could feel the stiff tips of her nipples. He couldn't wait to have the tight points on his tongue.

He opened his eyes and the first thing he saw were the roses next to the bed. The sight sobered him, reminding him of what he was trying to accomplish.

Romance.

"Raina. Hey, let's slow down for a minute," he whispered.

"Uh uh." She shook her head and tightened her legs around his waist. "Don't want to." She made the sexiest little sound, like a whimper, in the back of her throat before she took his bottom lip between her teeth and nipped gently. It was all he could do to stay upright when she was kissing him like she wanted nothing more than his tongue in her mouth.

"I just want to light the candles, sweets. I can't have you telling your friends how unromantic I am."

She pulled back and then looked around the room in surprise. "Nick, what in the world?"

She hopped down and walked over to inspect the rose petals sprinkled on the bed and the bottle of champagne chilling in a bucket on the dresser. He'd arranged for their room to be prepared while they were gone. It was hard to be romantic when they'd had such a tacky ceremony but he was determined that at least their wedding night could be up to his standards.

He wanted her to cherish the memory of their first time making love as husband and wife.

Raina's eyes were wide with wonder as she looked back at him. "I can't believe you did all this for me."

"Of course I did. I hope there will come a day when you won't find it unusual for me to surprise you like this." He walked up behind her and pulled her back against his chest. She relaxed against him and he kissed the soft skin behind her ear. Her right hand came up and caressed his neck, holding him closer as she pushed back against him.

He breathed in deep as he nuzzled her throat. How long had he imagined this? If he was honest with himself, he'd probably been dreaming about having her beneath him since the last time. He took deep breaths, trying to calm down, but her scent was intoxicating, warm and rich like vanilla.

"Nick?" she whispered.

"Yes, sweetheart?"

She turned in his arms and took his face between her hands. "This is beautiful. Thank you for making this special for me." She stood on tiptoe and kissed him softly.

Then she turned her head and gently bit the lobe of his ear. "Now, get your clothes off before I rip them off."

Instant molten arousal raced through Nick's veins at her words. She made quick work of the buttons on the front of his shirt, then stepped back and pulled her blouse over her head. Any blood that was still left in his brain flowed south as she pushed her khaki shorts down. She stepped out of them and stood before him in another lacy panty set, this one a bright, fire-engine red.

"You're trying to drive me crazy, aren't you?"

She pushed him and they tumbled onto the bed in a jumble of arms and legs. She rolled over and climbed on top of him, running her hands over his chest.

Then she reached behind her and unhooked her bra. *Mercy.* Looking at her would never get old. She was beautifully built with small, perky breasts and dark, tight little nipples. With her long hair wild around her shoulders, she was a wet dream come to life.

"You are so beautiful. You stagger me." He took one of her hands and pressed it between his legs. Even through the denim there was no doubt she could feel his arousal. She massaged him through the fabric and then helped him push his jeans and boxers down. Once he was naked, Raina took him between her hands, lust in her eyes as she caressed him. The tip of her tongue came out to wet her lips a second before she dipped her head.

"Oh my God," he breathed. Her warm, wet mouth danced over his flesh, teasing him with quick little laps of her tongue. She giggled and moved away so she could pull her tiny panties off.

He tried to use the time to get his sanity back, but before he could even breathe, she straddled him again.

"You feel so good." She skimmed her palms over the tips of her nipples. It excited Nick just to watch.

There was nothing in the world so arousing as a confident, sexually aggressive woman. Raina never played coy or pretended to be bashful. Their one night together was seared in Nick's brain not just because of how electric their connection was, but because he couldn't forget how erotic it was just to *watch* her. She was a living siren, an entrancing creature that was completely aware of her own sensual power.

Her hands stroked lower until she gripped him firmly, stood him straight up, and then sank down until he slid deep.

"Oh shit." Nick couldn't hold back as she rocked against him, taking him deeper and deeper each time. "Give me your hands," he ordered. She grabbed his hands and used him as leverage to hold herself steady as she worked him.

He squeezed her hands, rewarded when she met his gaze. Her mouth fell open and she moaned as he rocked up under her, meeting her motions until they moved together in perfect rhythm. As overwhelming as the physical sensations were, he didn't want to close his eyes. He didn't want to miss the moment when she let go.

He wanted more than just to have her for a tumble. He wanted to possess her. He wanted everything she had to give.

It was a heady thing to realize that he already possessed her in the legal and moral sense.

She was his *wife*.

"Please, please…" Her soft chant faded into incoherent mumbling as he reached between their bodies and stroked her in time with his thrusts. She shuddered over him, her body clamping down on him like a tight wet fist.

"*Jesus*." He slowed down, determined to draw out her orgasm, but the tight contractions of her body were impossible to ignore. He felt the familiar burn of his own release. He didn't want to go without her.

Nick realized she was trying to avoid looking him directly in the eye. He growled. His lovely wife was in for a wakeup call if she thought she could keep their lovemaking impersonal. She didn't love him yet, but Nick refused to accept anything less than everything she had to give.

She didn't have to love him, but she wouldn't hide from him.

He let go of her hands and pulled her down so he could look in her eyes. She looked alarmed and tried to sit back up. "Nick. Wait—"

He held tight and anchored a hand in her hair. "I love you, Raina."

Her eyes softened at his words and he could see the answering response in her eyes.

That broke him. His orgasm shattered him into a thousand pieces as he came harder than ever before, like he was filling her with the feelings he could no longer deny.

The knowledge that she could soon be pregnant with his child made his orgasm even stronger. He was giving her an essential piece of himself, and he realized he wanted a child just as much as she did. He was going to be there for her and show her day after day that she could trust him to keep his promises. Starting with the most important one he'd ever made.

To love her until the day he died.

Chapter Seven

~

THE SEXY SMILE on her husband's face was Raina's first clue that she'd grossly miscalculated.

His enormous erection was the second.

"You're ready again? So soon?" Raina couldn't keep the astonishment from her voice. She'd taken control before, determined to keep their lovemaking as sexual as possible. It was enjoyable for her to be on top and seemed less intimate somehow. Like she was just having a good time.

Especially since she'd immediately rolled off him and

elevated her hips.

Nick stalked toward her, a confident smile on his face as he knelt next to her. "You didn't honestly think that was it, did you?"

Raina just stared at him as he took the glass of water she held and placed it on the nightstand. Dating an older man had definitely lowered her expectations when it came to recovery time. Her eyes dipped lower and a deep throb of arousal gripped her core. Nick looked painfully erect, almost as if he hadn't come just five minutes ago.

Clearly she was going to have to adjust her thinking about how to manage her new husband.

"See something you like, my love?"

She looked up to find Nick watching her from beneath lowered lashes, his eyes lingering on her mouth. How many nights had she dreamed a scenario just like this one? Nick, on his knees before her, kissing her, caressing her.

Telling her he loved her.

She flushed, the heat spreading from her cheeks down to her toes. It was bad enough to have these fantasies about him. It was unbearable for him to know about it. A man like Nick could have any woman he wanted and no doubt had plenty, probably more than one at a time.

But he didn't marry any of them, did he?

"I probably shouldn't move yet. I'm supposed to..." She motioned toward where her hips were elevated by a pillow. Nick's eyes followed her hand. He looked back at her and winked.

"I like to be thorough in everything I do. So I'm not convinced once is enough."

His lips rubbed hers once, then again, before she opened for him. His taste flooded her senses. He took her mouth slowly, savoring, drawing out the anticipation.

He moved the pillow gently until she was flat on her

back. When she started to protest, he said, "Trust me, okay?"

She nodded, shakily. He got on the bed and turned her until she fit in the curve of his body, her back to his chest, her bottom snug against his hips. His hand trailed over her rib cage and came to stop over her heart. Her breasts tightened in anticipation.

He squeezed the stiff tip of one of her nipples between his fingers and the sensation shot straight to her core. It had been so long since she'd been touched. Her skin was aching for it, practically crying out for more. She turned her head slowly and their eyes met. He looked golden in the fading sunlight coming in through the window.

Part of her wanted to turn away. Being with him like this in the soft light of early evening seemed too intimate. They were here for one purpose and one purpose only. To make a baby.

Him touching her like this, gently worshipping her with his hands, was more than she could handle.

"Nick, make love to me," she cried. Anything to stop the torturously slow motion of his hands over her skin.

"I am making love to you." He lifted her leg and hooked her ankle gently over his calf. In this position she was completely still but her body was open to anything Nick wanted to do.

He held her anchored to his chest with his right arm, his fingers playing gently with the tips of her nipples. He thrust into her from behind, going all the way deep on the first stroke. The sudden shocking invasion sent her headfirst into another orgasm.

"Sweet," he breathed in her ear. "Just the feel of you around me is so sweet."

Raina shuddered in his arms as he held her closer, not allowing her to retreat at all from the shocking intimacy of being bared to him so openly.

She'd thought she knew what to expect. After all, she was hardly a virgin and it wasn't like she hadn't had sex with Nick before. But she hadn't expected him to want to hold her. To caress her.

She hadn't expected him to love her like this.

"I love the idea that I'm filling you up when I come. Just the thought that I'm coming inside you, giving you my child, makes me crazy." Nick growled and held her tighter, pulling her leg up slightly so he could get in deeper.

"I love it, too." She reached back and grabbed his ass, tugging him up higher, encouraging him to thrust deeper. "Give me everything, Nick."

Her hands on him seemed to drive him wild because he took the lobe of her ear between his teeth and tugged.

"You already have it. You already have me."

When he came he clutched her tighter to his chest. She could feel him swell inside her.

It was carnal; it was dirty and wet and messy. But it was also real. Raw and beautiful. Something that she'd never shared with anyone else and never would.

It was undeniably Nick.

*　*　*　*　*

RAINA WOKE IN a haze of confusion. She sat up and pushed her long hair out of her face. The bed she was in was covered in soft, white sheets and a downy comforter. The rest of the room was still swathed in darkness but she could see the glow of daylight around the edges of the curtains.

Then she remembered. Nick. Vegas. *Wedding.*

"Nick," she called out. There was no answer. She held still and listened. Maybe he'd left to get them something to eat. If so, he'd probably left her a note.

She pushed back the comforter and climbed out of the bed, taking a moment to run her fingers through her hair. Even though she straightened it regularly, its natural inclination was so wild that she usually woke up looking like she'd been attacked. After she was fairly certain she wouldn't scare him with her appearance in case he was still there, she walked to the door of the hotel room and pulled it open.

The rest of the suite was bright. She walked out into the open living room. There was nothing next to the phone or on the minibar counter. Maybe he hadn't left after all. He might have just left her alone in the bedroom so as not to disturb her sleep.

"Nick, are you here?"

She listened but it was completely quiet. The curtains had been opened, revealing a stunning view of the Strip. She walked over and looked out onto the jumble of people, buildings, and neon lights. It looked like how she felt.

Out of control.

"I can't believe I got married."

Her handbag sat next to the couch. She remembered dropping it near the door when they'd gotten in yesterday. She groaned and covered her face with her hands. "I was so busy ripping my husband's clothes off that I forgot all about it." Nick must have picked up her things and put them back inside.

The door slammed behind her and she turned to see Nick at the door.

"Good morning, my beautiful wife."

Raina couldn't seem to stop smiling. "Oh my God. You're a morning person, aren't you?"

He crossed the room to her and kissed her on the forehead. "This surprises you more than anything else I've done?"

Raina smirked. "Well, I already knew you were a freak in bed."

"This is true." He set his keycard, a tray of coffee, and several brochures on the coffee table.

"I picked up a few pamphlets about things to do while we're in town. I figured we could check out a few clubs or maybe see a show." He gestured to the brochures. "There's some famous magician who does a show here, an erotic ballet that looks interesting and—"

"*The Phantom of the Opera*!" Raina exclaimed and snatched up one of the fliers.

"Yeah. That one's at The Venetian hotel. It's supposed to be pretty good but we don't have to see any of these shows. I just picked up a stack of pamphlets downstairs from the concierge."

Raina waved it back and forth. "I want to see this one!"

He laughed at her obvious delight. "Then I'll set it up. We can have dinner there, too."

Raina clapped, already imagining what the show would be like. She'd read Gaston Leroux's novel many times and seen several film adaptations over the years, but never seen it performed live. "I can't wait! It's one of the most romantic stories ever."

Nick raised an eyebrow. "A creepy guy stalking you and then kidnapping you and holding you underground is romantic?"

She stuck out her tongue. "Didn't you kidnap me? Besides, he's not stalking her. He's just consumed by his love for her. It's very complex. And *very* erotic."

"Oh, well. Maybe I need to give this show a chance after all." Nick leered and made a grab for her. She shrieked and fell back on the couch, giggling.

"How do you feel?" Nick sat next to her and stroked the back of her hand with his thumb.

"I'm fine," she replied. "Why wouldn't I be?"

Nick shrugged. He didn't meet her eyes when he said, "I just wanted to make sure I didn't hurt you. I thought you might be sore."

Raina sat up straighter on the couch, suddenly aware that she'd instinctively leaned into him. God, this keeping her distance thing was no easy feat. Just that quickly, she'd forgotten their purpose. She wasn't here to go to shows and gallivant around the Strip. They were supposed to be making a baby.

"Crap! I didn't take my temperature." Raina groaned and let her head drop back against the couch. She turned to Nick. "I should be ovulating today. I forgot to bring a thermometer so I could take my temperature, but I'll just have to hope that everything stayed on track."

"I can call down to the concierge and ask for one."

"I was supposed to take it first thing in the morning. Once you've been moving around, it's not accurate. For the purpose of pinpointing ovulation anyway." She reached down into her bag and pulled out her cell phone. She had a missed call from Ridley and five from Sam.

"Oh boy. He's pissed at me," she muttered.

Nick looked over at her. "Who's pissed at you?"

She held up her phone. "Sam's been trying to get in touch with me. I texted him before we got on the plane." After heaving a great sigh, she called Sam back. He answered immediately and after several very pointed questions about her sanity, she assured him that she was fine and would be back after the weekend.

After hanging up, she looked over at Nick. His jaw was clenched tight.

"Is he satisfied now that I haven't chopped you up in little pieces and buried you in my backyard?" he asked.

"Sam's been a part of my life for a long time. He looks out for me and keeps me safe while I travel around to different shoots. It's his job to be worried about where I am. But it's nothing more than that."

He looked at her finally. "I believe you."

"Good. Now, as to the reason we're here, I think we should stay in tonight."

"All night?" When she nodded, Nick whistled.

"Damn, girl. Not that I mind at all but were you going to let me out of the bed to eat?"

"Nick! Stop teasing me."

"We have to go out sometime. So it might as well be to a show that you want to see." He pulled her into his lap. "I don't mind making love to you before and after the show."

He reached into the bag in his lap. Raina hadn't even noticed he carried something. "I brought you a croissant and some coffee. We can go downstairs and get something else if you want. Or we could order room service." He fed her a small bite of the croissant. Raina sighed as it melted on her tongue like butter.

"Why are you being so accommodating? I feel like you must have an ulterior motive."

"I do have an ulterior motive." Nick broke off another piece of the pastry and held it to her lips. "My ulterior motive is to get you to fall in love with me. Because being in love all on your own isn't nearly as much fun."

Raina almost choked on the bite she'd just taken. After a few swallows, she sat back and glared at him. "Not fair."

"It's not fair to tell my wife I'm in love with her?" he asked quietly.

Raina pushed away and looked him in the face. "Oh my God. I thought you were just saying that to get a reaction. You're serious."

"I told you I loved you last night. Over and over again, if I recall correctly."

"That was pillow talk," Raina stammered. "Everyone knows you don't trust what a man says in bed."

Nick stared at his hands. "I always say what I mean. Even in bed."

Raina stood up and faced the window. "Nick, I know things got a little… intense last night but my feelings haven't changed. Well, they *have* changed. I've seen a different side of you. One I like a lot. But I don't want any more than that. This is why I wanted to keep emotion out of it. It's too easy for us to forget why we're here. If you don't feel you can stick to our original agreement, then we should stop this now before it goes any further."

She held her breath, waiting for his reply. What if he decided to renege? Technically, she could already be pregnant with his child. What a mess. The seconds that passed before he answered seemed to take eons.

"No, I don't want to stop this."

She didn't turn as he walked away. A moment later, the door shut with a decisive *click*.

She whirled around, shocked to see that he'd actually left the hotel room. Her shoulders sagged and she sat on the floor right where she stood.

Way to be sensitive, Raina.

Hurting him had never been her intention. She was trying to prevent either of them from being hurt by getting too involved. It was better if she went into this without any unreasonable expectations. What he thought was love was more than likely just the novelty of finally hooking up with one of the few women who'd ever turned him down. She imagined he wasn't used to being denied.

Which made protecting her heart even more essential.

Nick was gorgeous and brilliant, but he was also immature and selfish. He didn't mean any harm but he had the power to crush her whether he meant for it to happen or not. When he was tired of her, Nick would move on to the next available woman. Raina would be left heartbroken, raising their baby alone. Something she couldn't let happen.

Nicholas Alexander could love any woman he wanted, except for her.

* * * * *

NICK SCRUBBED HIS hands over his hair and blinked through the curtain of water in his face before picking up one of the tiny bottles of shampoo provided by the hotel. He dumped a glob in his hand and soaped his hair. After he rinsed it out, he used some of the conditioner. He was contemplating using the conditioner again—anything to prolong the shower—before he finally shut the water off.

He'd been in the shower so long his skin was starting to prune up, but it was preferable to what was waiting for him on the other side of the bathroom door.

Another dose of Raina telling him that she didn't want his love, just his sperm.

"Damn it all to hell."

He'd spent the entire afternoon hanging out in the casino. He'd wasted a large sum of money and made a new friend named Gino, all while replaying their argument over and over in his head.

"You just couldn't play it cool, could you?" he muttered. If he weren't in the shower he'd kick something. Clearly experience had taught him nothing when dealing with Raina. He kept making the same mistakes over and over again. Most guys would be happy with a woman who didn't seem to want emotional involvement. It was the main reason he'd avoided any talk of marriage with his prior girlfriends. Just the thought of being with any of them forever had seemed so final. Like he was giving up something.

With Raina, he didn't feel he was sacrificing anything since she was the only woman he thought about anyway.

His dick seemed not to care whether he was happy or not because it filled and stood straight up at just the thought of his wife. It seemed his body was ready to perform on cue even if his mind wasn't.

He toweled off quickly and didn't bother getting dressed. What was the point if he was just going to have to get naked again anyway? No more trying to find things that would please her. No more dressing up and trying to look good. He could just lay around all weekend stark-naked so she could jump on his dick and ride him whenever her temperature was right or whatever.

"If a stud puppy is what she wants, that's what she'll get."

He yanked open the door to the bathroom. Raina sat on the couch looking out onto the sparkling lights of the Strip. It was an incredible view and he stood for a moment watching her, how peaceful she was sitting there, looking out into the night.

She looked back at him, then jumped to her feet when she saw he was naked. "Nick, what are you doing?"

He sat on the couch and patted his thighs. "Aren't you ready for me by now?" He ran a hand down his chest and gripped his dick. "Stud puppy, reporting for duty."

She winced. "Don't say that. This isn't what I wanted."

He leaned closer. There were pale streaks under her eyes like she'd been crying. The sight hit him like a fist. The thought of her up here crying her eyes out over him didn't make him feel any better. "I'm sorry. That was uncalled for."

"I don't want you to be angry with me." Raina sat next to him on the couch.

He wiped under her eyes with his thumb. "I hate that I made you cry."

Nick sighed. He was the one who'd changed the rules of the game after the fact. She'd warned him up front that she wasn't looking for love. If he was going to change her mind, he couldn't stalk off in a snit every time she hurt his feelings. The question was did he think it was worth it to endure a few blows while trying to change her mind? He looked over at Raina and his heart rolled over in his chest.

Hell, yeah.

"What do you say to a compromise?" Nick leaned back against the couch, pulling her with him until she relaxed against his chest.

"What kind of compromise?" She looked up at him warily.

"I'll accept that you just want sex if you can accept that I feel more. I don't think I can hide my emotions and I don't think either of us should have to. Isn't the point of this for us to communicate openly?"

She nodded slowly. "Yes, I guess so."

"Well, then I'll accept how you feel and you'll accept me caring for you. Can you do that, Raina? Can you let me care for you?"

She stared at him like she was trying to figure out what the catch was. "Okay. I can try."

It was obvious when she remembered he was naked. Her gaze dropped to his waist before she looked back up at him, her eyes suddenly soft. Her breathing sped up a little. He probably wouldn't have noticed if she wasn't lying on his chest. But the little hitch in her breathing told him she was affected.

Nick groaned when she turned and placed her hands against his chest. She pushed lightly but when he didn't move, she made a soft sound in the back of her throat and grabbed at his chest, her nails leaving little scratches on his skin. Before he knew it, she was pulling him down to her, threading her fingers through his hair.

She bit his bottom lip and sucked it into her mouth and he stopped thinking. He picked her up and carried her back to the bedroom. When he placed her gently on the bed, she got up on her knees and tried to pull him down on top of her.

"We have to get your clothes off," Nick managed to say in between her kisses.

It was pure chemical reaction between them, her skin scorching him through her clothes. He yanked at the fastenings to her shorts, nearly tearing them off in his haste before returning to stand in the cradle of her thighs, pressing against the heat of her mound.

At the first touch of her lips against his chest, he groaned and grabbed her by the ponytail. She seemed to like the pain because she arched her back and cried out.

Which set him off like a match being lit.

He helped her pull her shirt over her head and it fell to the floor in a heap. Immediately she wiggled her hips to get out of her panties and in moments she knelt before him naked.

"Scoot back."

She looked at him with narrowed eyes as if she wanted to protest. But she backed up slowly until she reclined against the pillows. He crawled over her, the dim light of the lamp throwing his shadow over her.

"Lay back and put your hands over your head." He pushed her shoulders gently until she lay flat, spread out like a feast before him. She looked good enough to eat with soft, dewy lips and buttery skin from head to toe.

Brushing a knuckle over the damp skin between her legs, he was pleased to feel her clench against his hand. Her body bowed into a beautiful curve as she arched at the contact. He chuckled as her eyes hungrily followed his movements when he sat back to look at her.

"Touch me, Nick. Please." She trailed a hand down her stomach. When he didn't move, she stroked lower.

He leaped forward and gripped her wrist. "Aren't you a naughty girl? I didn't say you could touch what's mine."

Her chin jutted upward in defiance. "Is it yours?"

"You tell me." He rubbed his thumb over her cleft, the scent of her passion enveloping him, drugging him. Her eyes fluttered shut as he curled two fingers into her heat. Her body clenched him so sweetly, contracting around his fingers.

He had to get inside her. *Now.*

He lifted one of her legs onto his shoulder and pushed inside, her wet heat sucking him in. He took his time, stroking slowly, willing her tight body to accept him. Her mouth fell open as he fed her his length inch by inch until their bodies finally met again.

She grasped at his shoulders, her nails digging in deep as she held on. He thrust deeply, joining them skin to skin, reveling in the crash and slide of their bodies. He kissed her hard, swallowing her cries of delight. Her head fell back on the pillow and he licked the curve of her collarbone and the soft skin of her neck. He loved having her taste in his mouth, her sweat on his skin, and her flesh in his hands. He wanted to get lost in her and never come back.

"Nick, I can't..." She lost her words, her hands grasping at his back as her orgasm consumed her. Her hands tangled in his hair, holding him to her breast, her nails digging into his scalp.

"Oh God. It's so good. Nick!"

His name on her lips was the stuff of fantasy. He turned his head and latched onto her breast, tonguing her nipple until it tightened in his mouth and her inner muscles clamped down on him. He reared up and took her mouth, tracing her lips with his tongue. He wanted her crazy for him, wanted to invade her in every way possible.

Wanted her hungry for him.

"I love you, Raina." He held her head in the palm of his hand so she couldn't look away. "And I am going to tell you every day until you believe it."

"Nick! Oh God, I can't..." She let out the sexiest little whimper. She was taking him so deep, clenching around him hard, and he knew she was coming again.

It was enough to send him over the edge, his release rocketing through him. It stunned him, the force of his orgasm causing him to shake. He clenched his fingers around her waist hard enough to leave bruises.

"Damn, Raina." He pressed his lips against the soft skin of her breastbone and laid his head against her breast. He could feel her heart hammering beneath her ribs. It gave him a very masculine sense of satisfaction to feel her fingers clench and unclench on his leg as she rode out the final pulses of her own release.

Chapter Eight

RAINA KNEW THAT the time of reckoning was coming, starting with the lecture she would get from Sam and ending with the teary-eyed questions from her sister. It was cowardly but she couldn't help wishing they could put it off a little longer.

After their intense lovemaking on Friday night, they'd spent the next day alternating between dining at each of the hotel's fine restaurants and doing dirty, unbelievably erotic things in bed. He'd taken her to *The Phantom of the Opera* on Saturday night and Raina had adored the show. It was too bad she'd only paid attention to half of it because Nick had spent the second act with his hand up her skirt.

He'd tortured her with slow, feathery strokes for almost half an hour before he'd finally thrust two fingers inside her, capturing her cry with his mouth as she'd come hard enough to almost lose consciousness.

Sunday had been more of the same. They'd eaten breakfast in bed and hadn't gotten out of it for more than a few minutes at a time the rest of the day. Well, she'd asked Nick to get her pregnant. There was no way she could accuse him of not being thorough.

But they'd had to come back to the real world at some point.

She placed a hand against her lower abdomen. Although, hopefully she was coming back to the real world with something more than what she'd left with.

"I think it's best if we take some time apart now that we're back."

Nick set her bags down next to the couch and then turned to face her. The set of his jaw told her he wasn't going to go easily. But after three days of constant contact with him, she needed a break from his support, his smile, his sexalicious *smell*. Everything about the man called out to her on a basic biological level.

If she was going to have any chance at keeping her heart protected, she was in desperate need of some Nick-free time.

"Are you pulling away from me, Raina?"

"No, I'm really not. It's just that I know things are going to be hectic for me and I'm sure they will be for you, too."

"Yeah, I pretty much just left my office in the lurch, but it was worth it."

His smile did funny things to her, making her want to

drop this whole separation idea and yank him by the collar back into the bedroom. But her fertile window was over. She was either pregnant now or she wasn't. If she wanted to have even a prayer of keeping her emotions unentangled, random afternoon delights with her hunk of a husband had to be off-limits.

Off-limits.

"Yeah it was..." She hesitated, unsure if calling their three-day sex fest "fun" was really the message she wanted to send. "I think it'll be worth it. I'll know in two weeks if we achieved our goal."

"Even if we didn't, then we'll just have to try again. I don't want you to worry about it. Stress isn't good for you, right?"

"Right. That's why I'm going to rest for a while. I know you'll probably have to work late a lot this week, so you don't have to worry about coming back here and checking up on me."

Nick pulled her by the hand until she looked him directly in the eye. "If I know you, your idea of resting is answering emails and calling a bunch of people. That doesn't sound very stress free to me."

"Sam won't let me overdo."

Nick's face darkened. "Sam isn't your husband. *I am.* Which means that I will see you at dinner tonight, Mrs. Alexander. My parents rarely spent a night apart. I don't have any intention of us doing so, either." Then he kissed her on the forehead and left.

Raina stared after him long after the door closed. It would be so much easier to be pissed if she wasn't glowing from him calling her "Mrs. Alexander."

"Ugh. I'm like a teenage girl writing his name on my notebook in sparkly glitter ink." She pulled out her cell phone and called her sister. After a brief conversation, they agreed that Ridley would come over in about an hour. Raina found herself strangely excited to talk to her sister. Usually Ridley was the one with cute stories about the things Jackson had done for her. Now it was Raina's turn.

She turned at the sound of the door closing. Sam stood in the doorway watching her.

"Hey. We're back," she said when he didn't speak. It occurred to her after she said it how stupid that was. He wouldn't be here if he didn't know she was back.

"I see that."

"I know you're really mad—"

"Mad? Raina, I think I lost about three decades of my life this weekend. You think you can just ditch me and fly off to Vegas? You hired me to protect you, but you have to let me do my job. I should quit and let you figure out your own shit."

Panic lanced through her at his words. It wasn't like she was some major celebrity, but with all the travel she did to foreign countries, it gave her an incredible peace of mind to know that she had Sam watching her back. More than that, he was someone she'd grown truly fond of over the last five years.

"Don't leave me, Sam."

Something in her voice must have gotten through to him because he crossed to her and picked her up in a bear hug. Startled, she held stock-still until he set her on her feet again.

"You'd better not ever do that again." The red strips of color on his cheeks betrayed his agitation.

"I really scared you, didn't I?" she whispered.

He coughed. "Yeah. You did."

"I didn't mean to. Everything just happened so fast. Nick makes me do things I shouldn't do."

"I'm starting to think that Alexander is the only one who can get you to act based on emotion. Which is not a bad thing, except when it involves running off to another state without letting me know. And a text message is not how I define letting me know. Anyone could have sent that. I need to hear your voice."

"I am so sorry." A wave of shame washed over her. It had felt incredibly freeing to run off and do something spontaneous, but looking at things from Sam's perspective, she could see how selfish it had been. She would probably quit in his place.

Sam scowled at her. "Uh huh. Don't think I'm letting you off that easy. You missed our Saturday workout and it's time for you to get back on track. Go get changed!"

Raina knew she was forgiven if he was willing to hold the heavy bag for her. "Thanks, Sam."

She grabbed the small suitcase she'd taken to Vegas and carried it upstairs to her room. Her room had always been her personal oasis. Now she would be sharing it with Nick.

Was she really ready for that?

She dropped the suitcase on the bed so she'd be forced to unpack it before going to sleep that night, then quickly changed into shorts and a sports tank and pulled her hair up into a ponytail.

It was weird to be doing the usual things, knowing that Nick would be coming home to her in a few hours. It was almost like she was living in some alternate dimension where everything looked the same but nothing was.

It was time to figure out what her new reality would be.

*   *   *   *   *

AT HIS OFFICE, Nick was trying hard not to let his mind wander to what Raina was doing. He knew exactly what her game was. She was hoping that by pushing him away as soon as they got back to their real lives, she could write their newfound intimacy off as part of "what happens in Vegas, stays in Vegas."

But he wasn't going to make it that easy for her.

"I brought the new bids that we were supposed to do Friday," Kay said. "Also, I need to head out a little earlier than usual today. Jackson wants to record tonight. I sent you a message Friday as soon as he told me about it. Sorry for the late notice."

"No problem. I thoroughly enjoyed my time off and I certainly don't begrudge anyone else theirs."

Kay looked relieved. "Thanks, sir. I'd better go now or I'll be late."

"Good luck with the recording."

He listened with half an ear as Kay gathered her things and shut down her computer. He heard her call out when she finally left, but his mind was still on the scene that morning. How was he supposed to romance his wife when she wanted them to live in separate houses?

All the usual things wouldn't have any effect on Raina. She probably received flowers all the time, and considering that she was a model, clothes and jewelry weren't going to be much of a thrill, either. If he was going to give her a gift, it needed to be something she wouldn't think to buy for herself. Something that showed her how committed to this marriage he really was.

Basically a miracle in a box.

He did an Internet search for "gifts" and browsed several pages of images. He considered a package for a luxury island vacation, then quickly moved on. Raina traveled all the time. Plus, the point was to keep her stress level low so she could get pregnant. Putting her through the rare torture of airport security and a long flight was probably counterproductive.

"This being in love stuff is harder than it looks," Nick muttered.

The problem, he realized, was that he was trying to buy her something to convince her that he was a nice guy. But there was really no product in the world that could do that. She needed to see that his intentions were pure based on his actions, not something he bought.

His eyes went to his briefcase. The top of the pregnancy book he'd picked up at the bookstore on the way in stuck out of the top. It was a heavy tome, easily six hundred pages of tiny text and weird, black-and-white charts and diagrams. He'd tried to read a little of it in the bookstore but the pictures of tiny bloblike cells had creeped him out a little. He felt incredibly juvenile being squeamish about a book.

"I can do this. Let's read about pregnancy." He flipped it open and paged past the initial sections about conception. No grown man should need a primer on that part, he reasoned. He stopped at the section entitled *The First Trimester*. After several pages, he had to wonder if getting Raina pregnant was such a good idea. Nausea, mood swings, fatigue, and tender breasts sounded like the symptoms of a disease, not pregnancy.

By the time he'd finished the whole section, he was almost afraid to read any more. What the hell had he been thinking? He'd gone into this assuming it would just be having a whole lot of sex and then bringing Raina ice cream and pickles for nine months. But there were all these warnings and rules that he'd had no idea about. They weren't supposed to have sex with her on her back. And then what if he penetrated her too deeply? They hadn't even talked about a birth plan.

He had no idea what he was doing!

"Hello, anyone here?"

Nick looked up at the deep voice echoing from the

reception area. "I'm in my office." A few seconds later, Elliot walked in.

"You haven't gotten a new assistant yet?"

Nick accepted his handshake and then they bumped shoulders. "She had to leave early. This one is actually working out. She's a singer in Jackson's new group."

"You're not banging her, are you? That could get sticky."

Nick recoiled. "No."

It wasn't an unfair question, considering his past, but just the thought made him feel wrong. What a change. It wouldn't have even registered a little while ago and he would have just shrugged it off. But now he had to wonder if this was what Raina thought of him. Did she think he just slept with anything that moved?

Was she worried about him being faithful?

"So what brings you by in the middle of the week? Mom will be excited to see you." Elliot owned and operated a security firm a few hours north in Washington, D.C. They usually only saw him on the weekends.

"Oh, I think she's already excited. You've just made her the happiest woman on the East Coast probably."

Nick stared at him blankly. "What did I do? Not that I'm complaining. It's better to be on her good side."

"Did you really think you could get married and we wouldn't find out? What is wrong with you?"

Nick lost his breath. "You know about that?"

"This is not the 1990s. Technology has ruined the ability for people to do stupid shit without anyone finding out. A fan of Raina's saw the two of you entering a chapel in Vegas and posted the picture on Twitter. I'm sure you can imagine my surprise this weekend when someone asked me about your wedding."

Elliot stopped talking suddenly. Nick followed his gaze

to where the pregnancy book lay open on his desk. A large diagram of a fetus was clearly visible.

Elliot looked back at him, no longer joking. "Well, I didn't see that one coming. You've been busy, little brother."

Nick covered his mouth with his hand. "You have no idea."

"When were you planning on filling us in?" Eli asked quietly. His brother wasn't usually chatty and he was hardly the sensitive type, but if Nick didn't know better, he'd think Eli's feelings were hurt.

"I was going to tell you all today, I swear. It all happened so fast. I saw that Mom left me a message but I didn't even listen to it. I was planning on stopping by later."

Elliot popped him on the back of the head.

"Ouch! Damn, Eli. What was that for? I already apologized."

Eli shook his head. "That was on behalf of your poor wife. Do you really think Mom is going to just sit back and wait for you to bring Raina to the house?"

Nick thought of Raina alone at her house, opening her front door to a crowd of Alexanders.

"Oh no."

Elliot nodded. "That's right."

Nick whipped out his cell phone and dialed Raina's number. It rang several times before voicemail picked up. "She's not answering. This is about to be bad. Really bad."

Elliot snorted. "You haven't seen bad. I hope your bride is ready for the invasion. Let's go rescue her."

* * * * *

"Harder. *Harder!*" Sam grunted when Raina punched

the heavy bag three times in quick succession. "Just because you disappeared for three days doesn't mean you get to ignore your workouts. Vacation time is over." He patted the bag and waited until she punched again, this time with enough force to knock it back against him.

"That's more like it."

Rock music blared from the speakers behind her as Raina channeled every bit of her rage at the face she was imagining on the bag in front of her.

Thwack. That was for being so convincing. *Thwack.* That was for invading so much of her mental space. *Thwack.* That was for being so damn good-looking.

She stopped in mid-punch at the thought. God, she was supposed to be using this time to catch up on things and gain some perspective. Instead, she was just daydreaming about him. How was she supposed to think of anything but him when he looked at her like that, like their marriage was real? Like she was his whole world.

The man was pure evil.

"Any other man would take offense to that." Sam raised an eyebrow when her eyes met his.

"Oh. I wasn't actually talking about you." Raina stopped punching and blew out her breath.

Sam slapped the bag. "If you've got enough energy to daydream, clearly I'm not working you hard enough. Come on. Go again."

Raina groaned. "I take it back. I was talking about you. You are evil."

"But you look good, right?"

Raina punched the bag once more, satisfied when he jumped at the sudden movement.

"You bet your ass I do." She stretched her arms overhead, reveling in the burn of her muscles.

Building a fully quipped home gym was one of the first things she'd done when she bought the house. Modeling was a career where women had a much shorter-than-average shelf life as a rule. Raina was smart enough to know her days were numbered, but she was determined to stay in the game as long as possible and then transition over into several side projects she was working on. Now that she'd gotten a network to carry her reality show, she was hoping it would do well enough for her to land a book deal. If everyone from Snooki to those housewives on TV could get publishing contracts, then why not her?

Sam walked over to the small cooler in the corner of her home gym and pulled out two bottles. He handed her one and then took a deep swig of his.

"Yuck. What is this stuff?" Sam held the bottle of bright green liquid away from him as if it was toxic.

"It's called Grenade. Remember the ad I did for the vitamin supplement? Well, one of the marketing guys sent me some free samples of their newest product."

Sam shook his head and placed the cap back on his bottle. "I can see why they're giving it away."

They were interrupted by a loud chirping sound. Raina had just taken a big sip of her own drink, so she just pointed toward the treadmill where she'd left her cell phone. Sam walked over and picked it up. After a quick glance at the screen, he smirked.

"It's Alexander. You want me to answer?"

Raina gulped down the mouthful of bitter juice and held out her hand. As soon as he gave it to her, she hit the button to silence the call. Sam narrowed his eyes.

"What? I'll just call him back after I'm done working out."

Sam shrugged. "Okay. Whatever you say. But just tell me one thing. And you have to promise to tell me the truth."

Raina sighed and put her bottle back in the

refrigerator. She didn't meet his eyes, just went back over to the heavy bag and waited. When he didn't follow, she let out a loud, exasperated sigh.

"I have many faults, but I've never been a liar. Ask me anything. Maybe then you'll finally stop worrying."

Sam waited until she came back and stood next to him. "Do you love this guy?"

Raina bit her lip. "You know I don't believe in love. He's a nice guy and I think he'll make a great dad. I love that about him."

"Don't tell me you don't believe in love. If something bad happened to him, how would you feel? Would you be sad for a few minutes and then move on?"

Raina picked at the edge of the boxing glove she held. She didn't have to be in love with him to miss his smile. His laughter. His way of talking her off the ledge when she was worried about something. Even in the abstract the thought of anything happening to Nick made her heart race.

"No, I wouldn't just be sad for a few minutes."

She had a feeling that if anything happened to Nick, she'd be sad for the rest of her life.

Chapter Nine

~

RAINA TURNED AT the sound of the bathroom door banging open. After finishing her workout, she'd immediately come upstairs to shower and wash her hair. Sam wouldn't bother her unless it was important. She pushed the glass shower door to the side slightly and called out, "Sam? What's wrong?"

"It's not Sam. It's me."

Raina pulled the door open a bit more and stuck her head out into the cold air of the bathroom. "Ridley? What are you doing here?"

Ridley was wearing a pair of leggings with a hole in the knee and the ugliest sweatshirt she'd ever seen.

"And what the hell are you wearing? I hope no one saw you dressed like that."

Ridley glared at her and pulled her towel off the rack. "I'm trying to save *you*. Mrs. Alexander came by the house. She heard about your marriage and wanted me to bring her to see her new daughter-in-law. She's downstairs. Right now!"

Raina squeaked and slammed the shower door shut. "Oh my God. I can't meet my mother-in-law looking like a drowned rat. I am going to kill Nick! I thought he was going to wait to tell everyone."

"Raina, it's all over the internet that you got married."

"It is?"

"Yes. *Everybody* knows now. Come on, it's time to face the music."

"Can't you stall her?" Raina whined. It was cowardly, yes, but dammit, she wasn't good with parents. They wanted nice, sweet, daughters-in-law who baked cupcakes and stuff. Not girls like her who were better at pouting on a sexy ad campaign.

This is going to be a disaster.

Ridley pulled open the shower door, letting in a blast of freezing air. "You're saying that because you don't know Julia Alexander. Trust me, if I don't come down there with you in a few minutes, she'll come up here and find you herself."

Raina pushed her wet hair off her face and shut the water off. "Okay, I'm coming." She took the towel her sister handed through the open door and wrapped it around herself, trying to stop the shivers wracking her body.

"I'll go pick you out some clothes." Ridley left, leaving the bathroom door wide open.

Raina toweled off quickly, then wrapped the towel around her body and knotted it under her arm.

Ridley came back in with her clothes and dropped them on the counter. "Okay, I'm going back down there to help with dinner. Hopefully cooking will distract her."

Raina's head shot up. "Dinner? I don't have any food in the house."

"She brought it all with her. I guess this is your 'welcome to the family' dinner. Now hurry up!"

As soon as Ridley left, Raina yanked off the towel and pulled on her clothes. She pulled out a wide-toothed comb and gently detangled her hair section by section. There was no time for blow-drying and flat-ironing. She'd have to just put it back in a braid.

The doorbell rang downstairs and she paused. Had Mrs. Alexander gone to get something from her car and gotten locked out? When it didn't ring again, she figured Ridley must have opened the door for her, so she hurriedly applied tinted moisturizer and swept a single coat of mascara on her lashes. She surveyed herself in the mirror.

She looked terrified.

"Here goes nothing," she muttered.

As soon as she descended the stairs, she could hear them. *How can two people make that much noise?* It sounded like a circus troupe had set up shop in her kitchen. She rounded the corner and stopped at the sight of the full room.

"There she is," someone said.

The entire room went silent and what felt like a million pairs of eyes fixed on her at the same time.

A short woman in a lacy blue dress came forward and grabbed her hands. "Raina, we're all so glad to meet you. I'm Nick's mother, Julia."

She'd met Steven's mother once when she'd been in

New York for the symphony. She was tall, thin, impeccably dressed, and just as stuffy and formal as her son.

Julia Alexander, on the other hand, was a short plump woman with a café-au-lait complexion. She wore her dark hair in a bob of pin curls that made Raina think of the old-fashioned pink rollers her mother used to wear.

She looked *warm*, Raina decided.

"Hello. I'm so glad to meet you, Mrs. Alexander."

"Oh sweetheart, just call me Julia. Or Mom. After all, you're Mrs. Alexander now, too."

Raina felt like her head was spinning as she was enveloped into a warm hug.

Julia pulled back and preened. "Oh, just look at you. Just as pretty as a picture! Of course, we knew that already. Come, come and meet the family."

Raina followed silently as she was led over to the group. She was hugged by Nick's father, Mark, first. Then she said hello to Nick's older brother, Bennett. He shook her hand and smiled politely. Then Mark introduced her to his younger sister, Maria. Next was Maria's daughter, Laura, her husband, Peter and their two children, Isabelle and Annabelle. She placed a hand over her racing heart. What if she couldn't remember any of their names? By the time they circled around to where Jackson and Ridley stood, Raina felt like her head was spinning with faces.

Ridley pulled her in for a hug and said in a low voice, "I had no idea she invited the whole family!"

Before Raina could respond, the front door opened. Nick stood in the doorway, breathing hard. "Raina!" he called out. He took a few steps then stopped short when he finally noticed everyone in the kitchen. "Oh boy."

Raina walked over to him and hugged him.

"I am so sorry," he whispered. "When Elliot warned

110

me, I came as fast as I could."

He looked like he'd run from the car to the house. Her earlier annoyance vanished as he struggled to catch his breath. It was kind of sweet that he'd come so quickly to "rescue" her.

"It's okay," she said. "I think I can handle a little family time."

"You might not say that after an hour of this," Nick warned.

Raina watched as everyone moved around her kitchen, following Julia's orders to set the table and carry the food out. It was so odd to see the dining room table her decorator had ordered filled to overflowing with platters and bowls of food. There was macaroni and cheese, chicken, both baked and southern-fried, and the most delicious potato salad she'd ever tasted. It was also *loud*. Everyone talked over everyone else in a delightful jumble of sound.

"So, Raina. You have a reality show now," Bennett asked. He was seated on her left side. They were the only people at the table not talking.

He spoke slowly and Raina noticed that he stumbled and stuttered over several of his words. He was different from the rest of his brothers who all seemed so confident and outgoing. He also looked different than the rest of his family. He was the palest one of them and his brown eyes were lighter with a sprinkling of green through them. He was also the only one who wore glasses. She thought he must have always been the oddball in such a boisterous, loud, confident family.

She liked him immediately.

When he noticed her watching him, he lowered his eyes. A slight blush tinged his cheeks. "S...sorry if we weren't supposed to ask about it. Mom told us."

"No, no. It's okay. It's public knowledge now. I signed

the deal a few weeks ago, so it should air early next year if all goes to plan. I'm really excited about it."

She looked around at everyone else. There were several conversations going on at once and a heated argument at the end of the table between Mark and Eli about football.

"Sorry if I'm not the best company."

Bennett glanced at her. "We can be a bit much to take at times. Mom's not normally this pushy. It's just that we thought you were a friend of Jackson's. When we heard you and Nick got married... She just couldn't take the suspense of waiting to find out. She thought he'd never settle down. Sorry if we bombarded you all at once."

"It's okay. I'm just not used to all... this." She gestured around the table. "I can't even imagine belonging to a big family."

Bennett smiled at her. "Well, you're Nick's wife, so you belong to one now."

That, it seemed, was all it took to be accepted.

* * * * *

A MONTH LATER, Raina stood at the window looking out into the backyard of Jackson's house. Jackson's sons, Chris and Jase, romped outside, chasing each other through the sprinklers. Every few minutes they would fall to the ground, rolling around in the wet grass. Her sister was going to have a disgusting pile of clothes to launder later, but they were having a great time. Happy shrieks and giggles filled the air.

"Raina, are you okay?"

Ridley stood behind her, putting the finishing touches on the spicy spaghetti casserole dish she was making for that night's dinner.

She'd started to feel guilty that Nick handled most of

their meals on the nights they didn't order takeout. He was a great cook and didn't seem to mind, but she'd asked Ridley to teach her to make a simple dish. Once it became clear that Raina was hopeless though, Ridley had abandoned the lesson.

She put a hand against her lower abdomen and turned to face her sister. "I'm okay. I'm just not pregnant."

It had been a chaotic month, filled with the awkward dance of two individuals set in their ways trying to learn to compromise.

Nick liked the left side of the bed but so did she. He had given in on that one, but since he slept cuddled up to her back, it didn't really matter anyway. He was kind of a slob and Raina liked things neat. She'd been the one to make concessions there. A stray shoe in the middle of the floor or a shirt hanging over a chair in the bedroom wasn't the end of the world.

She'd been disappointed upon discovering that their time in Vegas hadn't yielded the desired results, but not that surprised. Nick had been more than anxious to try again a few weeks later. She blushed remembering just how excited he'd been.

"Oh, Ray. I thought you looked sad."

Ridley dropped the bag of shredded cheese she held and came from around the kitchen island. "I'm really sorry. I know how much you wanted to be."

Raina took a deep breath. "Yeah, I did. I'm trying not to hear the doctor's voice of doom and gloom in my head. But the fact is that every month that goes by where I'm not pregnant means it'll be that much harder for me to get there."

"It'll happen. This was just your second month trying, right?"

"I know. I'm determined to stay positive. Plus everything was kind of chaotic with the whole running off to Vegas thing. Then there was the stress of trying to adjust to living together. This time, I'm ready."

"I just hope *Nick* is ready. You have to let the poor guy out of bed at some point."

"You have an incredibly dirty mind since hooking up with Jackson, you know that? I was referring to the fact that I'm calmer this time. Too much excitement can throw off your ovulation. I should be able to pinpoint my ovulation date with more accuracy this time."

Ridley wrinkled her nose. "Oh, that doesn't sound like fun. All that charting and temperature taking and whatever. I like my way better. Just chain my handsome brother-in-law to the bed and have your way with him until the deed is done."

"Is this what you two talk about when we're not around?"

They both jumped at the sound of Jackson's voice. He stood in the doorway that connected the kitchen to the family room. He raised his eyebrows at Ridley's shocked expression.

"Um, hey baby. How long have you been standing there?"

Jackson came behind her and wrapped her in his arms. "Long enough to know that your version of 'girl talk' differs vastly from mine."

Raina laughed. "She used to blush when I even mentioned sex. Apparently you've corrupted my sister, because she never talked like this before. "

Jackson nuzzled Ridley's neck and held there, like he was just breathing her in. "I certainly hope so," he whispered against her neck.

It was easier to be around them lately, even when they were being so openly affectionate. Nick had stuck to their agreement. He didn't hide his feelings but he didn't pressure her to return them. Over the past few weeks, they'd settled into a comfortable rhythm. He didn't seem bored or confined by married life, either.

Not yet, anyway.

She knew it was dangerous to get attached to the way Nick treated her, but it was hard not to enjoy it. Even couples who'd been deeply in love for years admitted the feelings you had in the beginning didn't last. Their honeymoon phase would wear off just like anyone else's, but in the meantime she was just going to soak up the attention. She'd have to be a total ice queen not to enjoy having a handsome man at her beck and call.

She hugged herself and remembered how Nick had kissed her until her eyes almost rolled into the back of her head before leaving for work that morning. The whole lovey-dovey thing was a lot easier to understand from the inside looking out. Feelings this strong had to have an outlet. When she was around Nick it took active thought on her part *not* to touch him or look at him or grin like a fool.

How ironic was it that all the things she used to scoff at were the things she most looked forward to now?

Ridley pursed her lips. "It just took the right man. And a couple of the erotic novels that I ordered online."

Jackson popped her on the bottom playfully. "Let's hope I had more influence than a book!"

"I would say yes but I think you are greatly underestimating the power of a hot book."

"Did you tell her the good news?" Jackson motioned toward Raina.

Ridley shook her head. "I didn't get a chance yet." She turned to Raina and grinned. "We've decided to move up the date of the wedding. To Labor Day."

Raina did a quick mental calculation. "Labor Day as in two weeks from now?"

Ridley nodded. "I know it's crazy but Julia said the

115

pastor was performing a wedding out of town that weekend but they just found out that wedding was canceled. We'd mentioned to her before that we kind of wished we'd just run off and gotten married like you and Nick did. So when she heard about that cancellation, she immediately asked Pastor Robbins if he would consider marrying us that weekend instead."

"Wow. That's amazing. But what about all your plans? Your dress and the flowers and everything."

Ridley closed her eyes and leaned back against Jackson. "We decided we didn't care about all that. We're going to have it at the farm and I don't care if I'm holding wildflowers when I get married. As long as I'm Mrs. Jackson Alexander at the end of it."

Ridley looked behind Jackson to the empty doorway. "Anyway, where is everyone? I thought the guys were coming over tonight."

"They are. Everyone's just running a bit late." Jackson reached around her and snagged a stray piece of pepperoni, popping it in his mouth before Ridley smacked his hand.

"Not until everyone else gets here," she chided.

Raina pushed away from the window and walked over to the chair where she'd left her bag, trying to hide her disappointment. "I forgot it was poker night. I'll get out of your way so you can get ready."

She pulled her phone out of her bag and then rolled her eyes when she saw that Steven had called. He'd been calling lately and even though she'd been ignoring him so far, she had to wonder if it wouldn't be easier to just answer and get it over with.

"Is everything all right, Raina?" Jackson pinned her with a stare. "Do you want me to call Nick?"

"No!" Raina pasted on a smile when he didn't look convinced. "I'll just see him at home later."

She was getting way too used to leaning on Nick. It would be that much harder to deal with things on her own once they went their separate ways. Enjoying the attention he gave her was one thing, *needing* him for comfort was another.

It was time for her to get used to comforting herself again.

*　*　*　*　*

"MR. ALEXANDER? YOU have a call waiting on line one." Kaylee's voice came over the speaker, jolting him out of his daydream.

"I'm not taking calls now, Kay. Take a message."

He still hadn't had any luck finding a present for Raina. They'd gotten pretty close over the past few weeks. He wanted to get her something that was special, but everything he found seemed trite and impersonal.

She seemed to be opening up to him, sharing her hopes for the future. He'd even been able to see a few episodes of her show before they went to postproduction. Raina had asked his advice on which scenes to cut and seemed to really value his opinion. It was exactly what he'd hoped for. The only thing that she wouldn't do was talk about their future child.

"I tried to, sir, but he keeps calling back." Kay sounded flustered. Her confidence level had increased dramatically over the past few weeks as she adjusted to her position. She'd gotten used to handling his clients with aplomb.

"Don't worry about it, Kay. I'll take care of it." Nick picked up the phone. "This is Nick."

"So, it seems you're still just as sleazy as ever, Nick." The voice on the other end of the line was only slightly familiar.

"Who is this?" Nick demanded.

"You must have a lot of enemies if you can't even identify them. This is the one that's calling to find out what your game is in marrying Raina."

Nick gritted his teeth. "What the hell do you want, Silvestre?" He practically hissed the name. "I saw your picture in the paper. I hope you're not calling to invite me to the wedding."

"No, I'm definitely not inviting the bastard I had to chase out of my wife's bed to anything."

"I told you then that I had no idea Marisol was a married woman. I don't do that."

"Funny how whenever I have woman trouble, it seems to circle around to you. First you sleep with my wife, now, according to my sources, you married my fiancée less than twenty-four hours after I last spoke with her."

"She's not your fiancée," Nick managed to say from between clenched teeth. "She's not your *anything*."

Silvestre sniffed. "When I heard the initial reports I was sure it was a hoax. Raina's way of getting back at me for embarrassing her in the press. Then I figured it must have been one of those drunken mistakes that would be annulled just as quickly."

"Oh, there won't be any annulment. Our marriage has been thoroughly consummated."

"Always so crude. How Raina could have made a mistake of this magnitude I can only imagine. I knew she was desperate to get married, but this is just absurd."

"Raina ceased to be any of your concern when you decided to play tonsil hockey with your ex-wife in broad daylight."

"You don't know anything about what happened with us. Raina and I would have worked things out. I regret hurting her, but I was going to honor the engagement. This *thing* with Marisol was a misunderstanding."

Nick shook his head in disbelief. Silvestre seemed to think he'd committed a minor transgression like forgetting to send flowers on Valentine's Day. It was absolutely amazing that this was the same man who'd lectured him about sleeping with his wife when Nick hadn't known she was married.

Apparently Marisol hadn't felt her marriage was worth mentioning.

"Look, Silvestre. It doesn't matter whether you like me or whether you believe me. This conversation is a waste of both of our time. Raina and I've been married six weeks already so the fact that you waited this long makes me wonder. Did Marisol leave you again already? Starting to wonder if you made a mistake, huh?"

"You think you're so smart. You always know what to say, don't you? But I'm guessing even you won't be able to smooth talk your way out of it once I tell Raina what you're really like. She may have been desperate enough to marry you, but I know she wants a good role model for her future children. Character is important to her."

Nick seethed with rage. "Listen up. Because I'm done playing nice. You're not the only one who can carry a tale to the right ears. Your new nightclubs are opening soon and you're negotiating another deal to acquire even more, right? This is probably not the best time for bad publicity."

"You can't touch me. You're a tiny fish in *my* pond, Alexander. I could buy and sell your operation with my pocket change."

"That wasn't enough to make Raina choose you, was it?" Nick chuckled at the harsh breathing on the other end of the line. "Raina covered for you, but I have no problem telling anyone who'll listen the truth. I'm sure your Japanese investors will love the story of a man who cheats on his fiancée with his ex-wife. Especially

119

considering the importance they place on honor and the value of a man's word."

There was a long pause, then Silvestre said, "Do what you want, Alexander. But for Raina's sake, I wonder if you'll have any more respect for your own marriage than you did for mine."

Chapter Ten

RAINA TIPPED THE watering can she held, dousing her flower bed with a spray of droplets. Before she'd left Ridley's, her sister had asked when she'd last watered her plants. The blank look on her face had probably been all the answer her sister needed. Ridley knew her too well.

"What are you doing out here?"

Raina turned to see Nick standing in the back doorway. "I'm just enjoying the last bit of sunlight and doing a little gardening."

He'd already pulled his tie off and his hair looked

slightly rumpled, as if he'd rubbed his hands over it a few times.

She turned back to her plants. How much water were they supposed to get, anyway? How was it that flowers seemed to do just fine in the wild with only the rain to rely on? She scowled when she noticed the small puddle at the base of the plant.

What kind of mother was she going to be if she couldn't even keep a stupid tulip alive?

"What are you doing home so early? I thought it was poker night with the guys?"

"Jackson said you were at the house earlier."

Raina rolled her eyes. "I also told him *not* to call you. Geez, men are the real gossips."

"Why didn't you stick around?"

"I'm not pregnant, Nick." She kept her back to him and doused the next section of plants with water.

She felt more than heard him come up behind her. He pulled her back against his chest.

"Why do you always do that, sweets?"

She looked up at him, sharply. "Do what?"

He pulled her closer and kissed her gently on the forehead. "Pull away from me when you think you're getting too emotional. Or cover your eyes if you think you might cry. I don't want you to hide your emotions from me, no matter what they are. I want the good, the bad, and the ugly. You have the right to be upset, Raina. I know how much you wanted this."

"I figured you'd be happy to have an excuse to have more crazy sex."

Nick tilted her chin up so she was forced to meet his eyes. "I will never be happy about anything that causes you pain. Besides, you can just breathe and I want you. I don't think we'll ever need an excuse to have crazy sex. "

He pulled her close and rested his chin on top of her

head.

"What are you doing?" She tried to pull back, but he tightened his arms until she couldn't move.

"I'm loving you. Sometimes when things aren't going so well, you need a hug. I used to see my parents doing this and just gag. But I understand it now. When life is heavy, it helps to know that someone is there for you. Even if they can't fix things or make them better." After a few moments, he pulled back. "You know what? We're going to take this trying thing more seriously."

She watched in surprise as he paced back and forth and put his hands on his hips. It was rare to see Nick so worked up about something.

"We *are* taking it seriously."

Nick pointed at her. "I know you've made a lot of changes in your life, but I haven't. I've been reading this book about pregnancy—"

Raina pulled back in surprise. "You have?"

"Why do you look so surprised? I care about what happens to you and I want to know what's going on. I started in the middle because I figured I already know how to make a baby, but I just went back and realized I've been doing *everything* wrong."

"What do you mean?"

"I've been wearing my boxers too tight, I've been riding the stationary bike downstairs, and I haven't been eating well. No wonder my swimmers aren't doing their job!"

Incredibly touched, Raina tried to suppress a smile. "Nick, those are just suggestions. More for men with low sperm counts. You probably don't need to worry about any of that."

"But just in case, I bought some of those loose boxers. I can deal with feeling a draft until we get the job done. And I can jog instead of riding the bike. I need to ask

Sam about those healthy protein shakes he drinks, too. My point is, I probably need to make some changes in my routine as well." He came back over to her and took her in his arms. "This is about both of us, so it doesn't make sense that all the preparation should be on your side."

Raina melted against him, allowing herself to draw comfort from his strong embrace. It felt so right to be in his arms just then. He wasn't just spouting platitudes to make her feel better—he was really sharing in her disappointment.

It was probably one of the first times that she realized how much he wanted a baby, too.

"You're going to be a really great dad, you know that?"

Nick pulled back and smiled down at her. "Thank you. That's probably the nicest thing you've ever said to me."

"Well, you're already a pretty great husband. This is so much more than I ever imagined having."

"I want us to have it all and there's no reason we can't."

*　*　*　*　*

"WHICH IS MORE romantic? Red velvet or the French vanilla?"

Raina had to refrain from rolling her eyes as she sat with Ridley in the catering office of New Haven's premiere wedding bakery. Premiere meaning it was the only one.

She still secretly thought it was lunacy to try to arrange a wedding in two weeks, but somehow, Ridley and Jackson had managed to pull most of it together. It helped that Julia knew almost everyone in town. A friend of Julia's owned this bakery and had agreed to supply them with plain sheet cakes that Julia would decorate. They only had to pick what flavor they wanted and she'd promised to fit their order in as a wedding gift.

Since the Alexanders were so active at church, they had been able to borrow chairs, tables, and tents that were normally used at the church's annual summer picnic. They'd found a florist who was going to bring out seasonal bouquets to decorate the tables.

It was all coming together.

"I'm probably the worst person to ask, Ri. I'm not exactly romantic. I think the red velvet tastes better." She took another bite of her sample of cake. It was sweet, moist, and the icing tasted like pure cream.

"How can you say you're not romantic? You and Nick have really inspired us."

"We have?" It was hard to believe that she and Nick, odd couple that they were, could inspire anyone.

"I know how things started between you but you're clearly perfect for each other. Seeing the two of you so happily married makes me realize that being with the man you love is more important than the right venue or having the perfect dress. I want to just seize the day. I'm so ready to be Jackson's wife."

Ridley sighed and took another bite of cake. "This red velvet is really good." She put her fork down. "I think this is what we'll go with. Besides, red is romantic."

"It's hard to believe you'll be married in two weeks. Summer will be over soon."

Ridley made a soft sound of agreement, then turned toward her. "I need to ask you something important." She took a deep breath. "It's about our father."

Raina pushed away the rest of her cake. "You can talk to me about anything, Ri. I know I haven't been so supportive about you meeting with him, but I don't want you to feel that you can't talk to me about things."

"I just don't want to stress you out. Especially now that you might be carrying my little niece or nephew." She leaned over and patted Raina's flat stomach. "But I wanted to invite our father to the wedding. I'm not going to ask him to give me away because it's not like he ever had me. Pretending that he did would be rather pointless."

"You don't have to get my permission to invite someone to your wedding. This day is about you. You should invite anyone you want."

"But I can't enjoy myself if having him there will bother you. Just because I'm marrying Jackson doesn't mean you're not still my other half. I think Jackson understands that. It's just part of being a twin. We shared uterus space. That's kind of hard to beat."

They both laughed.

Raina grabbed her sister's hand. "It's not going to bother me. I've been thinking about it and I've decided that I do want to meet him. At least once."

Ridley squeezed her hand. "Do you want me to introduce you? Or you can meet him alone. I won't be offended if you'd rather have time with him by yourself."

"No. I don't think I can do it if you're not with me."

Raina's heart thumped at the thought of meeting her father. She wasn't sure how she was supposed to feel about him. Worried, nervous, excited, or angry. Sometimes she felt all those things at once. She was so tired of constantly feeling conflicted.

"The more I think about my child, things look different to me than they did before. I realize that things aren't always black and white. I'd like to understand why he wasn't there growing up. We can't go back, but maybe we can move forward without bitterness. Mom was never able to let it go and it stole her whole life. I don't want even a trace of ugliness from the past to touch my child."

"It won't," Ridley stated. "We had no part of what happened in the past, but we can control what happens now."

*   *   *   *   *

AFTER A LOT of discussion, they'd decided that inviting William to Sunday dinner at the Alexanders was the best move. There would be a lot of other people around which would take off some of the pressure to make conversation.

Raina wasn't really worried about the small talk. She was just hoping they wouldn't hate each other on sight.

They drove past a sign that read "The Alexander-Bennett Co-Op" and drove down a long, dirt-packed road leading to a two-story ranch house. The sky was just starting to turn the colors of twilight; purples and reds and golds splashed along the horizon in bright smudges of color.

"I've never brought anyone home for Sunday dinner before," Nick stated suddenly.

"Never?"

"No. That isn't to say I never introduced my parents to anyone. New Haven isn't that big, so I've actually run into my parents while out on dates before. Which was awkward." He grinned. "But I never felt compelled to show any of those women where I grew up."

"I'm honored to be the first," she whispered. After the past few weeks with him, she'd come to know a totally different side of Nick than what she'd ever imagined. It would be interesting to see where he'd lived as a boy. Part of her was fascinated with everything to do with her sexy husband.

They got out of the car and stood staring at the front of the house. Nick came around the car and stood next to her. He leaned over and whispered, "Here comes one of my dad's ranch hands. He's worked here forever."

An older man, his pale skin smudged with dirt, ambled toward them. His gray hair stuck out in scraggly spikes that he'd halfway covered with a floppy, battered straw hat.

Nick raised a hand in greeting. "Hey, Grady. Is everyone inside?"

"Yup. Your mama was upset about sumthin'. You better get on inside. Evening, miss." He tipped the bill of his hat at Raina.

"Grady, this is my wife, Raina."

"Hi," she said and held out her hand. Grady shook it slowly.

He glanced at Nick. "This one looks the same as the other one. You boys never did share well." Then he ambled on down the lane, shaking his head the whole way.

"Well, that was interesting," Raina remarked.

Nick took her arm. "The fun is just beginning. Let's go inside before they send out a search party."

Nick knocked twice and then used his key. They stepped into the small entryway and he called out, "Mom! Dad! We're here."

Raina followed him into the family room. Most of the furniture looked brand new and the room was done in airy blues and greens. The stone fireplace looked like one of those ancient ones that could burn anything.

She leaned closer to see one of the pictures on the wall near her. It was Nick, wearing a basketball uniform. He had his arms crossed in the picture and a smug smile on his face like he'd thought he was so cool. He looked about fifteen.

She glanced over at him with a smile. "Wow. Seeing you this young is so weird. I can't even imagine you as a teenage boy."

Nick stuck his hands in his pockets and rocked back on his heels as she examined some of the other pictures on the wall. "Trust me, you don't want to know what I was like then. Our poor parents had to deal with teen-boy attitude four times over. Jackson is going to have his hands full with his in about ten years."

Raina thought about the child they would soon have. She could understand why his mom kept all these photos visible. She already couldn't wait to see what their baby would look like and she was going to document and cherish every moment of their life.

Their baby was going to know it was loved.

They crossed through the family room and into the kitchen. Music and voices flowed through the open back door and into the kitchen.

"Everyone must be outside." Nick pushed open the screen door and Raina followed him out onto the back deck. A tiny body bumped into her leg and she looked down to see Jase watching them, his thumb bobbing in his mouth. He took it out only to say, "Hi, Unca Nick."

"Are you still sucking on that thumb, little man? I thought we had a talk about that. That look is ruining your swag. How are you supposed to impress the lady babies with your thumb in your mouth?"

Raina smacked him in the arm. "Nick! He's a toddler."

Nick pretended to jump away from Raina and Jase giggled. "Help me, Jase! Auntie Raina is assaulting me!"

Jase just laughed harder and pointed at Nick. "Get him! Get him!"

Nick shook his head. "My own nephew isn't even on my side. I guess a pretty face trumps family when you're three, huh?"

Raina sent him a scathing look and then knelt down next to Jase. "Can I have a high five, Mr. Alexander? I've missed having you jump in the pond in my backyard. You and Chris need to come visit me again."

Jase gave her a high five and then immediately stuck his thumb in his mouth again. He glanced up at Nick, then took it out and slowly put it behind his back.

"That's better, my man."

A blur of motion passed by them and then Jase took off running. They watched as Chris ran across the deck and down into the yard with Jase struggling to catch up. Laura's little girls were already there, blowing bubbles with a long wand. Before long all four kids were chasing and tagging each other.

He turned to look at Raina. "One day ours will be out there, too."

"I hope," Raina replied.

He pulled her close and kissed her on the forehead. "It'll happen. Hopefully tonight." He leered at her and she poked him in the side.

Ridley appeared at her left side. "I'm so glad you came."

"Did you think I wouldn't?"

"It occurred to me," Ridley admitted.

She looked toward the other end of the porch where Mark and Julia stood with an unfamiliar man. He was older with pale skin and dark hair, silvered at the temples. He turned slightly and she recognized him from the pictures she'd seen.

"There they are!" Julia walked over to them, arms outstretched. Mark trailed behind her with an indulgent smile. She hugged Raina and then kissed Nick on the cheek. "I figured you were on your way." She turned to Raina with a hesitant smile. "Are you ready to meet your father, honey?"

Raina nodded. Then she changed her mind and shook her head.

"What if he doesn't like me?"

She didn't want to care what he thought of her but in that moment, when he was only a few feet away, she was overcome with anxiety.

"Oh, honey," Julia exclaimed. "Of course he'll like you."

Mark put a gentle hand on her shoulder. "As a father of four I feel completely qualified to say you're the kind of woman any man would be proud to call his daughter."

Raina let out the breath she was holding. "Thank you. I guess I'd better go meet him then."

Ridley took her arm and tugged her over to where William stood, looking extremely uncomfortable. Julia, Mark, and Nick all trailed behind. *Great, just what I need. An audience,* Raina thought.

"William, this is Raina. Raina, William."

Unsure of what to do, Raina stuck out her hand. He accepted it with a small smile.

"Hello, Raina. It's nice to finally meet you."

Raina smiled but didn't respond. Was that a criticism for refusing to meet with him earlier? He didn't seem upset when he said it so she just nodded.

"I want to thank you all for inviting me to dinner. You have a lovely home," William added.

"Thank you so much. We're happy to have you here with us." Julia took control of the conversation and motioned for her father to go inside. "Dinner is ready, everyone."

The rest of the evening went much the same. Even though dinner was just as lively as the one Julia had hosted at her house, Raina's eyes kept going to her father seated a few places away. He ate slowly and methodically, one food at a time.

Raina looked down at her own plate in astonishment and noticed she'd just finished her corn salad. She hadn't met too many other people who liked to eat all of one food before moving on to the next.

She noticed that Ridley made an effort to include their father in the conversation. William was perfectly polite but only spoke when spoken to, and though he seemed perfectly composed, there was something about him that was a little... awkward. He didn't seem all that comfortable socializing.

Like me, Raina thought. It was odd to see where so many of her own character traits had come from.

After dinner, Ridley shoved a basket at her. "William, why don't you show Raina the blackberry bushes? She loves them as much as you do. Bring back a lot for me, okay?"

Raina gritted her teeth at her sister but it was too late to get out of it. She glanced behind her at Nick. He nodded slightly as if saying *go ahead.*

"I remember where it is." William led the way to the back door. They stepped out into the humid evening air and walked down the deck steps to the backyard. The air was just warm enough to feel like a caress as they walked across the springy green grass. William led the way toward the long wooden fence at the back of the yard.

"Here they are." William gestured to the bush. "You don't have to pick them if you don't want to. I can do it. That was just Ridley's way of throwing us together. Subtle she is not."

Raina was startled into laughing out loud. She clamped her lips together and handed him the basket. "I've been trying really hard not to like you."

He looked up at her with knowing eyes. "I know. You

have every reason not to."

Before she could stop herself, Raina was asking, "So why did you leave then?"

He pulled a few berries from the bush. They were so juicy they left bright smudges on his fingers.

"I was afraid," he said finally. "I was also selfish. I didn't want to give up the excitement of being able to run off at the drop of a hat and party all night and do drugs." He looked over at her. "I'm not going to try to spin some story to make myself look good. I was messed up. All I cared about was sex, drugs, and rock and roll. Not necessarily in that order. The racial difference also played a part. My parents aren't the most progressive people. When I married your mother, they never really accepted it and I wasn't strong enough to stand up to them. I'm not proud of that."

Raina couldn't imagine your new family ostracizing you just because of the way you looked. What if Julia and Mark had decided not to accept her just because she was biracial? She felt a pang of sympathy for her mother. It was easier to understand why she'd been so bitter.

"Do they even know about us?" Raina moved closer and yanked a berry off the bush. He held out the basket so she could put it on top of the others.

William nodded. "They do. Things have changed a lot in the world over the past two decades. I'm not asking you to meet them. I know I don't have the right to do that, but I want you to know they regret how they treated your mom. I do, too."

They worked side by side, filling the basket with the plump berries. Raina looked at him from the corner of her eye. He had a long, straight nose and an angular jaw. It was surreal how many times she'd wondered what her father looked like growing up. Now she was standing here picking berries with him.

"So, you're clean now?" she asked.

He nodded. "Now, yes. But I was only able to get there when I was truly ready. I tried so many times to clean up my act and failed because I wasn't doing it for the right reasons. Your mother tried to reform me and nearly destroyed herself in the process. That's the only part I truly regret. I don't regret leaving, because I think if I'd been there, I would have just passed my problems on to another generation."

Raina thought about the changes she'd made in her life recently. She didn't miss the hectic pace of her prior schedule and had started to wonder if going back to modeling after the baby was born was really what she wanted to do. But she'd come to that decision all on her own. No one had forced her to make those changes. Nick probably hadn't realized before he made his offer just how different his life would be.

He came home to her every night and they watched television or relaxed on the couch and read. It was a far cry from the lives they'd both led previously. No wild parties. No traveling. No excitement. But he hadn't given her any indication that he missed his old life.

Yet.

She gave herself a mental shake. Nick wasn't anything like her father. He was his own man. And he would never leave her to take care of their baby alone.

William continued talking, oblivious to her thoughts. "Trying to go on the straight and narrow for someone else never works. You can't escape who you really are."

Chapter Eleven

∽

A WEEK LATER, Nick was ready.

He was *R-E-A-D-Y*.

He'd been wearing his new loose boxers so his boys wouldn't be squeezed. He'd started drinking raw fruit smoothies and taking his vitamins. His swimmers should be at their fighting best.

Because he wasn't sure he could stand to see Raina disappointed again.

This night was going to be about romance, he decided. They'd been focusing too much on the end goal. He didn't want their child conceived out of worry and stress. Their child should be born to parents who'd made love because of how they felt about each other.

He'd ordered a bottle of Raina's favorite champagne, which was currently on ice in a bucket on his dresser. He'd brought up candles to set the mood. He'd even purchased a pair of silk boxers for himself.

He was lighting the candles on his nightstand when Raina entered the room from the bathroom. His hand stilled when he saw what she was wearing. She leaned against the doorframe and gave him a smoldering look. Her lithe body was encased in a tiny scrap of a black lace bodysuit. It covered everything but managed to somehow make her look even *more* scandalous than if she were just naked, if that was possible.

He groaned when he immediately hardened then sent a mental command to his dick to take a seat. He wasn't going to be sidetracked by how mouthwatering his wife looked in lingerie. Or without lingerie.

"Come here, sweetheart." He held out a hand to her and she skipped across the room and launched herself into his arms.

They fell back onto the bed, laughing. Nick pushed her hair back and looked up into her bright, mischievous expression. He'd never laughed so much during sex before. Something he wouldn't have thought could be such a good thing.

"You're not going to distract me this time, Raina. I want us to go slow. Take our time." He moved back and pulled the covers down.

"Right. Slow and romantic," Raina breathed. She slipped between the sheets and looked up at him with a naughty expression on her face.

Nick got in next to her and stroked his hands over the soft skin of her arms. She decided to return the favor and caressed his chest in slow, sinuous strokes. Then she disappeared beneath the covers.

"Raina, wait a minute." His mouth fell open when she tongued him through the fabric of his boxers. *"Oh God."*

A giggle floated up from beneath the covers. She was giggling while he was inside her mouth. He reached down and pulled her up before she made him embarrass himself by coming too soon.

Before she could withdraw her hand, he captured one of her fingers in his mouth and laved it with his tongue. She wasn't giggling anymore, he thought smugly.

"I can see that I need to take control." He pushed her back gently and then maneuvered her so she was on her stomach. The line of her back and the curve of her ass were the most beautiful scenery he'd ever seen. He blanketed her with his body, his front to her back.

"Do you have any idea what you mean to me?" Nick growled, pressing deeper, pinning her to the bed beneath him. The position put him firmly in control, giving her very little room to move.

She was helpless to take what he had to give.

The delicate line of her spine was revealed in this position. Nick touched the points of her vertebrae with the tip of his index finger, then trailed his finger firmly down her back.

As she arched under the contact, he entered her, gliding slowly through her tight muscles. Her nails clutched at the sheets as he slid home, then pulled out just as slowly. Inch by torturous inch.

She tried to push back on him but he held her still, forcing her to wait. After struggling for a moment, she finally accepted it and lay beneath him, moaning and crying out his name.

With a firm hand, he urged her up on her knees. *I*

could look at this view all day, he thought.

His head fell back on his shoulders as he powered into her, the curves of her ass providing lush padding for him every time their hips met. The sight of his length entering her and then emerging covered with the slick evidence of her arousal was a fuel to his already overhyped libido. She panted and shuddered as he took her with deep strokes. Her skin gleamed with a fine sheen of sweat. He touched his tongue to the middle of her back.

That must have set her off because she tightened around him and screamed. "Nick, please! I need, *oh God*, it's too much."

He leaned forward, pressing deeper. At this angle, her breasts were neglected and he knew she enjoyed it when he played with them. Something he enjoyed just as much.

He pulled out. "Turn over, sweetheart."

She rolled over so she was flat on her back. There were tears on her cheeks but he knew they weren't from pain. She looked down his chest, her mouth falling open as her eyes stopped between his legs.

"That's right, sweets. Look how hard I am for you."

She bit her lip as he covered her body with his and entered her again. When she buried her fingers in his hair, Nick knew he couldn't last much longer. The sensation of her delicate fingers stroking over his scalp while he was surrounded by her tight, wet walls was a double whammy he couldn't resist. He turned his head and latched on to her breast, tonguing the nipple until he felt her shuddering beneath him again.

"Yes, just like that. Come for me just like that." He came in an explosion of sensation, feeling like he was surrounded by her. Her body, her scent, and her love.

When he finally became aware of himself again, he raised his head to find her watching him with a tender expression.

"That was intense," she whispered.

Raina whimpered as he took her mouth, kissing her so deeply that it got him aroused again almost immediately. He hardened inside her and she arched underneath him.

"Nick. *Nick!*" She clutched his back as he made love to her again with thick, forceful thrusts.

"I'm not leaving your body this time. I don't want to. This is where I always want to be," he growled in her ear. He made love to her over and over again, never leaving her body until they fell into an exhausted sleep.

*   *   *   *   *

THE DAY OF the wedding dawned sunny and clear. After spending the morning checking in with the florist and Julia while Ridley bathed and gathered her things, Raina was more than ready to head to the Alexander's farm.

She made sure Ridley's honeymoon bag was packed and then they gathered up the simple white off-the-rack wedding dress Ridley had purchased. Raina put her white pumps, hair pins, hose, and corset in a separate bag. She'd brought her own makeup kit with her. Her sister barely owned any and the stuff she'd buy wouldn't be as high quality as what Raina had.

As they were driving over to Julia's house she said, "You know, there's something really special about just jumping in and doing it this way."

Ridley looked at her from the passenger seat of her car. "There is?"

"Yeah. Since you planned everything in such a short time frame, you kept all the stress contained."

Ridley looked over at her and then squealed. "I'm getting married today!" They giggled all the way to the Alexander farm.

As soon as they pulled up, the front door opened and Julia came out. "Here she is! Come on in, honey."

Ridley got out of the car and Raina followed, scooping up Ridley's dress bag and her makeup kit.

"You can take the second guest bedroom on the left to get ready. That used to be Jackson's room." Julia winked as she said it. They followed her inside and down one of the hallways.

"Here you go, girls. I'll be back in a little while. I'm waiting on Lonny Wilson to bring the flowers. He's an hour late." Julia threw up her hands and made a face. "That boy would be late to his own funeral, bless his heart."

Raina suppressed a smile. Since she'd grown up mainly in D.C., she was still amused by the uniquely Southern tradition of insulting someone and then bestowing a blessing on them. She'd kind of prefer to just say "screw you" and be done with it.

"Let's do my hair first. I have a feeling this is going to take a while." Ridley sighed and then pulled out the band holding her ponytail.

Raina worked for the next hour, meticulously twisting sections of her sister's hair and then pinning the coils high on her head. Next she spritzed several tendrils around her face with water and wound them around small rollers. She used the blow-dryer to get them mostly dry and then left the rollers in while she worked on her sister's makeup.

By the time Julia came back, Ridley was just stepping into her dress. It was a simple A-line with a sweetheart neckline and lacy cap sleeves. Simple but perfect.

"Oh my goodness. You are so beautiful." Julia fanned at her eyes, blinking back tears. "Wait until my son gets a look at you."

Raina agreed. Considering that Jackson couldn't keep

his eyes off her sister on any given day, she had a feeling he was going to be knocked on his ass when he saw Ridley coming down the aisle.

The next hour was a blur as she rushed around getting her own dress on and doing her hair. Ridley had decided that just Raina, Laura, and her friend Katie would stand up with her as bridesmaids. They were all wearing simple blue sheath dresses that they'd gotten at the same discount bridal store where Ridley had found her dress. Laura and Katie arrived and after the requisite *oohing* and *aahing* over Ridley's dress, they were all changed and lined up with their escorts, waiting to go down the aisle.

"You look beautiful," Nick said.

"Thank you. How's Jackson holding up? Is he sweating yet?" she teased.

"Like a hooker in church. He looked like he'd just run a marathon."

"Nick!" Raina glanced around to make sure Julia wasn't close enough to overhear. That was when she realized Julia and Mark had already gone down the aisle to be seated.

The music changed and Raina looked over to one of Julia's church friends, standing behind the table where Elliot's sound system was set up. Apparently he'd arranged everything so the music was on a playlist and all she had to do was press "Play." Elliot was watching her closely anyway.

Laura linked arms with Bennett and they walked down the aisle. After a few beats, Katie linked arms with Elliot and they followed. Raina smoothed down the front of her dress and glanced back at Ridley.

Mark had offered to stand in and give her away, but in the end, Ridley had decided to walk alone. She'd figured it was a fitting symbol of the way she'd found Jackson and Raina couldn't disagree.

"Are you ready to become an Alexander, Ri?"

After a brief pause, Ridley nodded. She glanced down the aisle to where they could see Jackson standing at the altar next to the pastor. Her eyes twinkled with excitement. "Yeah. I'm ready."

She smiled at her sister and then linked arms with her husband. "Well then, here we go."

* * * * *

NICK HADN'T FIGURED on leaving the house until that afternoon when the wedding was supposed to start. He quickly realized the error of his ways when Raina had woken him up early. Apparently, as Jackson's best man, he was supposed to keep his brother out of the way while she helped Ridley get ready.

He'd never been a big fan of weddings except, like most single men, as a way to pick up women, so the complicated goings-on involved in planning one were way over his head. Maybe it was a guy thing or maybe just because he'd eloped, but he couldn't understand what they needed to do that would take *all damn morning.*

Bennett and Elliott had met them at their parents' house and the four brothers had played poker and shared stories about growing up. They'd joked that they were going to gamble away Jackson's last hours as a free man. His brother had taken their teasing in stride and looked as happy as Nick had ever seen him.

He hadn't shown any nerves until he was in his tuxedo and they'd had to leave him to meet up with the bridesmaids. That was when Nick had been happy he and Raina had eloped.

But now as he watched his brother and Ridley dance in

the grass in his parents' backyard, he could sort of see what all the fuss was about. His brother had said his vows in a clear, sure voice. Nick had found himself mouthing the words, then looked over to see Raina watching him. It was a powerful thing to declare your lifelong commitment to someone in front of everyone you knew.

Ridley looked beautiful and was wearing makeup, something she rarely did. He looked down at Raina, swaying in his arms. They looked much more alike now, even though Raina had done her makeup in a much more understated fashion than usual.

"Do you regret that we didn't do this?" He was terrified she'd say yes but wanted to hear her answer nonetheless. It was an increasing need of his to make sure she had everything she wanted. To make her happy and keep her that way.

"No, not really. Even though it was so beautiful to watch them up there saying their vows, I kind of like how crazy our wedding was. Imagine the stories we're going to be able to tell our kids!" She grinned up at him. "We're going to be those embarrassing parents. I can't wait."

Nick laughed along with her. "I'm definitely planning on being embarrassing. That dad who tries to learn all the latest dances and talk in the newest slang."

"I bet you'll be the dad that the other kids think is cool." She was quiet for a moment and then said, "I can't wait, Nick. More than that, I'm really glad I'm going on this journey with *you*."

He leaned down and nuzzled her neck, mindful of all the relatives watching them.

"Whatever my cousin is telling you, it's all lies."

Nick looked up at the words drawled in a familiar deep voice. His cousin Grant was standing at the edges of the dance floor nursing a drink. Knowing his cousin, it was nonalcoholic. He was a doctor and was usually talking some nonsense about how his "body was a temple."

Nick considered his body to be a temple, too, as long as it was a temple that allowed drinking, dancing, and having a good time.

"Oh, is that right? According to who?" Raina raised her eyebrow and looked up at Nick. He tried to dance them in the other direction but Raina had already turned toward his cousin. Nick sighed.

The last time he'd seen Grant had been at Jackson's house for Memorial Day. The only time he ever saw his West Haven cousins was at Jackson's house since they weren't on speaking terms with anyone else.

Grant stuck out his hand and Raina pulled back to accept it. Nick kept a firm hold on her waist so she was forced to turn within the circle of his arms.

"Grant Alexander. Dr. Grant Alexander. And you must be the bride's twin sister."

Raina looked back at Nick uncertainly. "That's right. Raina Winters. Well, Raina Winters Alexander, now."

Grant, in the process of taking a sip of his drink, spluttered in surprise. He looked at Nick in shock. "You got *married*?"

"Nice seeing you too, Grant. Always a pleasure." Nick held Raina closer and danced her away a few feet.

"How many cousins do you have?" Raina asked. "Every time I turn around, there are more of you. So, how is he related to you? Is he Maria's son?"

Nick shook his head. "No, that's Langston. He lives in California. Grant is one of my Uncle Stewart's kids. We don't really see them that often."

"Oh. Okay," Raina replied. He could tell she wanted to ask him more about it so he was glad when the music changed to something slightly more up-tempo. He twirled her around. She suddenly clutched at his shoulders.

"Raina, are you okay?"

She blinked a few times. "I just got dizzy all of a sudden. I think I need to sit for a minute."

Nick led her off the dance floor. Before they could get to their table, she slumped against him. He swung her up in his arms.

"No, Nick, put me down. You're making a scene."

Nick ignored her and continued to their table. Once there, he lowered her gently to her feet. "You think I care about that?"

"No, but I do." She sat in her chair and put her head in her hands.

"Hey, is she okay?" His cousin Grant was no longer glaring at him but instead kneeling next to Raina. "How are you feeling?"

"Dizzy. I was fine, then all of a sudden I felt hot and sort of sick."

Grant looked up at Nick. "Let's go inside. I think a break from all the noise and excitement out here will help."

"For once, we actually agree on something." Nick offered Raina his arm and they walked toward the house.

Chapter Twelve

~

"HOW LONG HAS this been happening?" Grant held her elbow in a firm but gentle grip and led her to the couch in the family room. The party was still going strong, so no one seemed to even notice the trio leaving and going back into the house. She could only hope Ridley hadn't seen them. The last thing she wanted was to distract her sister on her wedding day.

Especially for something stupid.

"It just started today. It might be something I ate." Raina sat down and let out a relieved sigh. Maybe now the room would stop swirling around.

"Anything is possible. It's better to take it easy until you feel better."

Nick sat next to her and pulled her against his chest. She leaned into him and closed her eyes. "We've been trying to get pregnant," he said.

Raina's eyes popped open. Grant observed her reaction with a knowing smile. "Is that right?"

"She has endometriosis. Do you think the dancing could have, I don't know, strained something? Never mind, I feel stupid even asking that." Nick squeezed her closer and ran a hand gently up and down her back. "It's probably just stress. She met her father for the first time recently."

Raina closed her eyes again, this time in embarrassment. "Did he really need my entire life story, Nick? I got a little dizzy. I didn't pass out."

"It's okay." Grant laughed. "I'm used to it. Occupational hazard. Once people find out you're a doctor, they tell you all kinds of things. Some stuff that you really wish they wouldn't, actually."

He winked at her and despite her headache, Raina couldn't help smiling back. In a strange way, he reminded her of a more rugged version of Nick with his cocky attitude and devil-may-care way of speaking.

Not that she thought her husband would appreciate the comparison.

"Once you're done flirting, perhaps you could tell me if my wife is okay?" Nick scowled up at his cousin.

Grant crossed his arms and leaned against the wall nonchalantly. "I'm not an obstetrician, but did your doctor place you under any restrictions?"

Raina shook her head. "No. I've been doing all the same stuff I usually do."

He nodded. "Then more than likely the dancing was

fine. Even if you are pregnant, dizziness is quite common. It's probably best if you try not to do too much until you know for sure whether you are or not. Especially if you might be a high-risk pregnancy."

Raina nodded. "Thank you. I have to admit, I do feel better just being off my feet and out of the crowd. I'm probably still not used to this many people at once."

Grant glanced over at Nick with narrowed eyes. "Why wouldn't you be used to it? How long have you two been married, anyway?"

Nick scowled. "Why? Are you hoping the ink isn't dry on the certificate or something?"

Raina sat up and looked between the two men. "I'm surprised there's anyone in your family who doesn't know that we eloped. I thought all you Alexanders told each other everything."

"Aaah, Cousin Nick hasn't told you about the 'other side' of the family yet. Interesting. You guys really are newlyweds then."

Raina nodded but decided against saying anything else. Her head wasn't clear enough for her to navigate the strange undercurrents of this conversation.

He looked at Raina. "Our fathers don't get along, so most of us West Haven Alexanders are treated like black sheep. Jackson has always been pretty welcoming to us, so we visit him from time to time."

He didn't say anything else. Nick's hand clenched around her waist. *Okay, I think that's enough sharing for one day*, Raina thought. It was obvious from what Grant hadn't said that Jackson was welcoming but Nick, not so much. The last thing she needed was to have to referee a fight between two equally stubborn Alexander males.

This family politics stuff wasn't for the faint of heart.

"I really don't feel too well," Raina stated, hoping Nick would pick up on her hint. He glanced at her and

148

then back to his cousin.

"I think I'd better get her home. Thanks again, Grant." They shook hands and Raina waved without getting up.

Grant ambled over to the door. Just before he pushed it open, he looked back. "If you're ever on the west side of the city, come visit. The door is always open." Then he walked out onto the deck and they were alone again.

Nick didn't look at her so Raina placed a hand on his cheek. He looked at her, startled.

"Do I even want to know what that was all about?"

He shrugged. "It's ancient history, but I promise I'll tell you all about it. Later, after your head feels better." He brushed a stray curl back from her face. "Because trying to understand the intricacies of the Alexander family feud is enough to give anyone a headache."

*　*　*　*　*

RAINA EYED THE clock, wondering for the millionth time when Nick was going to show up. Waiting to find out if she was pregnant was agonizing, so she'd been scrambling to find ways to distract herself. She couldn't even hang out with Ridley since Jackson had surprised her with a trip to Paris for their honeymoon. They wouldn't be back for another week.

In lieu of having her sister to talk to, she'd started signing up for different social media sites. She'd stumbled upon a site filled with gorgeous pictures of arts and crafts and some of the most delicious-looking recipes.

The fact that she couldn't cook hadn't stopped her from downloading a bunch of them and forcing Sam to come with her to the store to stock up on baking supplies. Of course, disorganized as she was, she hadn't remembered to actually bring the recipes with her so she'd ended up buying almost everything on the baking aisle just in case.

Sam, to his credit, hadn't voiced a word of complaint.

The timer dinged and she stuck her hand in an oven mitt. She pulled open the oven door and a cloud of black smoke billowed out. A few seconds later, the smoke alarm let out a shrill cry.

"Oh no! No, No, NO!"

Raina grabbed the dishtowel next to the sink and fanned the opening to the oven frantically, dispelling the thick gray clouds of smoke.

"What the hell is going on?" Sam appeared behind her and took the dishtowel from her. He wrapped it around his hand and reached into the oven. A moment later, he dropped the pan on the stove top and closed the door.

"Um, I was baking." Raina would have laughed at his bewildered expression if she wasn't so embarrassed.

"I see that. When we went to the store, I thought you were just stocking up on stuff Nick asked you to buy." He looked down at the pan of cupcakes and then snorted. "Who were you baking for? A village of giants?"

Raina looked down at the pan and let out a small gasp. She'd followed the recipe to the letter and had filled each mold in the cupcake pan to the brim so they'd be nice and thick. She loved the big, thick cupcakes sold in bakeries.

Her cupcakes however, looked like they'd exploded out of the cups. Each one was melted over the edges of the pan while the tops stood up in a puffy mass. They looked deformed.

"Is everything okay in here?"

Raina turned to see Nick dropping his briefcase into one of the kitchen chairs.

"Uh, I'll leave you guys to it." Sam, the traitor, retreated back down the hall leading toward his rooms in the basement.

Raina turned around to see Nick eyeing the exploding cupcakes with barely concealed horror.

"Um, did your muffins get attacked by aliens?"

Raina's shoulders sagged. "They're supposed to be chocolate cupcakes. I don't know what happened." She sank down onto one of the bar stools next to the island and covered her face with her hands. "What kind of mother am I going to be? I can't even follow a stupid recipe."

Nick walked forward hesitantly. "It's okay. Maybe they just need a little icing. Or something."

Raina lifted her head and glared at him. "They look awful. It looks like the batter crawled into the oven and died."

Nick pulled one of the cupcakes loose. The bottom was charred black. "See, I'm sure they're fine. I'll taste it." He bit the top of the cupcake and then stilled. His face twisted before he shuddered. He looked like he was on the verge of throwing up.

Raina jumped up and grabbed a paper towel. She held it out to him. He spit the cupcake remains into it. "Um, it's not that bad. Maybe you just left out an ingredient. Like the sugar, maybe?"

Raina stared at the remaining cupcakes. "You don't have to be nice. You definitely don't have to eat these to spare my feelings. Geez, we've only been married a month and I'm already poisoning you with my terrible cooking."

It would have helped if she hadn't decided to finally answer one of Steven's calls while she was baking. He'd started calling a few weeks after she'd gotten married. She'd ignored him, hoping he'd go away, but he'd been calling intermittently since then.

The good news was she'd finally told him to stop

calling her. The bad news was she'd been so distracted that she'd messed up the recipe. Not that she could tell Nick any of that.

Nick pulled her into his arms. "Hey, it's not as bad as all that. I'm hardly poisoned. And I didn't marry you for your baking skills."

"Oh right, you married me for my DNA," she mumbled.

"No, I married you because I adore you. I knew you didn't feel the same way, but I didn't care. I figured if this was the only way I could have you, it was still better than what I had before—watching and loving you from afar. "

Raina looked up at him, stunned at the tenderness in his eyes. "Oh, Nick."

He covered her lips with his finger. "You don't have to say anything. I'm not pressuring you to feel the same way, remember? I just want you to get used to me loving you. Because I plan on doing it for a very long time."

Raina allowed him to pull her back into his arms and snuggled deeper into his embrace. Nick made her feel like she could tell him anything and he was always quick to defend her, even when she was criticizing herself. It was such an unexpectedly lovely feeling to have someone be her champion, but sometimes it felt like she was doing all the taking and not giving enough back.

Especially since every time he told her he loved her, it was getting harder and harder not to say it back.

* * * * *

OVER THE PAST few weeks, Nick and Raina had finally fallen into a comfortable rhythm. He rose at five a.m. so he could have an hour to work out before waking Raina briefly to give her a kiss goodbye.

She usually didn't get up until after eight, then spent the day catching up on all the movies she hadn't seen and books she hadn't read.

"You know, this vacation thing is pretty nice. I wonder why I haven't done this in so long," Raina said to Sam one morning over eggs and toast.

Sam looked up from his protein shake. "Because you're a workaholic, that's why. You and Alexander have that in common."

She'd been working nonstop since she was fifteen and had assumed that she'd be bored with so much time on her hands. She was surprised by how much she was enjoying herself. But the biggest surprise of all in the past few weeks had been Nick.

He returned home around six and changed out of his suit and tie. She'd only seen him in casual clothes a few times prior to their marriage. Even though they'd spent a fair amount of time together at Jackson and Ridley's house, he was always coming straight from work. It was strange to see him wandering around in gym shorts with bare feet. It was like seeing him go from Superman to Clark Kent. It didn't diminish her attraction for him at all. Rather, it felt like she was seeing a side of him that few people did.

After he'd changed clothes, he'd cook them dinner. Sometimes it was complicated and fancy like salmon-stuffed crab cakes with herbed dressing. Other days it was refreshingly simple like a tossed salad with grilled chicken.

But no matter what, they always ate together. She'd tell him about her day buying baby clothes and decorating the nursery and he'd share funny stories about his clients. They talked about everything from politics to popular music. He'd walked in on her one night jamming in her pajamas to the latest boy band and hadn't stopped teasing her about it since.

She'd come to look forward to those conversations each night.

"Don't you think it's time you stopped calling him by his last name? I mean, we're all living together now. One big happy family," she teased.

Sam slurped up the last of his shake. "This is the happiest I've ever seen you."

Suddenly self-conscious, Raina shrugged. "Well, I've got no reason to complain. I'm on vacation and I'm living with two sexy men. I'd say I'm doing all right."

Sam raised an eyebrow. "Being happy isn't a crime, Raina. You don't have to pretend like it's no big deal. Whether you're ready for it or not, I think you've found your soul mate."

"You know why we got married, Sam." Raina stabbed her fork into what was left of her eggs.

"I know what you told me and I also know that you feel more for him than that. We've been friends too long for you to fool me. I wasn't sure about him in the beginning, but I've seen the way he treats you. The way he looks at you. For what it's worth, you've got my blessing." With that, he kissed her on the forehead and went back downstairs.

Raina decided to put her earbuds in and listen to music while cleaning up the kitchen. After the embarrassing dancing incident, she was leery of playing her music out loud anymore. She was just lucky Nick hadn't thought to videotape her.

After everything was pristine, she went upstairs and flopped down on her bed.

It was time to see what other popular culture she'd missed out on. She scrolled through the list of movies available to rent. She'd already watched a lot of them but was hoping to find something different this time. There were several horror flicks available, but she figured they might not be the best choices. She was supposed to be relaxing, after all.

Finally she gave up and clicked on an old romantic comedy she'd already seen. She laughed along with all the hijinks and sighed at all the sappy romantic spots. It was completely unrealistic but it was the perfect diversion for a lazy afternoon.

She woke a few hours later, slightly disoriented and with an urgent need to use the bathroom.

"It's no wonder with all this water I'm drinking. I feel like all I do is take vitamins, sleep, and pee."

Still a bit sleepy, she stumbled into the bathroom and sat on the toilet. When she looked down, she blinked twice before standing and yanking her shorts back up. She went to the sink and took a few deep breaths, trying to hold back tears. It took a few minutes of deep breathing before she felt calm enough to move.

Then she reached beneath the counter and pulled out the box of tampons sitting next to her hairdryer.

Chapter Thirteen

NICK PULLED INTO the driveway and grabbed his
briefcase. He was running late and had little time to
think of what to make for dinner. Raina had been pretty
tired lately and he wondered if she was pregnant already.

Just the thought brought a smile to his face. It was
hard to believe, but he was more than ready to be a
father. He couldn't wait to see Raina swell up with his
child.

He opened the door and stopped when he saw Sam
standing there. It was still a little weird to have another

dude living with them, but he'd come to appreciate that Sam was there to look out for Raina when he couldn't. "Hey. Everything okay?"

Sam shook his head. "No. Raina needs you."

Nick dropped his stuff at the base of the stairs. "Oh, did she ask for me?"

"She doesn't know how to ask for help when she needs it. That's why I'm telling you. *She needs you.*"

"Okay," Nick said. Sam seemed to be a good guy but he'd never seemed all that interested in chatting with Nick before. For him to approach him now was incredibly odd. He glanced behind Sam. "Where is she, anyway?"

Sam pointed up the stairs. "In the nursery. Ripping all the decorations down."

"What? She spent days putting them up." Nick turned and took the stairs two at a time. He pushed the nursery room door open and peered around the frame hesitantly.

Raina stood on a small footstool, stretching up to reach the teddy-bear appliques on the wall. She peeled one off, then balled it up and dropped it on the floor. She got down, moved the footstool a little to the right, and then repeated the process. A small pile of crumpled liners lay at her feet already.

"Raina? What are you doing, sweets?"

She paused at the sound of his voice and then ripped another teddy bear down. "I'm taking all this crap down."

Nick walked farther into the room. "Why? We'll need it soon. Or did you decide you don't like it anymore? We can choose another theme."

"I got my period today, Nick. I'm not pregnant." She yanked off another decoration. "I'm never going to be pregnant."

His heart sank. Then he ached inside as he watched

her stroke a finger over the teddy bear she was holding before she balled it up.

"I'm so sorry, sweetheart. I know how much you were hoping this time was the charm. I was, too."

She looked at him then, her eyes bright with tears. "I know you were. I understand if you want to get a divorce. I understand—"

Nick crossed the room and snatched her off the stool. "Don't ever say that. Ever."

"Nick, it's time for us to face facts. I'm probably not going to get pregnant. It was a long shot anyway."

"You don't know that. This is only the third month we've tried. We just have to be patient. It takes time."

She shoved away from him. "Don't you tell me it takes time. People always say that like they have some crystal ball. It's *easy* to say that when you don't know how it *feels* to be disappointed over and over again. It's easy to say that when it's not your fault!"

She pushed away and went back to her step stool, tearing the last teddy bear down with a curse. Then she grabbed the edge of the border lining the ceiling and yanked. There was a loud, ripping sound as it detached from the wall.

"Raina, it is not your fault."

She didn't respond. She seemed to have forgotten he was even in the room. He watched, stunned, as she got down from the step stool and marched over to the white dresser filled with baby clothes. She yanked open the first drawer and pulled out all the neatly folded onesies. He knew it had taken her quite a while to launder and fold them all.

She picked up a big armful and dumped them on the floor at her feet.

"It's okay, baby. It's okay." He repeated the words but didn't seem to be getting through to her. Before long she was shaking as she grabbed more and more clothes. When he touched her arm, she flinched and then sat down on the ground. She wrapped her arms around her legs and didn't move.

Nick dropped to the ground in front of her and pulled her into his lap. She clung to him and buried her face in his chest as if she didn't want him to see her cry.

"Raina." He couldn't keep the pity from his voice. "Come on, sweets, let's get you into bed."

She shook her head frantically, her limbs trembling. The more he talked to her, the tighter she curled.

This is not working, Nick thought.

Talking wasn't getting through to her. It was time to take some drastic action. He leaned back slightly and shucked off his suit jacket. It fell in a heap behind him.

Then he stood, carrying Raina in his arms. At the sudden movement, she squeaked and tightened her hold around his neck until she was almost strangling him.

"What are you doing?"

"I'm going to have to pull rank on you, sweetheart. You're really upset and I think you need a bath and bed. So that's where I'm taking you, whether you want it or not." He pulled her closer and kissed the top of her forehead. "You can yell at me for this later."

*   *   *   *   *

AFTER STRIPPING HER clothes off, Raina sat on the side of the tub, watching Nick. He moved around the bathroom with quick, decisive motions. He'd turned the water on, adjusted the temperature, and then gathered all the bath stuff he could find. He'd pulled bath salts, bubble bath, and several types of scented body gel from beneath her counter and lined them up on the edge of the tub. When he started pulling out shampoo and conditioner, she finally put up a hand to stop him.

"I don't need all that. My hair's dry, so I don't have to wash it as much. I'll just put it up." She pointed to the counter where she'd left a hair band. Nick handed it to her and watched as she twisted her hair into a long coil and then wrapped it around itself until it formed a big bun on top of her head.

"I always like when you wear your hair up. You look like a naughty librarian," Nick commented. Then he turned back to the line of products on the edge of the tub. "I'm not really sure what I'm doing here so help me out, love."

She pointed at the bubble bath and the shower gel. "That's really all I need. My loofah sponge is in the shower."

He retrieved it and then helped her into the tub. Usually he would have made some racy comment or at least tried to cop a feel. But even though she was naked, his eyes didn't dip below her neck. There was something different about the way he looked at her. Like he was scared of doing the wrong thing.

She thought back to her hysterics. It was no wonder he was scared to say anything. He was probably worried she was on the verge of another mental breakdown. She sighed and sank down slowly into the hot water before turning to face Nick.

"I'm really sorry about all that. I don't know what came over me."

Once she was sitting in the middle of the froth of bubbles, he leaned over and kissed her softly on the nose. "Let's just relax for a while. We can talk later. What do you say?"

"Care to join me? I think I'll relax faster if you stay." She really hoped he would. Even though she felt calmer after her little fit, she really didn't want to be alone. She felt like she'd spent far too much time alone lately.

Nick nodded his assent and began shucking his own clothes. Since he'd already taken his jacket off, he yanked at the knot in his tie and removed his pants and boxers. He was about to drop them on the tile when he noticed her watching him. She'd been teasing him since they got married about living with a slob. With a sheepish smile, he folded them in half and put them on the counter.

"See, you're getting better," she teased.

His lips tilted up as he quickly unbuttoned his shirt and folded it as well. "Apparently I can be trained."

Raina would have responded, but her mouth went dry at the first sight of his flat stomach and well-developed pectorals. What dream was this that she was allowed to be with someone so magnificent? She got to wake up every morning with this amazing man and he came home to her every night.

When she'd started this journey, he'd simply been a gorgeous man offering her a lifeline. Now she knew without a doubt that he was more than just her savior.

He was the love of her life.

Nick climbed in the tub, facing her. They didn't talk for a few minutes. Then they both started speaking at once.

"I just want to say…"

"I want to apologize…"

Laughing, Raina shook her head and held out her hand for Nick to speak first. Apparently Nick had other ideas, though. Without another word spoken between them, he leaned forward and kissed her until she could barely think straight.

If this is how he apologizes, he's already forgiven.

He closed his eyes and pressed his forehead against hers. "I want to apologize for manhandling you in there. I wasn't sure what to do."

She pushed back a little so she could see his eyes. "I was freaking out, Nick. You did the only thing you *could* do besides slap me silly."

"I'm really sorry you're not pregnant. I know how much you want this. And I feel like a broken record saying the same things to you. I wish there was some way I could just fix it for you. All I want is for you to be happy."

Raina blinked back tears. "I don't know what happened. I know intellectually that it's not going to happen overnight just because I want it. But in that moment, it just got bigger and bigger in my mind until all I could see was failure. It kind of took over my brain. I think it's just me being afraid that it'll never happen."

The warmth of the water was doing its job, because she was suddenly more tired than she'd ever been. The emotion she'd expended with her meltdown had drained her. She added a little bath gel to her loofah sponge and inhaled the soothing lavender scent. When she felt Nick's arms circle her from behind, she pressed back onto him, enjoying the tortured groan that slipped from his lips.

They took their time in the bath, trailing damp fingertips over silken skin and enjoying the heat and scent of the fragrant water. She loved the way they fit together, like two halves of a matched set, and she felt herself relax, really relax, for the first time since she'd come back to the States. From Ridley's being shot, to her new diagnosis, to marrying Nick, it felt like she hadn't stopped worrying in a long time.

When her skin started to pucker, they got out. Nick toweled her off gently with a plush, oversized bath towel. Raina slipped into one of Nick's T-shirts and Nick dragged on a pair of shorts before gathering Raina in his arms and cuddling with her under the covers.

She rolled over to look at him, then raised her hand to

trace the angle of his strong jaw, the slightly uneven line of his nose, and the curve of his sensual lips. He was the epitome of masculine beauty to her. Not just because of his good looks but because of all the things others couldn't see. The things she couldn't touch.

His generosity, his spirit, and his unfailing determination to make her happy.

It dawned on her then that this was love. Love was the man who took care of her when she needed him to. The man who made sure she ate well, listened to her babble on about her show even though he probably had no idea what she was talking about, and who was disappointed right along with her when she was sad.

Love was the man who'd literally carry you when you were down.

* * * * *

NICK HELD HIMSELF perfectly still as Raina touched him. Her beautiful brown eyes followed the path of her finger as if memorizing the lines of his face. As many times as they'd made love and as intimate as they'd been, nothing had made him feel as self-conscious. He'd never been the focus of her attention so completely before.

She leaned closer and kissed him. Softly. Sweetly.

"Goodnight, Nick." Then she snuggled against his shoulder and let out a soft sigh, the warm puff of air tickling his skin. After a few minutes, her breathing evened out. He looked down and was startled to see that her eyes were wide open and locked on his face.

"You're still awake? I thought you'd fallen asleep." He stroked her cheek with the side of his thumb.

"I think I love you," she whispered.

Everything inside of Nick stopped at that moment. His

thoughts. The questions he'd been about to ask.

His heartbeat.

"I think *I'm* dreaming," Nick said finally.

Raina squeezed her eyes shut. "I don't have much experience with love. It made my mom so bitter. Most of my relationships have been more about sex than feelings. So I always thought how could I believe in something that I'd never seen? It just seemed like some fairy tale that couldn't possibly come true."

Nick's heart twisted at the raw pain in her voice.

"But these past two months with you I've *seen* it. I've seen a mother who dotes on each and every one of her children and loves them for their differences. I've seen brothers who stick together against the world. I've seen how you take care of me even when I've given you plenty of reasons not to want to. If this isn't love, I can't imagine how it could be any better."

Nick wanted to say something but everything inside him was still too jumbled for him to form a sentence. He'd loved her for so long but he didn't think he'd fully *understood* her until now. She projected the image of strength so convincingly that most people never saw how scared and vulnerable she was underneath. Afraid to try, afraid to trust, and most of all, afraid to believe in love because it seemed like too much to hope for.

He'd thought he'd come to terms with the possibility of her never returning his feelings. Love wasn't something that was based on a reciprocal exchange, he'd reasoned. Over time he'd hoped she'd develop fondness for him, but he'd started to think that's all it would ever be.

Which would have killed him slowly from the inside out.

But she was finally getting there. *Thank God.* He wasn't the most spiritual person but in that moment, he felt like he needed to say thank you to a higher power. *I think I love you* wasn't the declaration he'd hoped for, but it was a hell of a lot more than he'd been expecting when they hadn't even been married three full months yet.

If she could even think of loving him, then he was the luckiest man on the planet.

Raina was watching him and must have interpreted his silence as him being upset.

"I'm so sorry, Nick. I wish I could just say it. You deserve someone who can love as openly as you do. Someone who's perfect for you."

Nick pulled her against him and held her there, comforted by the steady beat of her heart against his and the soft scent of her skin. Raina seemed to be under the impression that he wouldn't want her love if it wasn't perfect.

But Nick knew that there were plenty of things that he'd done wrong in their relationship. Times when he'd been impatient or selfish or hadn't loved her as well as he could have. There was no such thing as a perfect love and he didn't want there to be. They'd worked hard to get from a place of distrust to where they could share their hearts without fear.

He'd take their messy, chaotic, disorganized love any day of the week because it was real.

"I do deserve that," he said finally. She tensed against him and then tried to push back. He tightened his arms around her, holding her still.

"But I'd like to think I also deserve to be loved by the woman I'm in love with. So, if it's okay with you, I think I'll stick around a little while longer."

Chapter Fourteen

～

A FEW WEEKS later, Raina woke up feeling like roadkill. October was usually mild in Virginia, but there had been a cold snap that had taken them all by surprise. The last week she'd been sick with a cold that left her a snotty, exhausted mess. She'd been worried about giving it to Nick, but he'd laughed at her concern.

"I never get sick," he'd claimed smugly, then promptly came down with it himself.

After a few days of them both being miserable, she'd finally started to feel human again. Until today. She tried to roll over and go back to sleep but she was too hot and agitated, so she finally decided to just get up. As soon as her feet hit the ground, she raced to the bathroom. She barely made it to the toilet before she threw up.

"Oh my God," she whispered. She stood staring at the mess in shock before doing a quick mental calculation. "I never thought I'd be so happy to barf."

She rinsed out her mouth and then retrieved her phone from her night table. She had to double- and triple-check the date before she believed it. Even then, she still didn't want to get too excited.

Her period could be late for any number of reasons.

She puttered around for the majority of the morning. Food was out of the question because just the thought made her nauseous again, so she read a little of a memoir she'd been trying to get into. She took a nap in the afternoon and when she woke, groggy and dizzy, book open on her chest, it was after three. Nick would be home in a few hours or so. Once he got here, she could do the test.

Her eyes jumped to the clock again. Three whole hours.

"Oh for crying out loud." She slammed the book down and marched upstairs and into her bathroom. Most pregnancy tests admonished you to wait until your period was several days late. But she couldn't take it any longer. If there was even a chance of finding out if she was pregnant now, she had to take it.

Otherwise she'd spend the day going slowly insane.

She pulled open the cabinet below the sink. She'd bought several brands of pregnancy tests when she and Nick had first started trying. After testing the first month, she'd always gotten her period early so she hadn't used any more.

This was the first time she'd been late in ages.

She went back downstairs for a cup. A few minutes later, she'd performed the tests (just in case one malfunctioned) and had them all lined up on the sink. Each had one pink line to show that the test was in process. She was supposed to wait and see if a second pink line developed. If it did, she was pregnant.

If it didn't, then... well, she'd cross that line if it happened.

The minutes ticked by at a glacial pace. When the timer on her phone went off, she knelt and peered at the first test. There was a second line but it was so faint that she thought she might be imagining it. But when she looked at the second test, two lines were clearly visible. She picked up the test and did a small jig.

She was pregnant. *Finally.*

After a fierce mental debate, she decided not to call Ridley yet. Nick should be the first person to find out. He'd been just as nervous as the weeks passed as she had been. She debated whether to call him at the office, then discarded the idea. Telling him over the phone wasn't as much fun. She wanted to see his face when she told him. It gave her an incredibly feminine sense of pride to be able to tell him he was going to be a father.

She went downstairs to wait for him to come home.

But when six o'clock came and went, she wondered if she should have called Ridley after all. She was *bursting* with the news and she wanted to talk about it with someone. Someone who'd understand how much it meant.

After another hour passed, she started to get mad. "Where is he?"

She stomped down the stairs to the main level. When she saw it was empty, she went down another level until she reached the basement. Sam looked up from where he was pouring himself a club soda at the bar.

"Is everything okay?" he asked.

She figured she must have looked just as pissed off as she felt. "Nick hasn't called, has he? I don't have any messages, but he's two hours late."

Sam shook his head. "No, I haven't heard the phone ring. It's only eight o'clock. He probably had a meeting run late or something."

Raina gripped her phone. "You're right. I've gotten spoiled with him coming home so early."

Sam gave her a pitying look. "I'm sure he'll be here soon."

Raina didn't even bother answering, just ran back upstairs. How desperate did she appear, acting like he was missing just because he was a little late? He was probably stuck with some overbearing client, trying to figure out how to get away.

As she passed the hall mirror, she skidded to a stop and looked at her reflection with distaste. "I can at least try to pretty up a little."

Maybe it was a good thing that Nick was late. It would be a nice change for him to come home to something other than a tired, cranky wife.

She bathed and shaved her legs, taking time to put on makeup and do her hair. She was in the middle of tying her hair up in a knot on top of her head the way Nick liked it when the bathroom door opened.

"There you are. I was looking for you." He crossed behind her and pulled her into his arms. "You look beautiful. What's the occasion?"

She turned around and placed his hand against her lower abdomen. "This is. I think creating life deserves a celebration." Nick's mouth fell open and he stood staring until she poked him in the stomach.

"Well, say something."

He let out a whoop and grabbed her in a bear hug.

"Oh, shit!" He put her down gently. "I shouldn't have done that. I forgot myself for a moment."

"Nick, I'm not made of glass. I've been walking around and doing all the normal things I usually do, including jogging and kickboxing. The doctor said I can."

"What kind of doctor is that? Kickboxing? We don't need to be kickboxing."

Raina crossed her arms. "*We* aren't doing anything. I'm just doing my usual exercise routine. But I'll switch to something gentler now. I already bought some pregnancy workout videos. I want to be careful now that I'm carrying little Nicholas Junior."

Nick leaned down and framed her face in his hands. "You have made me so happy, you know that?"

Raina closed her eyes. "You have, too. Just by being you."

"We do need to celebrate. As a matter of fact, why don't you come by the office tomorrow and I'll show you around? You could come later in the day and I'll take you to dinner. It'll give you a break from my cooking."

Raina squeezed him around the waist. "Are you fishing for compliments or what? Your cooking is amazing and you know it."

Nick grinned. "I'll talk to my assistant about rearranging my client meetings."

"That sounds nice."

"I want you to be a part of my world and I want to be there for you, too." He let out a shaky breath. "You're really pregnant. We're going to have a baby?" At her nod, he got down on his knees and lifted her shirt.

"We're going to have a baby," he whispered against her stomach.

*   *   *   *   *

IT WAS MORE than a week before Nick was able to rearrange his schedule enough to take an extended lunch break. On a humid Monday morning, Raina drove to Nick's building in one of the few commercial office parks in New Haven. She parked in the open lot designated for visitors and then took the elevator to the fifth floor. It opened into a modern, spacious reception area decorated in shades of cream and blue. The young woman behind the desk had her back to her, furiously pressing the buttons on a copy machine.

"Come on, I just want to send a fax. How do I get it off the scan function? I hate this stupid thing."

Raina wasn't sure if she should interrupt. It looked like the young lady was on the verge of declaring war against the machine. Just as she was about to call out, the woman turned and then jumped.

"Oh no. How long have you been waiting?" she cried.

Raina waved her away. "Just a second. Not long."

The girl's shoulders slumped. "Good. There was another lady who made the biggest fuss because I wasn't here when she got in for her meeting. I think she complained to my boss."

Raina leaned over and said, "She sounds like a bitch."

The girl giggled before she seemed to catch herself. She sat down behind her desk and looked up at Raina with a bright smile. "Um, sorry about that. You must be with Davis Development." She tapped a few keys and then shook her head. "I actually don't have your appointment until three p.m., but I'm sure Mr. Alexander will make time."

Raina took off her sunglasses. "I don't have an appointment, actually. I'm, uh… Well, I'm Nick's wife."

The girl's mouth fell open. "You're Raina. Ridley's twin. With the sunglasses, I didn't realize."

171

Raina looked at her closer. "You know my sister?"

"I'm Kaylee," she said, holding out her hand. "I'm in Jackson's newest group, Divine."

Raina accepted her hand with a smile. "What a small world. Is that how Jackson discovered you? Were you singing at the office Christmas party when he found you or something?"

Kaylee shook her head. "That would be a much cooler story than the real one. My friend Sasha asked me to sing backup for her group when one of the members dropped out. We did a few small gigs at clubs and several restaurants and Jackson's assistant saw us at one of them. That's how I met your sister. At the studio with Jackson."

"So how did you end up here?" Raina leaned a hip against the desk. She didn't get the chance to shoot the breeze that often. As weird as it was, it was surprisingly refreshing to just chat with someone.

"Your husband hired me as a favor to Jackson. Which was really nice of him since I've never done this type of job before." She gestured toward the copy machine behind her. "As you just saw."

"I'm sure you'll figure everything out."

Kay blew out a breath. "I hope so. Anyway, let me go peek in his office and see if he's still on his conference call. It was supposed to end twenty minutes ago but last I knew, they were still on." She got up from behind her desk and walked to a closed door a few feet away.

Raina closed her eyes and massaged her temples. She'd spent the morning reviewing more footage of her show. Now that she was taking a break from modeling, it was alarming to watch how hectic her schedule had been. She'd been doing it for so long that it had become second nature, but watching from an outsider's perspective, it didn't look as exciting and glamorous as it sounded.

The production technicians were trying to cut the material in a way that presented an interesting "story," they'd explained to her. But Raina was starting to get worried. The network had only picked up the first six episodes of the show. If they couldn't find enough interesting material to use, they wouldn't option any episodes after that.

Now that there was no wedding to film, there wasn't much left for future episodes. Her agent had already called and asked if she and Nick were willing to be filmed, which she'd immediately declined. Steven had been willing to go on air but somehow she doubted Nick would be interested in having cameras following him. He was very poised in front of the media but he also guarded his family fiercely. Having cameras following him would affect them, too.

Something she knew he'd never agree to.

Surprisingly, Raina felt just as protective about her in-laws. Julia wore clothes that were comfortable and fit her round figure, but they were definitely not designer fashions. What if someone made fun of her? Although when she thought on it, Julia would probably deal with a nosy camera crew by just feeding them until they were all good friends.

But what about Bennett? With his slight stutter and awkward demeanor, he could become a target of ridicule. Her hands clenched into fists. It enraged her to think of anyone targeting him because of his association with her.

"Raina, sorry to keep you waiting."

She turned at Nick's touch to her elbow. He looked stressed but handsome, as usual. Her eyes traveled over his dark blue pinstriped suit. By the time she got back to his face, his eyes were amused.

"Does my fashion sense meet with your approval,

sweets?"

She ran a finger down his tie, then moved the knot slightly to the left. "The suit is divine. What's in the suit is even better."

Nick pulled her close and whispered in her ear. "I'm supposed to be romancing you and taking you for a civilized lunch. You're making me want to forget my good intentions. There are so many other things we can do with this hour."

"Oh no. You aren't getting out of this that easily. You promised to show me around and then take me out. So..." She grabbed him by the hand and tugged him toward his office. "Show me your world, Nick."

*   *   *   *   *

NICK PULLED OUT her chair and Raina sank down into the wrought-iron seat gracefully. After a quick tour of his office, they'd walked down to a sidewalk café a few blocks from Nick's building.

"I never asked you this before, but what made you decide to open your office in New Haven? Wouldn't it have been easier to get clients in Norfolk or Virginia Beach? Or go up to D.C. like Elliot? Not that I'm not happy you're here." She turned and accepted a menu from the waiter who'd just approached the table.

Nick waited patiently as their server rattled off an impressive list of specials and took their orders. Once they were alone again, he picked up her hand that was resting on top of the table. He'd been touching her like that all afternoon. Just casual little touches, but he couldn't seem to stop.

He was doing his best not to push after her *I think I love you* declaration but at moments like this, when they were just hanging out and sharing their lives, it was so hard not to show how he felt.

"I thought about going to other, more metropolitan areas. I would have gotten more clients, twice as fast. But my family is here and I didn't want to go that far."

They sat in comfortable silence for a while. Raina seemed to be thinking about what he'd said.

"You know, I don't think I could have done what you did. Could I have stayed at home if my mother had needed me? Or if Ridley had been scared to be on her own? I want to believe that I'd be that selfless, but I probably would have gone anyway."

Their server returned then with her chicken salad and Nick's club sandwich. He immediately took the bun off his sandwich and rearranged the way the lettuce and tomatoes were stacked. When he looked up, she was staring, so he said, "I don't like too much lettuce."

"I didn't say anything," she said with a smile. "I just never noticed that you're almost as fussy about food as I am. Anyway, that was really nice of you, Nick. To stay in case your family needed you."

He took a big bite of his sandwich and shrugged. It was weird to have her congratulating him for sticking around. That was what you did for family. Did she think that he'd just run out on *her* if she needed him?

"I was raised to believe that when you need help, your family is there. I'm not sure how much you know about Jackson's story, but his late wife got pregnant while I was a senior in college. It took us all by surprise."

He figured she had to know bits and pieces about Jackson's life before he was widowed. Ridley had probably told her about the accident that had killed his first wife.

"I bet. What was she like?"

Nick considered his words very carefully. "Cynthia was a sweet girl. She was pretty quiet."

Raina watched him take a sip of his drink. "It's okay if you didn't like her."

Nick put his drink down. "I didn't say I didn't like her. She was really nice. Just perhaps not the best match for my brother."

"You don't have to mince words around me, Nick. I understand. Not everyone gets to have that picture-perfect movie love."

Nick took her hand. "It's not that rare. I see it in my parents, and Jackson has found his perfect match in Ridley." He looked at her long enough that he hoped she could hear what he wasn't saying.

And I have my perfect match in you.

She cleared her throat and looked away. "Anyway, I'm really glad Ridley has Jackson now. He and the boys are exactly what she needs. I worry about her sometimes."

"Why? What happened?"

"Nothing. It's just that Ridley's been communicating with our father a lot lately. I worry that he's using her soft nature to worm his way into her good graces. She's planning to go visit him in Maryland soon."

"You don't want to go, too?" Nick asked.

"I wanted to meet him, but that doesn't mean I trust him completely. Everybody seems to think I should just forgive and forget all those years he wasn't around," Raina snapped. Then she sighed. "I'm sorry, I don't mean to take it out on you. This topic just puts me on edge."

Nick pushed his half-eaten sandwich aside. "I think you're doing what's best for you by being cautious. After all, what if he decides to up and disappear again? There's nothing wrong with taking this slowly. He's been gone this long, so surely he can wait until you're ready to take the next step."

Raina relaxed back into her seat. "Thank you. That's

pretty much how I feel about it, too."

His phone vibrated in his pocket and Nick pulled back. "Sorry, I meant to turn this off." He looked at the screen for a minute and then looked up at Raina. "We need to go. Now."

He pushed his chair back and pulled out several twenty-dollar bills, tucking them under the salt shaker.

"Nick, what's wrong?"

Raina stood and followed him down the sidewalk. He turned into a little corner store and walked to the checkout aisle. *Where are they? Where are they?* He didn't read tabloids, but he knew they were usually sold right near the cashiers. He knelt down and grabbed one of the papers on the bottom row. The bold headline was easy to read.

FAMILY TROUBLE FOR LEGGY?

Nick handed the magazine to the cashier and a few minutes later they were outside on the sidewalk again. He flipped to the article and read it quickly.

"Whatever's in there isn't worth getting worked up about, Nick. Lies are what tabloids are known for." Raina watched him with a sad smile. "I'm just sorry that you have to deal with it now, too. Was it something about me or you?"

He looked up at her. "No, it's about my mom."

Raina choked. "What?"

He ran his hands over his hair. "Apparently one of my mom's friends sold a story to the press. They printed an email my mom wrote. I'm really sorry."

"Well, it's not her fault that one of her friends is a sellout."

"It's not that. The email was about you. Here." He handed her the paper. She skimmed the article quickly.

- - - *Family Trouble for Leggy?* - - -

Sources close to the Alexander family share their

worries about the marriage of Raina "Leggy" Winters to finance whiz kid, Nicholas Alexander. Nick's mother, Julia, is quoted in an email to our source as saying:

"We didn't hear anything from Nick, just some story on the Internet that he's married some woman we barely know. I don't know what to think! How do I know she didn't kidnap my son?"

Sources also confirm that Raina is not only persona non grata with her new in-laws, but she's not even on speaking terms with her own father! Leggy's dad was reportedly distraught when she refused to meet with him earlier this month. The honeymoon seems to be over for Leggy already.

Raina handed the paper back. "It's okay, Nick. I'm not upset."

"You aren't?" He peered at her closely. "I can understand if you are. I'm sure she didn't mean it."

She sighed. "Nick, the tabloids are a necessary evil in my life. But I *chose* this life. Your mom didn't. She should be able to vent to a friend about her daughter-in-law. She didn't even say anything that bad, just that she wasn't sure what to think. Although the fact that she was worried about *me* kidnapping *you* is pretty ironic."

Nick chuckled. "I'm glad you're taking this so well. Because the text I got was from Bennett. Mom is pretty upset about this. I think we should go smooth things over."

She slipped her hand in his. "Of course. When family needs you, you're there. Let's go."

Chapter Fifteen

⁓

RAINA TRIED TO ignore the feeling of dread that settled in her stomach as they drove down the dirt road leading to the farm. He'd said his mother was upset, but was she mad at Raina for bringing the tabloids into their lives?

Would his family even be happy to see them?

"Nick, maybe you should go talk to everyone first."

He looked at her in surprise. "Why would I do that?"

She looked at him in annoyance. "I'm sure they don't want to see me right now, Nick. Their lives were peaceful before I brought all this tabloid garbage into the mix. I'm probably the last person they want to see right now. Especially your mom."

He grabbed her hand and squeezed it. "I can guarantee you that no one is mad at you. My family adores you."

"That was before. Now they have people stealing their emails and publishing their private thoughts. I know how invasive it is when it happens to you."

"I know you do, sweetheart. That's why you're the best person to talk to them right now. You know what it's like better than anyone else here. You can help the rest of us get through it. You're an Alexander now and we stick together. So if it's a problem for you, it's a problem for us. None of us would have it any differently."

He opened his door and climbed out. Raina followed reluctantly. The front door was open, so they walked through to the backyard. Bennett, Laura, and Nick's parents stood at the railing, looking out onto the lawn.

"Hey, Dad. Mom. We came as soon as we heard," Nick said.

His mother turned to face them and Raina sucked in a shocked breath. Julia's eyes were puffy and red. She was filled with anger and shame all over again. Someone like Julia only wanted to help people, to show kindness to her neighbors and her family. She had no defense against mean-spirited journalism. She shouldn't have to guard herself against it, either.

"Mom, are you okay?" Nick asked.

She nodded then glanced over at Raina. "I'm fine."

Raina's heart sank. It had been a long time since she'd cared about what the tabloids printed about her. They were going to make up something to get their story no matter what she did, so she'd long ago learned to tune it out. What they did had simply ceased to matter in her world.

But it was totally different when people who'd been nothing but nice to her were being harassed. It *mattered* when the lies they spread hurt family. The Alexanders, she realized, weren't just Nick's family now.

They were hers, too.

"I have something I want to say." Raina turned to the rest of the group.

Laura reached over and turned the music off. "I'll just go supervise the kids so they stay out of the way." She gave Raina a sympathetic smile and skipped down the steps into the yard.

It was suddenly extremely quiet.

"I want to apologize for the invasion of your privacy," Raina said. "I'm so used to the tabloids that I don't even think about them anymore, but I remember what it was like in the beginning. It was awful. I really wish this wasn't happening." She didn't look at Nick as she said, "But perhaps if I go stay in my apartment in D.C. for a few months, it'll help. Maybe they'll focus on what I'm doing and not bother you if I'm not here."

Nick's head shot up and he looked like he was about to speak when his mother beat him to it.

"You shouldn't have to exile yourself because of those miscreants." Julia's chest heaved as she stomped her foot. "They're the ones in the wrong. We want you to stay right here with your family."

Raina twisted her fingers together. "But I'm the one they're targeting. You all didn't ask for any of this. I'm going to have my security guy look into how they got their hands on that email. I'm sure some laws have been broken."

Julia's eyes suddenly filled with tears. "I wrote that before I ever met you, honey. I would never say that now. I think you're the best thing that's ever happened to

Nick."

Raina stepped forward and then shocked the hell out of both of them by pulling Julia into a hug. It probably looked as awkward as it felt, like she was trying out a skill she rarely used. She was so much taller than her mother-in-law, especially in the super-high heels she'd worn that day, so she ended up patting Julia on the back clumsily while looking down at her.

But the smile on her mother-in-law's face was worth it.

Raina looked back at Nick and said, "I think he might be the best thing that ever happened to me, too. Partially because he comes attached to all of you."

* * * * *

IT NEVER FAILED. Whenever he really needed to be somewhere, a client wanted to ask questions. No matter what else was going on in the world, this was the one rule that Nick could always count on.

"So, I'm thinking about buying more investment property. I was going to wait until next year when I have more cash on hand. But I heard that congress might not extend the current bonus depreciation after this year. Should I buy now?"

Nick cleared his throat and tried to focus on Ian Williamson, one of his oldest clients.

"Oh, look at the time. We've run over."

Nick's head snapped up. "Yes, we have, and unfortunately I really do need to run. My wife is having her first sonogram today," he found himself saying. "We get to hear the heartbeat."

Ian looked shocked. "Well, congratulations, Nick. As you know, I have four with the missus. There's nothing like the first time you see your child. Go on. Go!"

Nick grabbed his briefcase and shot out the door,

yelling over his shoulder for Kay to put Mr. Williamson down again for next week.

Too impatient to wait for the elevator, he bounded down the five flights of stairs to the lobby and then another flight to the underground parking deck.

By the time he pulled up to New Haven General, he was pretty sure he'd broken several traffic laws. He pulled around to the side of the hospital where the medical offices were located. Not finding a space close to the door, he parked at the back of the lot and jogged up the path. He entered and walked straight up to the reception desk.

"Hi. My wife, Raina, is here and I'm late."

The nurse behind the desk smiled knowingly. "She asked us to keep a lookout for you, Mr. Alexander. She only went back five minutes ago."

He followed the nurse through another door and down a long hallway. She stopped at a room on the right and knocked briskly. He heard Raina's voice call out, "*Come in.*"

The nurse opened the door and ushered him inside.

"Nick!" Raina stood as soon as he entered. "You made it. I thought you weren't going to get here in time." She had already undressed and wore a light blue hospital gown. He kissed her lightly on the cheek.

"I'm so sorry, sweets. I was in the middle of a client meeting. I was on the verge of running out. Luckily, this guy has four kids of his own so he seemed to understand."

Her eyes sparkled as she looked up at him. Her pregnancy was already obvious in the glow of her skin and the flush on her cheeks.

"I'm just glad you're here. I'm waiting on the doctor now. I already filled out my paperwork and the nurses weighed me."

He sat in one of the uncomfortable blue chairs next to the utilitarian gray desk in the corner. Raina sat back on the paper-lined exam table. It was stark and slightly scary to be in such a medicinal environment.

Raina has to do this all the time?

Nick couldn't imagine having to come here on a regular basis, but Raina had already been once to confirm pregnancy. Now they would get to see the baby and hear the heartbeat.

There was another brief knock before the door opened. An older woman with salt-and-pepper hair stepped through the door.

"Ms. Winters, good to see you again."

Raina waved. "Hi, Dr. Waters. This is my husband, Nick."

The doctor shook his hand. "Hello, Mr. Alexander. Glad you could join us this time." She read over Raina's chart and then asked, "Any problems I should be aware of?"

"I'm just throwing up a lot. When is this part going to be over?"

"Usually it'll stop before the second trimester. Hopefully, sooner. If it becomes severe and persistent then we'll need to address it. But hopefully it won't come to that."

She pulled out a small machine and positioned it next to Raina. "Now it's time for the good stuff. We get to do another ultrasound so you can hear your baby's heartbeat. I'll also measure the baby to make sure he or she is growing properly."

Nick rubbed his hands together. While the doctor moved around the room gathering equipment, he leaned over and took Raina's hand.

"She can't tell whether it's a boy or a girl yet, right?"

Raina shook her head. "Not yet. We have to wait until

I'm twenty weeks along for that."

"You don't have a preference, do you? Because I should probably warn you, Alexander men mainly shoot Y chromosomes."

Raina put a hand over her stomach. "I don't care about that. I'll love them either way. And they'll love me right back." She said the last part so softly he wondered if she'd meant to say it at all.

The doctor came back to them with a large wand. "Now don't be alarmed, Mr. Alexander. Since your wife isn't that far along, we have to use a probe."

"A transvaginal ultrasound, right?" Nick supplied.

Dr. Waters looked impressed. "Very good. Not many fathers are that well informed."

He gave himself a mental pat on the back. "I've been reading this book about pregnancy."

Raina shot him a wry glance. "He probably knows more about it than I do."

"Okay, just lie back and try to relax, Raina."

Nick moved up closer to Raina's head. Her eyes latched on to his. He could hear movement below, but he kept his eyes on hers. She flinched, then he heard the doctor tapping away at the keyboard of the machine she was staring at.

"Okay, I'm measuring the fetus. Growth is on target. Now, just a second and we'll let you hear the heartbeat."

There was a pause and then the room was filled with a loud whooshing sound. Nick felt his own heart rate jump in response.

"That's our baby?" he whispered to Raina.

She nodded and a tear slipped down her cheek. "Listen to him! It's so fast."

"It does sound really fast. Is that normal?" He turned and repeated the question to Dr. Waters.

"It's a beautiful heart rate. It's normal for it to sound

fast like a horse's gallop."

Raina looked at the screen. There wasn't much to see, just a few white shaded areas and a small blob in the center.

"There's my little jelly bean," she said.

Dr. Waters hit a few keys and then handed them a strip of black and white pictures. "Here are some photos for your scrapbook."

Nick peered at the photo. There was a small circle around the blob in the middle so he assumed that was the baby.

"Now, do you two have any questions for me?"

Nick looked up. "I do. Is there anything that we should avoid? Like sex, for example?"

Raina winced. "Nick!"

Dr. Waters held up a hand. "The most common question I get about pregnancy is whether sex is safe. In your case, Raina, your difficulty in getting pregnant was due to the blockage in your fallopian tubes. Now that you *are* pregnant, I fully expect you to have a completely normal pregnancy and delivery. Which means that sexual activity is perfectly safe."

Nick leaned forward. "The book said no deep penetration though—"

"Nick! She said it was safe." Raina's cheeks flushed bright red.

Dr. Waters looked like she was fighting a smile. "It's perfectly all right. It's safe for you to do whatever Raina feels comfortable doing. Just listen to your body's natural cues. If anything feels uncomfortable or you start to feel dizzy or sick, then stop. Otherwise, it's perfectly fine."

Nick sighed. "Okay, then I have no other questions."

*   *   *   *   *

"YOU'RE WEARING THAT?" Nick stood in the doorway of their bedroom, watching as she smoothed down her dress.

"I'm pretty sure those words are in the 'what to never say to your pregnant wife' category. But yes, I'm wearing this. I have to wear all my nice clothes before I'm too big for them. Plus, I've been feeling so sick and gross all week that the only things I've worn are my pajamas. I want to wear something nice."

"You look beautiful."

"I can't wait until this horrible nausea stops. Baby bumps are all the rage now. I'm determined to be fashionable all throughout this pregnancy. I've already gotten a few offers for pregnancy modeling, but I can't take them when I'm barfing all day."

"You'll be as beautiful pregnant as you've always been." He was saying the right things but looking down at his phone. He'd been like this lately, distracted and distant.

Raina looked at herself in the mirror over her dresser. Was it any wonder? Throwing up for the past month and a half had robbed her complexion of its usual freshness. She snorted. Who was she trying to fool? *Freshness?* She looked like a hag. She was bloated even though she hadn't been eating much because even the smell of food made her want to upchuck.

They arrived at the ABC Farm and Nick ushered Raina quickly from the car into the house. It was much colder out now. The weather seemed to have gotten pissed off that summer was gone and had just snapped into the low forties overnight.

Julia greeted them at the door. "I'm so glad you're feeling well enough to come, Raina. Come on into the kitchen and keep me company."

Raina followed behind as Julia led her through the

family room and into the kitchen. It was a relief to leave the noise and chaos of the den behind.

Ridley and Laura were chopping tomatoes and dropping them into a big wooden bowl. A decorative plate of oranges sat on the table.

"Would you like something to drink, Raina?"

"I'd love an orange, actually." Raina stood at the counter and peeled the fruit. She popped a section in her mouth and the tart juice exploded on her taste buds. She wasn't able to keep much down, but everything she ate now just tasted better. She found herself eyeing the peel, wondering how it would taste. Before she could stop herself, she popped a small piece in her mouth.

Weird but good.

She looked up to find Ridley watching her in disbelief. "Did you just eat the orange peel?"

"I don't know why I did that." Slightly embarrassed, Raina continued eating her orange while Ridley and Laura carried the food out to the table.

"Weird cravings must be part of carrying an Alexander baby." Julia came over and stood next to her. "I never craved ice cream or any of the usual things when I was pregnant with any of the boys. I craved *really* strange things when I was pregnant with Nick. I wanted black pepper all the time."

"Well, that's not that weird," Raina pointed out.

"I wanted black pepper *by itself.* Not sprinkled on food but I would just shake it onto my tongue. It drove Mark crazy."

Raina looked down at the orange peel she'd been absently gnawing on and suddenly didn't feel so bad.

"I've been doing weird things more than anything else. I had just about given up on baking, but lately I've been craving chocolate cupcakes again."

"I bet Nick likes that. He's always had a sweet tooth."

"Well, he would probably like them if they didn't all taste like cardboard. I'm completely useless in the kitchen," she admitted. Every time she tried to cook anything, it was an utter disaster. She'd been feeling more and more useless lately. Domestic skills had never been at the top of her priority list, but now she wondered if she'd been too quick to dismiss their importance. All the things she'd thought were so boring and ordinary were skills that would come in handy now.

Julia rubbed her arm. "Everyone has different talents. What would be the point of chefs if everyone could cook? Besides, my son is a great cook. He'll take good care of you."

"He shouldn't have to do everything, though. I'm sure he's going to get tired of always having to do everything for me."

If he isn't already, Raina thought. Considering how distant he'd been lately, it seemed their honeymoon period was already over.

"All I know is that my son had a shadow over him for much of this past year. Until he married *you.* He was always making jokes so everyone else thought he was fine, but a mother doesn't miss these things. You'll see once yours arrives."

She rubbed Raina's belly. Raina warmed from the inside out. She had never been the touchy-feely type, but it was very easy to make an exception for her mother-in-law. Julia had a way about her that put everyone at ease.

"I know your own mother is gone and I'm so sorry, sweetheart. But I hope you know you can come to me with any questions you have or if you just need to talk. I wasn't blessed with daughters, but I feel like the good Lord is making up for it now by bringing you two sweet girls into my sons' lives. I've met their girlfriends before, of course, and I'm sure they were nice enough girls. But

Lord love them, some of them didn't have the brains God gave a turnip. My sons need strong women they can really talk to. Women who can be true partners."

"I'm sure I'm not what you wanted in your daughter-in-law," Raina said softly.

"I wanted him to have a wife who makes him *happy*. Look at him." Julia gestured with her chin to where Nick was holding Jase in his lap and feeding him cookies. He was talking to Jackson and gesturing with his hands emphatically. He looked up and met Raina's eyes. She smiled and he smiled back. It transformed his whole face.

"I've never seen my Nicky so happy," Julia commented.

Raina could only hope he was really as happy as he looked.

Chapter Sixteen

THERE WERE FEW things Nick enjoyed more than taking his motorcycle out for a ride. The wind in his hair, the zing of adrenaline as he took a tight curve. It was one of the only times he could let go of his worries and just fly.

There were several back roads that connected most of the older farms in New Haven. There wasn't much traffic, so he could ride for an hour easily just circling around his parents' property and then looping around their neighbor's spread and back again.

It was almost as good as sex.

Well, not quite.

He finally pulled up to Raina's house. Her garage had three bays. One held her Audi sedan and the other held a black SUV that looked bulletproof. The third had been empty since he'd moved in.

He cut the engine on his bike and rolled it into the third bay. Just as he was fastening his helmet to the back, he looked up to see Raina standing in the doorway.

Things were still tense between them. He'd had to work longer hours lately and even though he tried to bring work home, it wasn't enough. It was far too easy to get wrapped up in Raina when he was here. He often forgot to look at the files he brought home or he only completed about half of what he would have gotten done if he'd been in the office.

"You bought a motorcycle?" Raina stood in the doorway leading from the garage to the house. She wore her favorite faded purple pajamas and a pair of fuzzy pink slippers. He could see the lines of exhaustion bracketing her eyes and mouth. It must have been another bad day. She'd been nauseated more and more lately. And *extremely cranky*. Not that he couldn't understand why.

Nick took off his helmet and tucked it under his arm. "No, I already had it. I drove over to my condo today and picked it up. I haven't taken it out in a while and today was great weather for a ride."

Raina didn't move, just stood in the same spot, staring at the bike. He had a feeling she wasn't admiring it for its racing lines.

"I'm guessing you're not a fan of motorcycles."

"I'm definitely not a fan." She glared at the bike as if it had personally offended her. "Those things are dangerous."

Nick sighed. "Cars are dangerous. So are airplanes. But we use those regularly. Come here, let me show you some of the safety features."

Raina just stared at him. "So that's it? You're just going to ride it anyway?"

"Well, I doubt I'll be riding much now. It's almost winter."

She closed her eyes slowly, as if counting to ten. "I'm not talking about this season, Nick. I mean in the future. You plan on riding this deathtrap in the future? Even after the baby is born?"

"Of course I'm going to keep riding. I'm supposed to stop riding just because you don't like motorcycles?"

Nick was beyond caring about whether this was just her pregnancy hormones. He'd been busting his ass for weeks to show her that he was taking his impending fatherhood seriously. He'd read that massive book about pregnancy, he'd signed them up for Lamaze classes at the hospital, and he'd spent an entire weekend putting together the jigsaw-puzzle pieces masquerading as a crib.

None of that had seemed to get her attention. But him taking out his motorcycle for the first time in months was worth notice. Enough for her to decide he was unfit to be a father, apparently.

"I've been riding for years, Raina. I'm careful and I've never been in an accident," he assured her.

"You know what, never mind. I don't know why I'm surprised. I've seen the signs these past few weeks. You've been distracted and distant. Staying out later and later. I should have known you'd need to seek out some excitement at some point." She looked down at the bike. Her anger seemed to have evaporated.

Now she just looked tired.

His joy at taking the bike for a spin vanished. "Fine, I won't ride it anymore. Will that make you happy?"

Raina just blinked at him. "No, because if it's not this it'll just be something else dangerous. This is who you are. I shouldn't have expected anything different." She turned and trudged back toward the house.

"Raina!" he called.

She didn't look back once.

"Now you're not speaking to me?"

The quiet click of the door closing seemed to reverberate in the otherwise silent street.

* * * * *

"WHERE'S YOUR PRETTY wife? I hope she's feeling well."

Nick looked up to see his father observing him closely. He'd stopped by after work to drop off some information about individual retirement accounts for Bennett. He'd ended up sticking around for dinner and then following his father out to the garage where he was tinkering with the engine on his ancient pickup truck.

It wasn't like there was a warm welcome waiting for him at home.

"The truth is I think I might be in the doghouse with my wife."

"Already? That was fast. What'd you do?" Mark asked.

"Who said I did anything?" Nick crossed his arms.

"Son, the first thing you need to learn if you want a happy marriage is you've *always* done something." Mark chuckled as he pulled down a bottle from one of the shelves on the wall of the garage.

Nick stared at the tips of his shoes, debating whether to just make up something or tell his father the truth. After their fight a few days ago, Raina had been largely ignoring him. It was slightly embarrassing to have to admit that his marriage was on the rocks already.

He looked up to find his father watching him closely. He tensed under the scrutiny. There was no one whose opinion he respected more than Mark Alexander but he hated to tell his dad when he'd screwed up.

Disappointing his father was the worst feeling in the world.

"What's wrong, son? I hate to see you like this."

"Raina and I have been trying for a baby. It's kind of tricky because she has fertility issues. She was willing to marry me so I could get her pregnant, but she doesn't love me, Dad. I'm starting to think she never will."

Nick didn't look up but he could feel the weight of his dad's stare.

"I won't speak on what initially brought you together. I don't condone what you did, but what's done is done. It sounds like your lady is dealing with a lot of heartache right now. I can understand her fears about not being able to have children. It's a little different for women, I think, but as a man, I can tell you my life wouldn't be the same without you boys in it. The four of you are truly my greatest accomplishment. You are my gift and legacy to the world."

"I didn't think I'd feel this way. I thought of the baby as just a means to an end, a way to get Raina to agree to marry me. But I'm already attached to this baby. I can't stand the thought of her leaving me and not seeing her or the baby. But we fought and now she thinks I'm immature. Too immature to be a good parent. I've screwed things up so badly and I can't see how to fix the damage I've done."

"Nothing is unfixable. If I could win your mother's heart after making a sexist comment, then anything is possible."

Nick sat forward, suddenly intrigued. "You did

what?"

It was part of the family lore that his father had initially struck out with their mother after saying something stupid. He'd had to work long and hard that summer to regain her good opinion. Neither of his parents had ever said what the "stupid thing" was. He'd assumed it had been a dirty comment, so he'd never had any interest in hearing it.

But if his father had really said something sexist, he was definitely interested in how he'd atoned for it. Their mother had been a feminist for as long as Nick could remember. If his dad could change her mind after a strikeout of that magnitude, maybe there was hope for Nick after all.

Mark grumbled. "It wasn't that bad. I was trying to make a joke and she took it the wrong way."

Nick folded his arms and tried not to smile. "What exactly did you say?"

"We were talking about colleges and I may have said a pretty girl like her didn't need to worry about it."

Nick winced. "Nice, Dad. So she should have just gotten married and stayed barefoot and pregnant, huh?"

Mark hitched up his pants and circled the hood of the truck again. He wiped his hands on the old rag thrown over his shoulder. "It was a joke! I'm willing to admit it was a bad one."

Nick finally gave in to laughter. "Um, I can see how you might have thought you were complimenting her, but knowing Mom, I'm sure she wasn't amused."

"She let me know in no uncertain terms what I could do with my attempts at flattery. After that, she didn't even look at me when she visited Maria. No more flirtatious looks or conversations. She wasn't rude—she's far too classy for that. But I could see she thought I was an uncivilized oaf. She was pretty determined to keep me at arm's length after that."

The situation was eerily similar to where he found himself with Raina. She was unfailingly polite and she hadn't asked for any more space. But she didn't come seek him out when he got home anymore. She didn't complain about her nausea or her random food cravings. There were no more late-night cuddle sessions and no more monster muffins with the bottoms burned off.

No more of those sweet smiles that made him feel like he'd just come in out of a storm.

"So, what happened? What did you say to change her mind?"

"I didn't say anything. Her parents died and during the aftermath, I was there for her. I was willing to do whatever she needed. More importantly, I didn't just offer my help; I gave it without her asking. In the midst of tragedy, people have the opportunity to show what they're really made of. This is *your* chance to show your lady what you're really made of, son. That you'll be there for her no matter what. In good times and in bad."

Too keyed up to sit still any longer, Nick jumped up and paced. He might not be able to convince her that he was there for her, but he could show her. He was suddenly sure that everything would be okay. That was one of his favorite things about spending time with his parents. He always felt better after seeing them.

"Thanks, Dad. You're never too busy for us. Even now, when I'm clearly keeping you from your work."

Mark ruffled his hair. "I've always got time for you, Nicky. My own father used to say that the true measure of a man is how he treats the people he loves."

"You fixing this old thing again?"

"Just changing the oil." His dad stroked an affectionate hand over the hood of the truck "She's got years of life left in her."

"Well, I guess I'd better go. Thanks for the advice, Dad."

"Anytime, kiddo."

He hugged his father and walked back in the house. His mother stood next to the sink, washing a handful of berries.

"Nick! You're still here."

"Yeah, I was just hanging out with Dad."

She smiled. "I'm so glad. It's strange sometimes for us, having this big old place all to ourselves. You always think you'll enjoy the peace and quiet after your kids are grown, but sometimes I miss all the noise. All the laughter."

She gazed out the window at the backyard as if seeing all the memories of the nights they'd spent playing there. His mother was still a beautiful woman, just softened by time, the lines around her eyes and mouth a testament to a life well lived. As he watched her, it occurred to him that his parents were getting older and that one day, one terrible day, they wouldn't be there anymore.

"You know what, Mom? I think I'll stay a little longer. Do you mind bringing me a pair of Dad's old jeans and a T-shirt? I think I'll help him with the truck."

"I think he'd love that." She disappeared and came back with a pile of clothes, then stood on tiptoe and kissed his cheek. "I probably don't tell you enough, but I'm proud of you, Nick. You were a bit of a wild child but you've grown into a fine man."

"Thanks, Mom."

He ducked into the first-floor bathroom and changed clothes, hanging his suit on the back of the door. When he went back into the garage, his father had already gotten the truck up on the ramps. He looked up at Nick, startled.

"What are you still doing here, Nick? I thought you

were long gone to go sweet-talk your lady."

Nick picked up one of the clean rags on the workbench and threw it over his shoulder. "I'm going to help you with this old clunker before I leave."

"You don't have to do that. I know you're anxious to get home."

"I've got time. This really smart guy once told me that the measure of a man is how he treats the people he loves. Since I had the best role model in the world for what it means to be a man, I'm never too busy to help you out, Dad."

Mark swallowed a few times. Tears shone in his eyes as he nodded. "Well, I'll let you get down there then. You'll have an easier time getting back up than I will, that's for sure!"

*   *   *   *   *

WHEN NICK GOT HOME later that night, Raina was already in bed. She was snuggled up with a mountain of pillows. He almost wanted to laugh when he saw that she'd put so many pillows in the bed that it left very little room for him.

Well played, sweetheart, he thought.

"I spent some time with my parents tonight. Bennett's in the converted barn out back, but he mainly keeps to himself and does his weird science experiments. I think they're a little lonely in the house all by themselves."

Raina didn't turn from the show she was watching.

He yanked at his tie, then unbuttoned his shirt. He shrugged it off before pushing down his pants and tossed the pile of clothes in the hamper Raina had placed in his closet.

"My dad gave me some great advice. He said that the true measure of a man is how he treats the people he loves."

Raina didn't roll over but he could tell by the sudden stiffness in her shoulders that she was holding herself still, listening.

"I thought about our argument and whether I was treating you the way I thought a husband should. The way a man who's crazy in love with his wife would. I decided that I wasn't. Even when we don't agree on something, I don't want you to ever think I don't care about your feelings. So I wanted to apologize."

She rolled over and faced him. "I'm sorry, too. I know I was unfair. It just took me by surprise. I don't want to take something you love away from you. I just can't pretend it doesn't terrify me to think of you getting hit. Getting thrown." She closed her eyes and wrapped her arms around herself.

"I love riding. I love the freedom of it, the excitement. It's just a good time. But I don't love it enough to make you sick with worry every time I do it. I don't love anything so much that it's worth putting you through that. I can always sell the bike."

Raina watched him with her big brown eyes. "Only if that's really what you want to do."

Nick shoved several of the pillows off the bed and curled up against her back. "What I want is to make my wife happy. I don't feel like I'm doing too great a job on that score lately."

Raina rolled over so they were facing each other. "I am happy with you, Nick. I just want to make sure *you're* happy, too. You've been different lately."

He closed his eyes and breathed in her scent. It would be ridiculous to pretend he didn't know what she meant. He'd been completely consumed by his worries over the foundation the past few weeks. If he hadn't invested so heavily in the charity, it would be easier to distance himself from it. But he stood to lose quite a bit of money if he had to keep floating the operating costs and the building costs by himself.

When he'd married Raina, they'd done so on equal terms. He didn't want her to ever feel that he couldn't take care of her in the lifestyle she was accustomed to. She was used to nice things and he was sure her previous boyfriends, Silvestre especially, had been able to afford to indulge her.

"I'm sorry, sweets. I know I've been distracted with work lately. I've been falling behind because I'm so busy thinking and worrying about you. But it's nothing I can't handle. I promise."

"That's all it is? Work stuff?"

"Yeah. Once I catch up on the backlog, things will go back to normal. I promise."

She heaved a sigh of relief. "As long as that's all it is. You've been patient with me. Now it's my turn."

"It's your fault, you know?" Nick kissed her jaw. "If you weren't so beautiful, I wouldn't be so distracted all the time."

Raina chuckled. "I never thought I'd say this, but keep lying to me. I know I look awful because I feel like such a mess."

Nick kissed her neck and took the strap of her nightgown between his teeth. He moved it to the side so he could reach the soft skin on her shoulder.

"Nick? What are you doing?" Raina let out a soft sigh as he nipped her shoulder with his teeth, then soothed the spot with his tongue.

"I'm making love to my wife." Nick thanked whoever had invented spandex because the straps of her gown were stretchy enough for him to push them down over her arms. With a few more tugs, her breasts popped out. They already looked fuller. Rounder.

He licked the tips gently, aware that they might be more sensitive. Raina let out another soft sigh, her nails digging into his arm. "God, I love it when you do that."

He continued downward, tugging the gown with him as he went. She lifted her hips, allowing him to slide it off. He tugged at her white cotton panties next. Finally she was bare before him. He licked her and she reared up off the bed.

"You really are more sensitive, aren't you? Oh, the fun I'm going to have with you."

Nick moved closer, wrapping her legs around his neck. Her hands went into his hair immediately, which made him growl against her. She shrieked when he licked her again. Longer. Deeper. He looked up her stomach, loving the look on her face as he traced over her skin with his tongue. Her head fell back as she came under him, her flesh contracting against his mouth.

He pulled back slightly so he could get his boxers off. Remembering what the book said, he urged her over onto her knees. "We're not supposed to have you on your back. So I guess that means I get to look at your delectable little bottom for the next nine months."

She chuckled and pushed back against him, wiggling her bottom at him. "I hope you like the view, then."

"Oh, I love the view." He leaned down and nipped at the sexy indentation where her spine curved into her ass. Then he entered her slowly, gently, giving her time to adjust to him.

She arched her back and pushed back against him, taking him deeply. Nick barked out a cry at the sudden, erotic sensation of being surrounded by her. "Damn, do that again."

Raina looked over her shoulder at him and bit her lip. She leaned forward, allowing him to slip almost all the way free, then she pushed back against him again, taking his full length in one thrust. Nick gritted his teeth against the overwhelming need to come.

"You like being in control, sweets?"

She nodded, her tongue between her teeth as she watched him with a sexy smile. "I like taking you."

"Hell, yeah. You can take me anytime." He rested his hands gently on her backside and allowed her to set the pace. She took him slowly at first, each thrust forceful and deep. Then she increased the tempo, her motions becoming jerky as she got closer and closer to her own orgasm. He could tell she was getting near to climaxing by the sounds she made and the way her nails curled into the sheets beneath her.

"Help me, Nick," she moaned. She came with a cry, nearly collapsing beneath him as she tightened around him.

He reached beneath her and captured her ripe breasts, holding them in his hands as he thrust. With every motion he felt like he was giving her something more than just sex. He felt like he was showing her the depth of his feelings. As he came, he thought maybe she could hear what his body was saying.

This is my love for you. This is my desire for you. Take everything that I am.

It's all for you.

Chapter Seventeen

~

RAINA PICKED UP her phone. Another missed call from Steven. The calls had tapered off after she'd told him to stop calling the last time, but in the last few days, he'd started calling her again.

Before she could think whether it was a good idea or not, she dialed his number.

"You finally decided to stop ignoring my calls," he answered.

Raina rolled her eyes. "Leave it to you to make yourself out to be the injured party. I thought we'd already agreed that you wouldn't call me anymore? I hold no ill will toward you, Steven, but I'm happily married now. These calls need to stop."

"Happily married," he scoffed. "Raina, I think you forget who you're talking to. I know you only married Alexander because you wanted a baby."

"That's why we got married but that's not why we're still married now. We're happy together. I would think considering all the pain and embarrassment you've caused me that you could just be happy for me."

"That's why I felt compelled to call. I've been struggling with my conscience about lying to you," Steven said finally.

"I don't think you've had much problem lying to me in the past."

There was a grunt on the other end of the line. "I meant about Nick. Did he ever tell you that we knew each other?"

Raina stopped flipping the channels on the television. "You know each other? How?"

"I found him in bed with my wife. I actually had to chase him out of the house."

"Now you're just making things up."

Raina knew her husband had never been a saint, but the idea of him being chased out of bed by Steven with his pants around his ankles was too ridiculous to even consider. If anything, Nick had probably romanced some woman that Steven wanted and now he was bitter. That sounded a lot more likely.

"I'm not lying. I know you have reason to doubt my word after everything that has happened, but I have no reason to lie about this. I already know that we're over and you're not coming back. I'm just trying to keep you from getting hurt again. I figured I owe you at least that much."

"Well, I don't believe you."

"It's true. Ask him. If he claims he's so honest with you then ask him to tell you the truth."

Raina fought the urge to slam the phone down even as part of her wanted to ask more questions. What if this was really why Nick had been coming home late and been so distracted lately? Was the lure of his old life too strong to resist?

"Even if it's true, what does that have to do with me? I've done things I'm not proud of before, too."

"Everyone has, but I'm sure those were isolated occurrences. Not a pattern of behavior. I know Alexander has you convinced that he's this great guy but I don't want to see you hurt, Raina. Or being used by a man who only wants to exploit you for personal gain."

"Personal gain? What are you talking about now?" There was a pause and Raina's stomach tightened.

"You don't think it's odd that he was suddenly so anxious to marry you? Did he ever tell you that his foundation is struggling for cash?"

"No, he didn't," Raina whispered.

"Hmm. I'm surprised he's never asked you to donate." Steven sounded genuinely surprised. "Or to endorse it. I figured he'd have asked you to mention it in the press or on your website."

"I don't have time for this, Steven. I'm not going to sit here and listen to you slander my husband. I'm busy growing a human being. I suggest you get busy figuring out how to grow up. Nick would never use me."

"I just wanted you to know the truth about the man you married and to tell you to be careful. There's no way a man like that can be faithful. Especially considering our history. I admit that I made things difficult for him after I found out about the affair. Taking you away from me was Alexander's ultimate revenge. Now that you know, you can't say I didn't warn you."

Raina ended the call and dropped her phone back on the couch next to her. Her head throbbed even worse than it had before. It had been an incredibly stupid idea to call Steven. He was just trying to ruin things for her because he hated to "lose." He'd been like that ever since she'd met him. Competitive, territorial, and smug.

Why would he lie about knowing Nick?

Surely Nick would have told her if he was acquainted with Steven. Although if he'd really been sleeping with Steven's wife, maybe he wouldn't have told her? He'd been trying to convince her to marry him. He wouldn't have wanted to tell her anything negative.

There was undoubtedly more to the story. The Nick Alexander she knew valued family above all else. He wouldn't romance a married woman and he definitely wouldn't make Raina part of some twisted payback scheme. But back before she'd known Nick so well, would she have given him the benefit of the doubt? Probably not.

She didn't want to go rushing off with a bunch of wild stories and accusations. Nick had been by her side since the beginning, helping her when she was down and celebrating with her when she'd finally gotten pregnant. Was she really going to let Steven's accusations come between them?

What was Steven trying to prove by even telling her? Was he trying to paint himself as the victim or was he just trying to plant seeds of doubt?

There was only one person who could answer her questions.

"Come on, Jelly Bean. Let's go see Daddy."

*   *   *   *   *

NICK WAS IN the middle of an income projection for one of his middle-aged clients when the door to his office opened. Raina poked her head in and looked around. "Is it okay if I come in?"

"Of course." She looked so lost and alone standing in the doorway. "I didn't forget a doctor's appointment, did I?"

"No, nothing like that. I just wanted to see you."

Nick came from behind his desk and gathered her into his arms. She rested her head against his shoulder and took a deep breath as he rested his head on top of hers. It was corny, but his stress truly seemed to evaporate when she was around.

His job as a financial planner was to help people plan to fund their lives. He'd done it for his clients for years but it was only recently that he'd been thinking so much about his own financial future. Raina reminded him of what he was working so hard for. Not just to accumulate wealth for the sake of being wealthy, but to provide for his family's future. To take care of their children and provide them with a comfortable retirement. It wasn't just numbers on a page anymore.

Raina and his child made it personal.

"So what brings you out here in the middle of the day?" Nick led her to one of the chairs in front of his desk. He sat next to her instead of sitting behind his desk. Maybe it was time to consider getting one of those couches for his office.

"I was just feeling kind of down and wanted to see you." Raina stared at him intently and twisted the straps of her purse. "I have to ask you something. Please don't get mad."

He brushed a gentle hand over her hair. "Of course not. You can ask me anything."

She took a deep breath. "Did you sleep with Steven's

wife?"

Shock rooted Nick to his seat. *Shit.* He closed his eyes.

"You don't have to say anything. I can tell by your face. I was hoping it wasn't true."

"No, it's true. Although I had no idea she was married. Until he came home, that is. I still hate that I was involved in that. Which is why he was so happy to bring it to your attention."

"I knew there had to be more to the story. I didn't want to believe what he said but I had to ask."

Nick sighed. He was suddenly very tired. "I wish you hadn't needed to ask. I wish you'd known that I wouldn't intentionally do something like that without even having to hear me tell you."

Raina's shoulders slumped. "You're right. You've done nothing but be my champion and at the first opportunity I'm here interrogating you like you're some criminal."

"I'm not blaming you, sweets. I know exactly who's to blame here. Anyone would have asked the question. Especially given my past. I just can't wait for the day when you trust me so implicitly that nothing can shake you."

"I do trust you, Nick. It's just my hormones. This baby is making me exhausted and paranoid. I know I can't trust anything Steven says. He's just vindictive."

Nick squeezed her arms. "You can't always assume the worst of me. I'm doing the best I can."

"Sometimes this all seems too good to be true. I think that I must be missing something huge. That you haven't really changed, you aren't really this great, upstanding, moral guy who just wanted to marry me because he loves me. In my world, when things are going too well, there's always a catch."

"There is no catch. There's just us. Our love is what

we make it."

"It makes me nervous when things are too perfect."

"I *never* said it was perfect. I'm still the guy who leaves his shoes in the middle of the floor and squeezes the toothpaste in the middle. You still drive me crazy with that teenybopper music and of course, let's not forget the Monster Muffins. Neither of us is perfect. But we can be perfect for each other. Isn't that enough?"

Raina nodded. Her hand came up to her forehead and she rubbed her temple.

"Are you all right?"

"I've had this stupid headache since yesterday. It probably doesn't help that I'm still barfing so much. I really thought this morning sickness would have passed by now. I'm not sure why they call it morning sickness. It's more like all-the-time sickness."

Just then Kay's voice blared through the speaker on his desk. "Mr. Alexander. Mr. Simmons is here to see you."

Nick cursed under his breath. "I forgot that Matt was coming by to show me some of the listings he found for condos. He's finally narrowed down the area he wants to live in. I can cancel, though. He'll understand."

He offered her his arm but she waved him away as she stood. "No, don't do that. He's come all the way up here to see you. We can talk more at home. I should really go home and rest."

"Okay, I'll see you tonight."

He walked over to his desk and hit the intercom. "Kay, you can send Matt to the conference room. I'll be there in a minute."

* * * * *

MATT CURSED HIS forgetfulness as he skipped down

the stairs of Nick's building. He was supposed to be bringing Nick the new listings he'd found and he'd conveniently left them on the front seat of his truck.

He figured Nick had to be as tired of his house-hunting search as he was. They'd been looking for condos since summertime and he still hadn't found one he liked. They were all either too expensive or didn't have the features he wanted.

I think you have commitment issues, buddy.

It was something his sister would say. Not that he disagreed. He was used to going where Uncle Sam told him to go. It was hard to get used to the idea that his life was his own again.

He pulled open the heavy metal door leading to the parking garage. A young woman sat on the edge of the curb, her head in her hands.

"Miss? Are you all right?"

When she raised her head, Matt rushed forward. "Raina, what's wrong?"

She blinked at him a few times, then said, "I don't feel so good. I think I'm going to be sick."

Matt instantly sprang into battle awareness. He looked at her eyes to see if her pupils were dilated. Her skin was flushed, but that was to be expected if she was about to throw up.

"Okay, let's get you to the hospital. My truck is right here."

Raina shook her head. "No, I can't move yet. It's worse when I move. That's why I sat down." She closed her eyes suddenly and started breathing through her mouth. "It smells like burnt rubber down here."

Matt didn't smell anything but he kept that thought to himself. "Okay. Let's just take it easy. Can you move yet? Are you still dizzy?"

After what seemed like a million years, Raina nodded.

"A little. My head hurts."

Matt looked at his truck just a few feet away. "Raina, how about you let me carry you? We really need to get you to the hospital."

Finally she nodded. She stood slowly and he picked her up. She was light, too light for her height. He carried her swiftly to the truck and hit the automatic opener on his keychain. He shoved the papers on the seat in the back and helped her climb in. As he rounded the car to the driver's side, he pulled out his cell phone and called Nick. It went to voicemail so he left a quick message.

"Hey, man, I found Raina down here. She looks pretty bad so I'm taking her to the hospital. Meet us there."

He fired up his truck. Raina jumped at the loud roar of the engine. "Sorry. I'm sure that's not helping your headache any."

"No, it just startled me. I'm sure I'm fine. I just got dizzy. I probably just need to lie down."

He pulled out of the parking garage and raced through the streets until they reached New Haven General. "Either way, we're going to get you checked out just in case."

He left his car parked at the curb of the emergency entrance and then jumped out. Raina already had the door open by the time he got around to her side.

"Here, take my arm." He led her through the automatic doors and up to the nurse sitting at the reception desk. He leaned over and said, "She's pregnant and she's having dizzy spells. I found her collapsed on the ground."

The nurse pushed a form across the desk along with a pen. "Fill this out and we'll see what's going on." Raina picked up the pen, then before she could write anything, she slumped against the counter.

"Whoa!" Matt looped a hand around her waist and

held her upright so she wouldn't fall over.

"She's going down!" The nurse jumped up and ran around to the desk. Before he knew what was happening they were surrounded by nurses and Raina was being helped into a wheelchair.

"Are you her husband?" the nurse on his left asked.

He shook his head. "He's on his way."

"We're going to take her back now."

Matt watched helplessly as Raina was wheeled away. He pulled out his cell phone and called Nick again. When it went to voicemail, he hung up. Then he called the main office line and left a message with Kaylee, who promised to look for him.

"Where are you, Nick?"

Chapter Eighteen

⁓

"WE JUST KEEP ending up here, don't we? What is it about us and hospitals? It's like we have bad karma."

Ridley sat gingerly on the edge of Raina's hospital bed. After her embarrassing fainting incident, she'd been examined by one of the emergency doctors on call. They'd drawn blood and were running tests. But they'd already determined that she was severely dehydrated. They'd hooked her up to an IV bag of fluids to try to get her electrolytes back in the normal range.

Apparently all the throwing up she'd been doing

wasn't normal. But at least it didn't seem to have hurt the baby. That was all she was holding on to at the moment.

"I know. This is getting to be a habit. One I will be happy to break." She poked at the tube in her arm. It was positioned so that no matter how she moved, it tugged at her skin and made her uncomfortable.

It was truly a cruel twist of fate for her to have so many medical issues considering how much she hated hospitals. They were just harbingers of germs. Whose bright idea was it anyway to put all the sick people in the same place? She felt like she was going to be permanently contaminated by the time the doctor returned to release her.

Or at least she could only hope he would release her. She stopped messing with the tube in her arm. If whatever was in that bag could help her get better faster, then she was all for it.

"I'm just glad Matt was there. I hate to think what could have happened if he hadn't found you." Ridley's voice brought her out of her daydreaming.

"I know. Can you go check and see if he's still here? I want to say thank you." Raina also wanted to apologize for being difficult. He'd only been trying to help her and she was pretty sure she'd snapped at him.

Ridley left briefly and Raina used the time to close her eyes and rest her head. It was nice to finally understand why she was so tired. She'd figured it was just part of being pregnant. It had made her feel incredibly guilty because after all the time, stress, and worry that had gone into getting pregnant, she'd expected to enjoy it. To be glowing and healthy and excited.

Instead she'd just been barfing and miserable and sick.

At least there was something she could do now that would hopefully make her feel better.

Ridley came back in the room, Nick trailing behind her. As soon as he saw her, he pushed past Ridley and strode to the side of the bed.

"I came as soon as I got Matt's message. What happened? Are you okay?" He turned to Ridley. "Is she okay?"

"They said she's dehydrated. She's going to be just fine after she gets some vitamins and nutrients in her." Ridley leaned over the side of the bed and kissed Raina on the forehead. "Now that I know you're in good hands, I'm going to give the rest of the family a call and let them know you're okay."

"Thanks, Ridley. I should have called on the way here but I wasn't even thinking." Nick took the seat next to her bed. "I'm so sorry I wasn't here sooner."

"Where were you, Nick?"

"I went to get a soda from the vending machine and then I was in the conference room waiting for Matt. I didn't realize I left my phone on my desk. I waited for him to come back for about fifteen minutes before I went back to my office. Kay finally found me."

"I was so scared something was wrong with the baby," she admitted finally, giving voice to the fears she hadn't wanted to say aloud.

"Did the doctors say the baby was in any danger?" He placed a hand over her abdomen.

She wasn't showing at all yet and hadn't gained any weight. She'd actually lost weight. It was no wonder, considering she hadn't held down a full meal in over a month.

"Everything seems to be fine. The doctor is going to come back in a while to give me the results of the blood work. I think they're going to give me something to help with the nausea, too. I feel like such an idiot. Dr. Waters told me to report any problems I had, but I just thought throwing up was part of being pregnant. I hope I haven't starved our baby."

"It's not your fault, Raina. You couldn't know what's normal or not. At least we'll know something soon." His phone beeped and he pulled it out. "I wonder if this is Mom. Once everyone hears what happened, you'll probably have more visitors than you really want."

Raina ran a hand over her hair self-consciously. "Why is it that when people most want to visit you is also the time when you look your worst?"

"You look beautiful."

"Nick, I want to tell you something."

Nick put his phone down and pulled his chair closer.

"I love you," she whispered. "I'm tired of dancing around it and not being brave enough to say it. You've always been honest with me, even when it wasn't easy for you. How can I be any less brave for you? So, I love you. I love you so much."

He looked like he was in shock by the end of her little speech. His mouth fell open and he let out a little cough.

"You're going to make me cry in public, you know that?" He laughed softly.

She leaned to the edge of the hospital bed so she could be as close to him as possible. He leaned against the metal frame and pressed his forehead to hers.

"No more I *think* I love you?"

She grinned up at him. "Definitely not."

*   *   *   *   *

NICK SAT ON the edge of Raina's bed and watched as she tried to braid her long hair over her shoulder. If she felt well enough to be worried about her appearance, he figured she must be recovering quickly.

"I still can't believe that Steven made up all those lies.

He deliberately led me to believe that you tried to seduce his wife away from him. He never mentioned that you had no idea she was married."

"I think it makes him feel better to blame someone else," Nick replied.

"What if Steven hadn't been divorced when I met him but hadn't told me? That could have happened just as easily to me." Raina reached out and grabbed his hand. "I'm sorry that I didn't tell you he'd been calling. I just didn't want to upset you or make you think you couldn't trust me. He's not the one I want. He never was. Are you mad at me?"

"I'm not upset with you. I'm just upset that you didn't feel you could tell me. I don't want you to keep anything from me."

"I won't. I've learned my lesson. I know you wouldn't keep secrets from me, either. Especially about something as big as finances."

Nick stopped and looked down at her. "Finances?"

"Yeah. Steven said that your foundation was in financial trouble." Something in Nick's face must have changed because she suddenly stopped talking. "Nick?" He looked up at her and she sucked in a deep breath. "There's no truth to what Steven said is there?"

"I can't lie to you, sweets. It's the only thing that makes me who I am. I'll always tell you the truth."

"Then it's true. You're in financial trouble?"

"Not yet. But I probably will be if my foundation doesn't get more investors soon."

"Oh, God. I was really hoping he made that up just to be mean." Raina paled and let go of his arm.

Nick couldn't understand why his foundation was of any interest to her. Especially not enough to cause her to look like that.

"He didn't make that part up, unfortunately."

Raina's eyes swung back to his face. "He was so surprised that you hadn't asked me to donate. He thinks that was the reason you married me. That you had some master plan to use me to push your agenda."

Nick gritted his teeth. "I would never use you."

"So it never occurred to you before we were married that an association with me could help your foundation?"

Nick immediately thought of the day Matt had come to his office. It seemed like a million years ago that he'd had the idea of asking Ridley to convince Raina to help him.

"It occurred to me. I can't pretend it didn't occur to me. But that's not why I married you."

Raina scoffed. "Of course not. You married me because I've always been so *nice* to you."

"All I was going to do was ask Ridley to talk to you about doing some ads for us. That's all. I didn't need to marry you for that."

"I can't believe how stupid I am sometimes."

Nick's heart sank. "Don't say that. You can't honestly believe that I married you to take advantage of you?"

"I'm sure you didn't think of it that way. It was probably just a nice bonus. Marry the girl, have some hot sex, and instantly boost your public profile at the same time. A win-win-win all around, right?"

He hadn't been on the receiving end of her sharp tongue in so long that he'd lost his armor. Every word she said sliced through him until Nick was shocked there weren't holes straight through him.

"It wasn't like that."

"The thing I don't get is why would you do that? Why would you go to all this trouble to make me fall in love with you? I was willing to marry you without all that. I was determined to keep things neutral between us.

219

You're the one who kept pushing for more."

"I wanted you to fall in love with me because I'm in love with *you*."

Raina closed her eyes. "Steven admitted that he's been making things difficult for you. Did you marry me just to get back at him?" The quiet despair in her voice sliced his emotions in half.

"Oh, no. *Raina*. I've been in love with you all along and that never changed. I don't care what Steven said. You know what we have is real."

She stared up at him from tear-filled eyes. "No, I don't. That's the problem. I just don't know what's real anymore. I don't know anything at all."

That was when Nick got angry. It was utter bullshit that she'd believe her ex over his word. "You just told me you love me and now just ten minutes later, you're suddenly not sure? Raina, don't you see? You're just afraid. But you don't have to be."

"I do. I was afraid and it turns out I had good reason to be. This whole time I thought you were doing all this stuff for me but it's really been some macho pissing contest between you and Steven." She pulled the thin blanket higher on her chest, almost as if it could shield her from him. "You're like two toddlers fighting over a toy. A toy that neither of you actually even wants."

"That's not true, Raina." Nick wondered how they'd gone from her declaring her love to accusing him of using her. "Whenever I get anywhere close to touching your heart, you pull away from me. I've done everything I can to show you how I feel. There's a point where you just can't do any more without losing yourself. I love you, Raina, but you don't make it easy."

Raina let out a sob. "You think this is easy for me? I want *so much* to believe you. But I've seen you in action before. You're so used to doing whatever you want to bend the world to your will. When was the last time you did something with no ulterior motive? Something with no benefit to you?"

It hurt Nick more than he'd thought possible that he couldn't think of even one example for her.

"I hate that this is hurting you, sweetheart. I can't stand to see you cry. I've always only wanted you to be happy. I would never knowingly cause you harm."

"I know you never mean any harm, Nick. But sometimes even when you don't mean for it to happen, people get hurt. This hurts," she cried.

He tried to approach her bed but as soon as he did, she started crying harder. "I just can't believe it. I just can't." The monitor attached to her arm started going crazy.

A nurse came in a few minutes later. "What happened in here? She was doing so much better."

"I can't. I just can't," Raina cried. She kept saying it over and over until the nurse looked up at him in alarm.

There was nothing left for him to do but leave.

* * * * *

NICK PACED BACK and forth in the corridor outside Raina's room. His shoes made little squeaking sounds on the linoleum floor. Everything Raina had just said felt like it was replaying in his head.

Hadn't he thought many times over the past month that he should confide in Raina about his problems? She was a great listener and was great at coming up with creative solutions to problems. He certainly didn't doubt her intelligence. She was quite well versed in geography and world affairs due to all her traveling. If he'd confided in her, she'd have probably been able to help.

It had been his pride, his stupid pride, that had kept him from telling her. He hadn't wanted to admit that the whiz kid might have made a mistake. He never wanted her to think less of him or have her faith in him tarnished.

Now, her faith in him had been completely shattered.

He'd known that his complicated past with her ex was going to come back and bite him in the ass. He should have told her everything himself before Steven had a chance to put his twisted spin on things. But he hadn't wanted to take a chance on pushing her away when they'd finally started to get closer. He'd let his fear override his common sense. Now it was too late.

Even though he wanted to be pissed at Silvestre, he ultimately was just pissed at himself. There were so many ways he could have handled the conversation that didn't include telling her she was difficult to love.

When he looked up, the nurse was just leaving Raina's room.

"How is she?"

The nurse gave him a sympathetic look. "She's resting comfortably now. The doctor is on his way. He's going to explain her treatment to you."

Nick backed up so she could pass. "Thank you."

"Nick! What are you doing out here in the hall?" Ridley stood behind him, holding a small cup of coffee and a bag of potato chips.

"We had a fight. I upset her." He blew out a long breath. "I don't know what happened. We were talking and then her monitor started going off. The nurse had to come in."

Ridley didn't say anything, just handed him the cup of coffee. She disappeared into Raina's room. When she came back out, she didn't meet his eyes. "She's sleeping now."

Just then a tall, thin man with gray hair approached them. "Mr. Alexander?"

"Yes, that's me."

"I'm Dr. Parrish. I was the doctor on call when your wife was brought in." He paused and then glanced at Ridley.

"Oh, it's okay. This is my wife's twin sister." Nick motioned for him to continue.

"Mr. Alexander, your wife is suffering from hyperemesis gravidarum, also known as HG. Basically her morning sickness has become so severe as to endanger her and the baby. When she was brought in she was severely dehydrated, which explains why she complained of dizziness and a headache before she collapsed."

Ridley gripped his arm and looked up at the doctor. "Is my sister going to be okay?"

"She's only seven weeks pregnant, so we've caught it early and can take precautions to make sure she doesn't get this dehydrated again."

"Do we know why this happened?" Ridley asked. "Raina's been trying for so long to get pregnant, so I know she was doing everything she could to be healthy. She was taking her vitamins and eating right."

The doctor nodded. "I wish I could point to one thing as the cause, but unfortunately the medical community doesn't agree on what causes HG. It's been thought that low Body Mass Index could be a cause, but it's likely a combination of factors, including hormone levels and stress."

He looked down at the clipboard he held. "We're going to do rehydration therapy for her, so we'll need to keep her overnight. Then I'll give her a prescription to take at home. Here's some information about her condition."

Nick accepted the papers the doctor held out and thanked him again. When he turned around, he handed the papers to Ridley.

"I need you to do something for me, Ridley."

She accepted the papers and tucked them under her arm. "Of course. What do you need?"

He tipped his head toward Raina's room. "I need you to take care of her for me."

"And where are *you* going to be?" Ridley asked. Nick finally had to look away from her searing gaze.

"Anywhere but here."

Ridley's face fell. "I don't understand you, Nick. You've fought so hard for her. Look how far you two have come. Now you're just giving up?"

"You didn't see her face in there. She's so upset with me right now. Having me around is causing her stress. It's not in her best interest for me to be here. I think leaving is probably the most unselfish thing I've ever done."

Ridley crossed her arms and glared at him. "What am I supposed to tell her when she wakes up?"

Nick looked down at his shoes. "Tell her that I love her. Tell her that I'm sorry and I never meant to hurt her. I think it's best if I move out of her house so she doesn't have to see me when she comes home. That's her space. She shouldn't have to be uncomfortable in her own place."

"I don't agree with this. Not at all." Ridley looked behind her as if afraid that Raina would overhear.

"There's a time for retreat. This is it."

Chapter Nineteen

~

MATT FLEXED HIS shoulder and breathed through the pain that lanced up his arm. He gritted his teeth and waited for it to pass. It usually stopped if he kept it completely still. But then again, he usually wasn't carrying around pregnant women.

"Hey, I'm glad you're still here."

Nick stood just outside Raina's hospital room. He looked like a zombie. Matt cursed inwardly. Why had he spent so much time talking to Raina? He should have just picked her up and put her in the car. He could have gotten her here sooner. If she had complications due to this, he would never forgive himself.

"What can I do to help you? Do you need me to pick up clothes so you can stay here with Raina?"

"No. I won't be coming back here," Nick said softly, almost like he was talking to himself. They'd been friends a long time and he'd watched his friend grow from a party animal into a husband and soon-to-be-father. It was starting to feel like all his friends were moving on with their lives.

Leaving him behind.

Matt shook his head and refocused on Nick. His friend was dealing with a lot right now and he needed to be there for him, not feel sorry for himself.

"Why wouldn't you be coming back here? Raina is going to have to stay overnight, right?"

Nick started walking. Matt dropped the magazine he'd been reading and ran to catch up. "Nick, what's going on?"

"You drove your truck here, right?" Nick turned left at the nurse's station. Matt nodded to the nurse behind the desk as they passed.

"Yeah. It's parked out in the visitor's lot."

"Good. I need your help moving some stuff."

"Anything. Just let me know what you want me to do." Matt hit the button for the elevator when Nick didn't move.

"I need help moving out of Raina's house."

Matt glanced behind them. The hall leading back to the OB wing was empty. "Please tell me you just mean moving some old shit you don't want anymore."

Nick shook his head. Matt cut off the question he'd been about to ask. He'd never seen his friend look so dejected. So exhausted. Now probably wasn't the time to ask him if he was crazy. He looked like he needed a friend to support him right now.

"Whatever you need, Nick. I'll help you out. You've always helped me when I needed it."

Nick looked up at him, then crossed his arms. "Have I?"

"Of course you have," Matt answered. "Whenever I need financial advice, you've helped me. You've been helping me look for a place to live for like six months. I doubt anyone else would have hung in there that long. I'm getting tired of looking and it's *my* place."

Nick looked away. "I did those things because they were easy for me to do. Finances are my business. Real estate is sort of an extension of that. Have I ever helped you when it took true effort on my part? When it inconvenienced me or pushed me out of my comfort zone?"

"I don't know what you mean."

"She's right. I'm selfish. I've always done things my way and damn the consequences. I've treated the world like it was my playground and I never looked behind to see what collateral damage was left in my wake."

The elevator arrived and they stepped in. Matt could only be glad it was empty so no one else had to witness this strange conversation.

"Nick, you're one of the best guys I know. I'm not saying you haven't ever screwed up, but who hasn't? She could just be upset because she's hormonal right now." Women were unpredictable creatures. He barely understood half the things Mara did and they were twins.

"Either way, I have to do what's best for Raina and the baby. Having me around is just too stressful for her. She needs to stay calm. It's not about what I want anymore."

With that, the elevator doors opened into the lobby of

the hospital. Matt led them to his truck and they pulled out of the lot.

"Let's just take a suitcase, okay? She's upset right now but you don't know how she'll feel tomorrow. Or tonight for that matter. A fight doesn't mean your marriage is over."

At least he hoped it didn't.

*   *   *   *   *

RAINA WOKE UP to a soft beeping sound. She opened her eyes to a blur of color, the room slowly coming into focus. She was in the hospital, that much she knew, but she was temporarily disoriented. The room had been bright before and now it looked like it was nighttime. There was no light shining around the edges of the heavy drapes drawn across the window.

She sat up slightly and looked to her left. The *beep beep beep* sound turned out to be her heart monitor. There were several numbers displayed along the top of the screen. The angular digital line jumped along with her pulse. According to the machinery, her heart was fine.

Funny it didn't feel that way.

She hadn't been asleep that long. At least she didn't think so. There was a large bouquet of lilies in the corner. They were gorgeous, but not the typical arrangement, so she could only assume they'd come from Ridley. Nick usually got her roses.

Speaking of Nick, she looked around the room. Where was he? Tears sprang to her eyes when she thought about their fight. Of all the things Steven had told her, Nick being in financial trouble was the last thing she'd thought would turn out to be true.

Ridley's head poked out of the bathroom. "You're

awake!"

She tried to clear her throat to answer but her mouth felt like sandpaper. Ridley rushed to her side and held out a small Styrofoam cup with a straw in it.

"Here, have some water. You're still dehydrated."

Raina took several long pulls from the straw. Cool water rushed down her throat and she instantly felt better. "Thank you. That feels so nice." She looked around again. "I have to talk to Nick."

When Ridley didn't answer right away, Raina leaned back against the pillows. "We had a fight earlier. I need to see him."

"He thought it would be best if he stayed away for a while. The doctor said you need to stay calm. You were really upset before."

Raina stared at the ceiling, blinking back tears. Just thinking about her conversation with Nick made her feel borderline hysterical all over again.

He'd spent so much time romancing her, convincing her that he loved her. *Why?* He had to have known that she would still help him even without all that.

He could have just asked her to help his foundation in exchange for fathering her baby. In the beginning she'd been open to just about any type of arrangement *except* a love match. She'd known all along how they usually ended and she'd wanted no part of it.

She'd wanted to avoid feeling the way she did right now.

"Did he leave?"

Ridley looked at her. It was impossible to miss the pity in her voice when she said "I think he went home." When she didn't say anything else, Raina suddenly understood what she *wasn't* saying.

"He's not coming back, is he?"

When her sister shook her head, sadly, Raina turned

her face against her pillow and let her tears fall freely.

*   *   *   *   *

OVER THE NEXT two weeks, Ridley came over every day to make sure that Raina was eating, taking her medication, and drinking enough water. Sam willingly submitted to her authority and before long he was ignoring everything Raina asked him to do in favor of Ridley's instructions.

He'd even eaten meals with her, watching her like a hawk to make sure she kept down the bland broth and toast. He'd made the mistake of sitting in Nick's usual seat one day only to have to move when she'd started crying over her food.

It was unbelievable how empty the house seemed without Nick there. Even his side of the closet was depressing to look at without all his junk and clutter.

The empty space next to all her stuff just made her sad.

In the beginning, Ridley had asked her each day if she wanted to see Nick. Just the thought of him brought tears to her eyes, so eventually Ridley had stopped asking.

It was too exhausting to think about her husband. She wished she could go back to the days before she'd talked to Steven. Or if she had just not asked Nick any more questions that day in the hospital. It was cowardly, but she would rather have lived her whole life in blissful ignorance than have to face the facts that Nick had married her for monetary reasons.

But she'd slowly started to adjust to being alone again. It was easier if she didn't actively think about Nick and focused on the other things in her life. Which was kind of hard to do when Sam wouldn't bring her the laptop or her cell phone.

"I just want to check emails," she complained.

The doctor hadn't even given her this many restrictions but Ridley had decided that using a computer was "working" and asked Sam to confiscate Raina's electronics.

The traitor hadn't even hesitated.

"If you don't stop complaining, I'm going to tell your sister on you." Sam didn't bother to hide his amusement as she glared at him. This was probably going to be really funny one day in the future. In the distant, distant future when she was no longer heartbroken. Like in about a million years.

"This isn't funny. What am I supposed to do?"

"Rest. Drink all that water," he said, pointing at the water bottle resting on the table next to her, "and read your magazines. That's all."

"You guys aren't the boss of me," Raina muttered.

"And if you aren't good," Sam continued, "then Ridley has instructed me to call your mother-in-law to come over here and babysit you."

Julia wouldn't hesitate to come over, either. She'd called Raina every day to find out if she needed anything and had delicately avoided any mention of Nick. Which was particularly annoying because Raina really wanted to know where he was.

Jackson and Ridley had come over, together and separately, to keep her company. Elliott had called on the phone to ask if she needed anything. Bennett had even dropped by and brought her some movies and TV shows on DVD to watch. They'd been talking at a family dinner one night and discovered they both enjoyed British comedies. She was surprised he'd remembered that.

She'd been surprised all around to be treated so nicely by Nick's family. Even though she was carrying an Alexander baby, she was still the outsider. She had been expecting them to all take Nick's side. But no one had even mentioned Nick.

Raina picked up the water bottle and sucked down a few gulps. "I'm being good, see?" She picked up the first magazine on the stack he'd brought her. There was a smiling blue-eyed baby on the cover holding a bright red ball.

"Better. Read a magazine and then take a nap. That's an order." He tucked the throw blanket around her and then left her alone.

Later that night, Sam brought her a TV tray. He plopped down on the couch next to her and watched her take a small spoonful of broth.

"I have bad news," Sam said once her mouth was full. "I've been going through your backlog of emails. The network isn't going to buy any more episodes of the show unless they're able to get behind-the-scenes footage with you and Nick."

"I already told them I wouldn't do that."

Raina was suddenly really glad that she'd never agreed to allow them to be filmed. Not only would some of the most embarrassing moments of her life have been captured on film, but she'd then have to explain to the network that she was no longer speaking to her husband, so he wasn't available to shoot any more scenes.

"They're going to release the six episodes they already bought as a miniseries about the world of modeling. But if you want it to be a reality series with a full season, they need to follow you around."

"I understand. All the reality shows on now are like that. I can't understand why they're so popular. Watching people acting trashy just doesn't seem that entertaining to me. But clearly someone likes it." Raina finished as much of the broth as possible and then took tiny bites of the toast until it was all gone. She still felt mildly queasy when she ate, but the medication the doctor had prescribed was helping and she was able to keep it all down.

Sam took her now-empty tray and set it on the coffee table. "Put your feet up," he ordered. He waited until she obeyed and then retucked her throw blanket around her legs.

"I didn't bring it up to stress you out. You aren't supposed to be thinking about work, remember? Your only job is to take care of yourself and relax."

Raina watched him leave and dropped her head back down on the cushions of the couch. Sam meant well but he didn't have a clue.

How was she supposed to relax when she kept looking for the face that wasn't there?

Chapter Twenty

NICK REALLY DIDN'T feel like playing cards. He felt like drinking a fifth of scotch and then spending some quality time viewing the backs of his eyelids. The only thing keeping him from doing that was the knowledge that Raina could have a reversal in her condition at any moment. He'd made sure Ridley had his cell phone number so she could call him right away if anything changed.

Since oblivion wasn't an option, he knew he needed to spend some time with his brothers. Otherwise they'd end up staging some kind of intervention and drag him out anyway.

"How are things going up in D.C.?" he asked Elliot. Maybe if he asked everyone else lots of questions, he could avoid thinking about the fact that Raina was only a street away.

"Good. We're growing steadily. Thanks for that tax analysis you did for me, by the way."

Nick grunted. He'd been more than happy to take on extra work lately. All the work he hadn't had time for before was a welcome diversion now that he had nowhere to rush to each evening. He was completely caught up and looking for things to do now.

Ridley walked in from the kitchen carrying a tray of cold cuts, cheese, and fruit. Ever since they'd started having poker night at Jackson's house, the quality of the food had gone up considerably. He thought of Raina and her deformed monster muffins. He'd never thought he could miss bad cooking so much.

He sighed. So much for not thinking about her.

"Would you like anything, Nick?"

He looked up from his cards to see Ridley offering him the platter. She'd been calling to give him daily progress reports, but it was always done in a terse voice. She also hung up on him as soon as she was done.

"I thought you were mad at me."

"I am. But that doesn't mean you need to starve," Ridley replied.

The others looked up, surprised she'd mentioned it. They'd all been dancing around the topic all night. They'd asked him about work and talked about sports, but avoided all mention of his wife or his impending fatherhood. He should have counted on Ridley for getting right to the point.

Especially when she'd made no secret of the fact that

she didn't think staying away from Raina was a good idea.

"I'm not really mad at you, Nick. But I can't pretend I'm not disappointed."

Nick cringed. Her disappointment hurt more than if she'd yelled at him.

"How was she today?" Since they were already talking about it, he might as well get his daily update. The fact that his brothers were hanging on their every word didn't even matter. There were no secrets in this family anyway.

It was annoying at times, the way they all knew each other's business, but he was also glad for it. His parents had been calling and visiting Raina ever since she left the hospital and he'd even heard that Bennett had dropped by to bring her the DVD box set of some show they both enjoyed. It was reassuring to know that no matter what, his family considered her one of theirs.

He wanted that for her whether she forgave him or not.

"Well, she was able to keep her pill down. So that was a win. She's pissed that Sam won't give her back her cell phone. I told him to keep her away from electronics so she won't work. But I'm also kind of paying her back for stealing my phone when I was in the hospital. She even had my cell phone number changed so Jackson couldn't call me. Talk about overbearing."

Nick smiled, remembering. "That's my girl."

"Is she your girl? Because you're not acting like it." Ridley put the platter down on the side table against the wall.

"She thinks I don't love her. She thinks I was just using her. I'm not sure how to prove that love exists to someone who doesn't believe in it. I tried that already and you saw what happened."

He dropped his cards on the table. There was no point

playing a game of chance when he knew from experience that Lady Luck was definitely not on his side.

* * * * *

RAINA MIXED THE cupcake batter, watching with obsessive interest as the butter and sugar blended into the flour mixture. She turned the speed up on the electric mixer a little and then stopped it. She'd already prepared the cupcake pan with colorful pink and blue liners.

After swiping a bit of stray mix from the edge of the bowl with her finger for a taste, she poured the mixture into the cupcake pan. She was careful to leave room for them to expand at the top.

She'd learned her lesson about that the hard way.

A giggle bubbled up as she remembered the look on Nick's face when he'd seen her monster muffins. Just as quickly, her smile faded. Her anger at Nick had disappeared over the the last few days.

Or maybe she just missed him so much that she didn't care about being mad anymore.

It was only eight o'clock and she was already on her third batch of cupcakes. The past few days she hadn't gone out or responded to calls or emails. Sam respected her privacy and left her to stew, only bothering her to make sure she ate her three meals a day.

If it hadn't smacked of desperation, she would have asked him to hang out with her. He wouldn't mind, he'd even said so. But every time she was about to ask him she changed her mind. He was her security chief, not one of the girls. He shouldn't have to navigate her hormonal surges or placate her in the midst of her depression.

Maybe you deserve to be depressed.

Every time she thought about how she'd treated Nick, she wondered if her feelings were just what she deserved.

She'd accused Nick of being selfish but most of the time they'd been together, Nick had put her needs before his own. He'd rearranged his schedule and habits to try to help her get pregnant. He'd stopped riding his motorcycle because it scared her. Would a selfish guy do that?

Over and over again, he'd put her needs first. She'd accused him of using her for his own gain but how could he when he'd never even asked her for anything? He admitted he'd thought about it, but he'd never done anything to draw attention to himself or play off her fame while they were together. He'd had many opportunities to do that if he'd wanted to. But he'd been at home with her every night, cooking her dinner and making her laugh.

Raina stood in the middle of her kitchen, looking around at the mess she'd made as if seeing it for the first time. Nick had been wrong about a lot of things, but he'd been right about her.

I don't make it easy for people to love me.

Hadn't she reached for the phone several times that day to call Ridley, only to stop herself before she could dial? She'd reasoned that her sister was finally happy with Jackson and didn't need to be dragged down with Raina's problems. But those were just excuses.

Excuses not to reach out.

Before she could change her mind, she picked up her cell phone and hit the second speed dial.

"Raina! I'm so glad you called. I've been so worried about you. I've been calling and calling and no one picked up."

"I know. I'm sorry. I've been dodging everyone's calls."

"Are you all right?"

"No. I'm not. I think I'm not. I need you, Ri."

238

"Oh, sweetie. I'm coming over right now. See you in a minute."

Ten minutes later, Ridley knocked on the door. Raina pulled it open and gestured for her sister to come inside. "Hey. Sorry about calling you out of the blue like that. I hope I wasn't interrupting anything."

Ridley gave her a quick hug. "No, I needed to get out of there. It's poker night so there was way too much testosterone at my house."

They walked into the kitchen. Raina had forgotten that quickly how much of a disaster it still was. "Let me just clean up a bit." She moved some of the baking cups she'd used and the bag of flour from the kitchen island so Ridley could sit down.

"Um, Ray. What happened in here?"

Raina couldn't think of anything to say so she just blurted, "I'm making cupcakes."

"You are? I didn't know you could bake."

"I can't. Not really."

Ridley walked over to the oven. The timer only had a few minutes left. "They smell really good. I'm hungry, too."

"They're chocolate cupcakes. I have milk, too."

Ridley bumped her arm affectionately. "I'm really glad you called me. I feel like I'm always calling you and dumping my problems on you. It's nice to know you need me, too."

Raina laced her arm through her sister's and lay her head on Ridley's shoulder. "Of course I need you. I know I'm not the easiest person to love, but thanks for never giving up on me. I'm going to do better. I'm finally learning that it's okay to need help sometimes."

The timer went off and Raina jumped.

"I've got it." Ridley stuck her hand in the oven mitt Raina had left on the counter and pulled the oven open.

She pulled the cupcake pan out carefully and placed it on the stove.

"They look perfect," Ridley remarked. "Just like the ones you see in the bakery. I can't believe you made these. I'm so proud of you, Ray."

"I finally got them right."

In the days since Nick had moved out, she hadn't been twiddling her thumbs. She'd organized her cupboards and annoyed Sam with her obsessive cleaning. *Nesting,* it was called. Whatever the case, she hadn't been sitting around crying. She'd been strong. But in that moment, bonding with her sister over cupcakes, Raina started to cry.

Ridley dropped the oven mitt and raced to her side. "Oh no, sweetie, what's wrong? I thought you wanted to learn to make cupcakes?"

"I did. But he's not here. I finally got it right and he's not here." Somehow just the thought made her cry harder, in big gasping sobs that made her chest hurt.

Ridley enfolded her in a tight hug and rocked her back and forth. Raina felt like she was free falling off a cliff. Her sister was the only solid, stable thing in the avalanche of emotion and she held on with both hands.

"You miss your husband. That's nothing to be ashamed of."

"I love him," Raina wailed. Part of her wanted to curse these damn pregnancy hormones but a tiny, smug part of her knew that what she was saying had nothing to do with her pregnancy and everything to do with her heart.

Ridley cupped her face and grinned. "You think I don't know that? The two of you have been crazy in love with each other since you met. You just didn't know what to do with it then."

Raina shook her head. Just the thought of Nick made

her simultaneously happy and sick to her stomach at the same time. It was a cruel fate that her last memory of him was watching him walk away.

She wondered if he was still working himself into the ground trying to find funding for the Alexander Foundation. Was he eating right and getting enough sleep?

Did he miss her?

"I don't even know how he's doing. What if something bad happened to him? I wouldn't even know."

"Nick is at our house right now," Ridley said.

Raina gripped her sister's arms. "He is?"

"Yeah. He's been staying at his place in Virginia Beach. I'm not going to lie. He doesn't look good. He looks about the same as you do."

Raina sighed. "Then why did he leave? How could he do that? After everything we've been through I thought we would stick together through anything. But he never came back."

"He did that for you. He thinks your relationship is too stressful for you to handle right now. You *were* really upset." Ridley led her to one of the chairs at the kitchen island. "As a matter of fact, you should be sitting down. You're supposed to stay off your feet."

Raina sat and laid her head on her arms. "I just feel like everything is falling apart. Nick is gone. The network decided not to pick up any additional episodes of my show. I don't know what to do."

"Who are you and what have you done with my real sister?"

"Huh?"

Ridley crossed her arms. "I know you're going through a hard time but *this* is not you." She gestured at Raina. "Where's the girl who told me to seduce Jackson? Where's the girl who doesn't care what anyone thinks and was brave enough to start her own fashion column when she couldn't find work?"

"She's gone," Raina mumbled.

"I don't believe that. If the network is balking at picking up more episodes, then shop it elsewhere. If no one else wants it, why can't you produce it on your own? Put it on the *Legs* blog so people can watch online. I bet you'd attract enough advertisers to cover the cost."

"I could do it myself," Raina repeated absently. She sat up as she considered the idea.

Half of the reason she'd declined to film more episodes of the show was because she didn't really *like* reality shows. There wasn't much real about them. Just people with too much makeup on acting as outrageous as possible to attract viewers. That was what the networks wanted to see—drama and bad behavior.

She wasn't interested.

But if she did it herself, she could take it back to her original vision. If she filmed some candid video herself, she wouldn't even have to hire a camera crew. She could show her fans what her life was really like and share with them the things she was trying to do in the future.

A true behind-the-scenes look at her life.

"When did you get so smart?" she asked Ridley.

"I'm learning that sometimes if you take a chance, things will work out the way they're supposed to. Before Jackson came to see me after I was shot, I was on my way to go get him. I just never made it past the door. But I was on my way. Nick isn't going to come to you. He's gotten this crazy notion that you can't handle the stress of him being here. You have to fix this. This is real life. Strong women don't wait to be saved. Sometimes we have to do the saving."

Raina leaned against her sister and closed her eyes. "I am really proud of the woman you've become, Ri."

Ridley beamed. "Good. Then take my advice and go get your man!"

* * * * *

THE NEXT DAY Nick logged onto the Alexander Foundation website. He'd been getting email confirmations all morning for new donations. Usually donations came in at a trickle. It was rare to get more than a few in a month unless he'd been speaking at an event or had paid for advertising.

The main webpage for the site showed that he'd received twenty donations in the last hour.

He hit the button for the speaker on his phone. "Kay? Did we run the advertising in the *Virginia Chronicle* yet?"

"No, that's not slated to run until next week."

He glanced back at the webpage. Twenty donations wasn't anywhere near enough to get him out of the hole they were in, but it was quite a jump from the usual.

He went back to the investment plan he was working on but he left the website open so he could see if anymore donations came in during the day. Maybe one of the donators would leave a comment that would give him a clue where they'd learned about the foundation.

He worked on several client files and then checked the donation page of the website again around lunchtime. His eyes widened when he saw the visitor count. The page had received over ten thousand views since he'd last checked. He looked at the donation meter and his mouth fell open.

They'd received over thirty thousand dollars' worth of donations.

He scrolled through the comments. Most of them were pretty generic.

Happy to donate to such a good cause!

Here's my contribution.

Heard about this on the Legs blog. Happy to donate!

With trembling hands, Nick opened a new browser window on the computer. He did an Internet search for "Raina Winters Legs Blog" until he found it. Then he clicked on the page.

Just then Kay's voice blared through the speaker on his desk. "Mr. Alexander, your next appointment is here."

He fumbled with the button until he managed to engage the intercom. "I need a moment, Kay."

Then he scrolled through the entries on the site. The first page was an introduction from Raina with several pictures from her most recent modeling jobs. He clicked on a few of the menu items at the top. There was a gardening column and a guide to dressing for different body types. He clicked on the last menu item labeled "About Raina."

He heard his office door open but didn't raise his head. "Dammit, Kay. Not now! They'll have to wait," Nick snapped.

"Well, I hope that's not how you talk to the poor girl most of the time."

Nick spun in his seat. Raina stood just inside the doorway, her hand still on the knob. He could see Kay standing in the background.

"I told her not to tell you that I was your three o'clock appointment. I wasn't sure if you'd see me otherwise. Is it okay that I'm here?" Her voice was strong but she looked a little uncertain.

"Of course it is. I'm just surprised to see you." He stood and met her in the middle of the room. "How are you? You look amazing."

She was wearing a loose white T-shirt and denim shorts. She was still thin, much too thin, but her eyes were bright and the flush was back in her cheeks.

She'd never looked more beautiful to him.

"I'm doing much better. I've been eating the blandest food ever. I've never been so tired of chicken broth and toast but at least I can keep it down." She pressed a hand against her lower abdomen and a pang went through Nick as he thought of their child. He was going to miss seeing Raina's body change as the baby got bigger. He was going to miss everything. Like he missed her.

"Our baby is the size of a lime now," he blurted.

Raina smiled softly. "I see you're still reading that pregnancy book."

He looked at her until she met his gaze. "I still care about what happens to you. That hasn't changed. That will *never* change."

Raina crossed the room and launched herself at his chest. "I'm so glad to hear you say that. I've done nothing but think about the things I said to you. I was so stupid. You've never asked me for anything. All you've done is give, give, give. If anyone is the user in this relationship, it's me." She looked up at him, her eyes wet. "I *never* should have accused you of using me for money, Nick. That was vile."

"Nothing has ever hurt as much as thinking you didn't trust me. All I want is to be everything you need, Raina. From the moment we met, I've been trying to be a better man. For you."

"You *are* all I need." She put her arms around his waist and laid her head against his chest. "I realized how stupid it was that I ever listened to anything Steven said. It was just so much easier than trusting that this could be real. But he did have one good idea. He said he'd assumed you'd asked me to put an ad for the foundation on my website. Which was a great plan, actually. So that's what I did. See?"

She pulled him by the hand over to his computer. When she saw that it was already on her website, she looked up at him. "You already saw it?"

"No, I was about to take a look. That's why I was so impatient with the pushy client who couldn't give me an extra five minutes."

Her lips twitched. "Well, you might as well just watch it."

He sat in his chair and pulled her on his lap. She leaned over and used the mouse to scroll down the screen. Then she clicked on something and a video started to play.

Hello, Legsters!

If you're watching this you must have seen the email blast that went out this morning. I'm really excited to tell you that the second half of my new reality series will be broadcast right here on the Legs blog. Contact me for advertising opportunities. Also, anyone who makes a donation to The Alexander Foundation will win a free day of advertising here and the chance to win a trip to Washington D.C. to meet me in person.

The Alexander Foundation provides summer activities and programs for at-risk youth in Virginia. It's a great cause, so go to the website in the comments and donate now!

Smooches!

"You didn't have to do that, sweets. I don't want you to feel like you have to bail me out."

"I wanted to. Plus it's my family's foundation, too." She kissed him softly on the forehead.

He pulled her back against him and held her tight. "I'm never going to be as rich as Silvestre." Raina started to protest but he stopped her with a finger against her lips. "I need to say this."

It galled Nick to say it, but it was true. He was doing pretty well for twenty-seven but he was never going to reach the heights of someone like Silvestre who owned private planes, yachts, and probably islands.

He was never going to be a billionaire.

"I'm never going to be as steady and stable as most other guys, either. Ask my mom, she'll tell you. I was always the one she called 'the wild child.' I'll probably always drive you crazy with my sloppiness and my need for speed. I'll never get it completely right."

Raina looked up at him, a fierce love in her eyes. "I don't care about any of that. Look at everything you've done for me. Who else would do the things you've done?"

Nick stroked her cheek with the tip of his finger. "I love you. There's no end to the things I'd do for you."

Raina leaned forward and whispered against his mouth. "Loving me is all I want you to do. Because I know I love you right back."

THE END

AUTHOR'S NOTE

If you've enjoyed this book, *please* consider leaving a review. I love to hear what my readers think!

Did you miss Book 1?
Keep reading for an excerpt from *One More Day*

Chapter One

"YOU DIDN'T BRING your hot-ass sister with you?"

As soon as the words left his mouth, Jackson Alexander dodged the punch that came sailing his way. A chorus of laughter rang out around him as he playacted dodging blows while his friend, Matt Simmons, growled at him.

"I should give you the ass-kicking you've been waiting for since freshman year."

Matt shoved the side of his lawn chair and Jackson tumbled out. He was laughing so hard by the time he hit the ground that it barely hurt.

Hanging out with his boys was his new favorite way to spend his weekends. After producing several platinum albums, suddenly everyone—from the kid who'd sat behind him in high school English class, to the receptionist at his gym—wanted to be his best friend. Just a year earlier he wouldn't have believed the things people would do for a piece of the spotlight. His *real* friends kept him sane.

Giving one of them a hard time was just part of the fun.

"Man, you know I'm just messing with you." Jackson righted his chair and flopped back down. He kept a healthy distance from Matt though, just in case.

His brother, Nicholas, and their friend, Trent, stifled their laughter when Matt looked at them.

"You know we love Mara. Mainly because she keeps your crazy ass in line. She's coming to the barbecue, right? Or is she visiting your parents for Memorial Day weekend?" Nicholas asked. That was his brother, always the mediator.

They could have passed for twins with their golden brown skin, dark eyes and curly black hair, but they couldn't be more different in personality. Nicholas craved excitement whereas, more and more, Jackson just wanted solitude. It was hard to believe that his playboy brother was actually twenty-seven, two years older than he was.

Matt took a swig of the beer he held. He rolled it through his palms a few times before answering. "Ask Trent. He sees more of her these days than I do."

All eyes swung to Trent. He shrugged but the look in his eyes was like that of a cornered animal. "She's great. She said to tell everyone hi."

Jackson picked up his lawn chair and then straddled it backward so he'd be facing the group. "Damn, you two aren't just playing with me? If I'd known she wasn't off limits..." He stopped at the murderous expression on Matt's face.

Nicholas leaned over. "If I were you I wouldn't finish that sentence."

Jackson shook his head as he looked back at Matt. "You are pathetic. I was going to say I would have married her. Mara is one of a kind."

Matt snorted. "You? Married?"

A hush fell over the group. Matt cleared his throat a few times before speaking. "Sorry, man. I shouldn't have said that. I wasn't thinking."

"You aren't saying anything that isn't true. I'm glad for once you aren't walking on eggshells around me." Jackson looked pointedly at Matt, then the other guys in the group.

"I gave up my chance to have a solo career when Cynthia got pregnant. I'll never regret that choice. She gave me the two best things in my life. I just wish she was here to see how amazing our boys are."

He stopped, frightened for a moment that his throat would close and he'd confirm their image of him as the tragic, broken widower. He just felt such anger, such impotent rage, that one twist of fate could take away his entire world.

"It's not too late. You could put out an album now," Nick suggested.

"I could. But it would mean a lot of time on the road away from the kids. I've let that dream go and I'm okay with it. Producing may not have been my first love but it's been good to me and I'm grateful. As for the marriage thing… Look, I know you guys think my life is just one party after another but I'm not making anyone any promises. I only date women who know the score and want the same thing I want. No strings and no drama."

"You're only twenty-five, Jack. You can't think you're going to be alone the rest of your life," Nicholas pointed out.

"I loved Cynthia more than life and when she died… well, let's just say I'm not signing up for that kind of pain ever again."

It was so hard to remember his vibrant wife in that hospital bed, broken and bruised. Especially since he'd been as much at fault in the accident as the drunk driver who'd plowed his SUV into her car.

He'd gotten there before they wheeled her into surgery. There'd been just enough time to tell her how sorry he was and how much he loved her. She'd made him promise that no matter what happened, he wouldn't stop living. For their boys' sake, especially, that he not close himself off.

He ran a hand over his face wearily. It was the only time he'd ever consciously lied to her. But in that moment he'd have done anything, promised *anything,* to give her peace. Including the one thing he knew he couldn't do.

Love again.

"So, anyway, my point is that it doesn't make me an asshole because I'm not signing up for the whole 'til death do us part deal again. I just don't believe you can find that kind of connection more than once in a lifetime."

He looked at the ground, not meeting anyone's eyes. He couldn't stand the looks of pity. He was a composer not a lyricist. He didn't have words to describe what it felt like to have the perfect family and then have it ripped in pieces. All he had were emotions that made him feel about as big as an ant and a sense of humor to keep his mind off the things he couldn't change.

He leaned closer to Matt. His friend clapped a hand on his shoulder, his expression grave. He almost hated to play a joke on him when he looked so serious but this conversation was way too kumbaya for his taste. And joking around was easier than putting his emotions on a platter for everyone to rifle through.

"But I would definitely make an exception for your sister because she is fine as hell!"

He barely had time to duck when Matt swung on him this time, but hearing his friends laugh was worth a few blows.

∼

"FINAL STOP—PORT of New Haven!"

Ridley Wells leaned her forehead against the bus window and gazed at the boats bobbing in the water. The small shops lining the pier still had the same bright red awnings. Fat seagulls still swooped down from above, ready to waddle their way up and down the boardwalk begging for food. Everything looked exactly the same as it had the last time she'd been here. Fifteen years ago.

After waiting a few minutes so the other passengers could disembark, she grabbed her backpack and stepped down into the warm, briny air. She took a deep breath and closed her eyes, enjoying the cool breeze coming off the water.

She'd been traveling for two days and was more than ready to take a hot shower and sleep in a real bed. *If Raina doesn't slam the door in your face.* With her sister's temper, it was a distinct possibility.

"Is this your first trip to the peninsula, too?"

A middle-aged woman wearing a bright pink "Nowhere Like New Haven" tee shirt and a faded blue visor stood at her elbow. A group of other women, all wearing the same bright pink shirt, milled nearby chatting excitedly. *Tourists*, Ridley thought. Come to enjoy the beaches and the world-class seafood restaurants.

"No. I used to live here. A long time ago."

She smiled politely at the woman before walking past the others and pulling out her phone. She'd mapped out the distance from the New Haven, Virginia bus station to her sister's house while on the road. At less than a mile it should be a relatively easy walk and a nice one. She hitched her backpack higher on her shoulder and set off to the south, toward the center of town.

The late spring breeze carried the scent of salt water and something slightly tangy, like someone was having a clambake. It brought back memories of the two years she'd spent in New Haven back in middle school. After years of moving around, an old friend of her mom's had told her about a waitressing position in the diner where she worked and offered to rent out her basement.

Ridley and her twin sister, Raina, were used to the schools in Washington, D.C. so moving to some backwater town in the south of Virginia seemed like banishment. Back then the town hadn't even had its own movie theater.

But their mom's friend, Miss Ruth, fixed up the basement so nicely it looked like something in one of the fancy design magazines Raina had always liked to flip through at the corner store. Their beds had been covered in pillows and not just the kind you slept on. Pretty little decorative ones with lace at the edges. Miss Ruth had told them she'd done the lace edging herself. It was the first time Ridley had realized everyone didn't live the way they did.

Her mother didn't do much after work that didn't involve a bottle.

They'd stayed there longer than just about anywhere else. Long enough for Ridley to get completely attached to Miss Ruth, her friends at school and the sleepy, little town itself. Driving away in their secondhand Buick had just about broken her heart.

College had become an obsession after that. If she had enough money, she could afford to make her own decisions. To make a place for herself somewhere, something no one could ever take away. Her sister had been just as driven. Raina had started modeling right after high school and never looked back. After years of working nonstop and traveling all over the world, she'd finally bought a house in the one place they'd lived that had felt like home. She'd sent Ridley a message containing her address, the security code and a simple sentence.

You are always welcome.

Those four words had let her know that no matter what happened, her sister would always be there for her. When she'd found herself scared and in need of a place to stay, this had been the first place she'd thought to come. She'd always known she'd come back to New Haven at some point.

But not like this.

All she'd wanted was to locate her father. After her mother's death she'd become obsessed with finding the only family they had left. The private investigator she'd hired had *finally* gotten a lead. If only she'd pushed him to tell her what it was. Images of charred wreckage flashed through her mind and she shivered. She pulled the diamond pendant she'd been wearing since the accident from beneath her shirt and stroked it.

What had he found out that was bad enough to make someone sabotage his car?

Whoever it was had to have been planning for him to die in the accident. They just probably hadn't counted on her witnessing the whole thing. She pulled back her sleeve to reveal the mottled bruises and scars on her forearms.

"You're just here to hide out until the police figure out what happened."

The officers working the case hadn't told her much, but she could tell something was up by what they hadn't said. When she'd asked directly, they couldn't tell her what she wanted to hear: that the accident was *truly* an accident. She planned to stay under the radar until they figured it out.

The arrow on her phone pointed to the left so she turned onto the next street. An ornate wrought iron sign spelled out:

HAVENSBROOKE

Ridley walked past towering houses with lush manicured lawns. Raina had been trying to convince her to move back to Virginia for ages and had claimed her new neighborhood was the perfect place for Ridley to launch her landscape design business now that she was done with school. As she turned onto her sister's street, she gasped at the first sight of the house.

As girls, they'd always talked about what kind of houses they'd buy when they were rich and famous. It looked like her sister had managed to find a house that fit both their childhood dreams to perfection, a stately three-story red brick with wide Palladian windows along the front.

"You really did it, Ray."

It made her sad that she hadn't been here when her sister moved in. They'd always been there for each other during major milestones like this. Until recently.

Until David.

She knocked on the door and then rang the doorbell. It was completely quiet in the house. Raina had told her there were two security panels, but to use the one on the back so she could get the spare key. As she climbed the stairs to the back deck, she peered through the back window into the kitchen. There was a long, oak farmers table covered with a cheerful, red gingham tablecloth. It looked cozy and inviting.

She walked over to the deck chair farthest from the door and squeezed the edges of its cushion until she felt a hard lump.

"Gotcha."

She unzipped the side of the cushion and rooted around until her fingers closed around the key. The alarm panel was mounted on the side of the door. She dropped her backpack on the deck and then punched in the security code. Three red lights flashed.

Access Denied.

"Okay. Let me try that again." She wiped her hand on the leg of her jeans and carefully typed the numbers in again.

Access Denied.

"Crap. I know I'm typing this right." She tugged her ᵖʰone from her pocket and pulled up the email from her sister. It was possible she'd forgotten something. It had been a few months since she'd gotten the email.

- -
From:Raina Winters (rwinters@modelco.net)
To: Ridley Wells (riri7@gigimail.com)
Subject: Just in case
- - - - - - - - - - - -
Here's my address:
1616 Crescent Drive
New Haven, Virginia 23665.

The security code is our birthday
(4 digits, the month and day).

You are always welcome.
xRaina
- -

The message had been pretty straightforward, so Raina must have forgotten to tell her one of the steps. Her sister hadn't responded to any of her text messages and calls since she'd left two days ago.

Probably still mad at me, she reasoned. Not that she could blame her. Their last argument had been one for the record books.

"I guess I'm on my own."

She let out a breath and pulled out her cell phone again. It was getting close to lunch time. It was already pretty humid and she wasn't even in direct sunlight. Her shirt clung to the damp skin between her breasts. She couldn't wait to take a shower.

As soon as she figured out how to get in the house.

Maybe she was supposed to hit the Enter button or something afterward. She walked back to the security panel and typed the code followed by Enter.

Access Denied.

"Great."

A door slammed next door and she shrank back out of sight as an older man came out on his back deck and walked around the yard. He looked over her way but didn't seem to notice her. After a few minutes, he went back in his house.

"How do I always get myself into these situations?"

This was the kind of neighborhood where everyone looked like they belonged in a golf advertisement. Her rumpled tee shirt and well-worn jeans made her look like a reject from one of those Survivor-style reality programs. With her luck, her sister's neighbors would call the police if she hung out too long, and she'd had enough of dealing with the police to last her a lifetime.

She looked back at the yard. The house directly behind was just as imposing but made of a beige brick. There was a wide patio on the back and a gorgeous little gazebo. Their yards were separated by a small creek.

Water.

The grass was spongy beneath her feet as she crossed the lawn. Half-convinced she was imagining the sight like a delirious desert traveler; she dropped to her knees and cupped her hands in the cool, clear water.

Multicolored fish darted beneath her hands as she scooped up handful after handful and rinsed her face. She'd been traveling with single-minded determination and hadn't made many stops. A proper shower was going to feel like nirvana. Water dribbled down her chin and across the front of her shirt but she didn't even care. Nothing had ever felt so good.

"Hey, what are you doing?"

She whipped around. Two little boys watched her curiously from a few feet away.

"My daddy said we're having a cookout. That means I get hot dogs!" The older of the two boys spoke hurriedly, all his words running together in one large breath. The smaller boy just stood watching, his thumb bobbing up and down in his mouth as he sucked on it.

The oldest boy took a tentative step forward. He reached into his pocket and produced a ragged napkin, which he offered her with a hesitant smile.

She took it and used it to wipe the water from her face. "Thanks. A cookout sounds like fun. What's your name?"

"It's me. Chris." He frowned. "Are you okay?"

"Oh, I'm…" A wave of nausea made her double over.

She took a few deep breaths. After two days of constant travel, she needed to rest and eat something that didn't come wrapped in cellophane. She'd done her best to travel without leaving a trail but she was hardly a super spy. It was time to face reality. Whatever David had discovered had been enough to get him killed. If she didn't want to be next, she had to get it together and fast.

She would try the security code one more time and if it didn't work, she still had enough cash left to pay for a night at a hotel. It wasn't ideal but it would do for now. It would keep her out of sight until she could get in touch with Raina.

"I'm fine…" She stood and the world spun crazily.

Tiny squiggly lines passed through her vision. God, it was hot. *Why was it so hot?* She dimly felt it when she hit the ground but didn't feel any pain. The last thing she saw was two tiny faces peering down at her.

Then everything went gray.

~

JACKSON MOVED HIS chair further away from his friend. "I couldn't resist! If we sit around talking about our feelings too long someone's going to come and take my man card."

"Oh, that's right. I forgot you have an image to uphold. Mr. Big Shot Producer." Matt started clapping. The other guys chimed in and chanted his name.

He shook his head and then took a mock bow. It didn't bother him when they teased him about his sudden fame. They'd been with him since college when he was still using a closet as a makeshift recording studio. They'd earned the right to clown him a little.

"Daddy! Daddy! Miss Raina ate the fish!" His youngest son, Jase, ran up and jumped in his lap. "She's in the water!"

Jackson gazed down at his son affectionately. His sons were the best things that had ever happened to him and he knew his late wife had felt the same way. Cynthia had gotten pregnant their second year in college, derailing her plans to be a lawyer. She hadn't agreed that getting married was the best option, but the idea of only seeing his child on weekends and holidays had left him cold. He'd done everything he could to convince her that he was worth taking a chance on.

Cynthia had finally agreed, after a lot of influence from her mother, and they'd been married in a civil ceremony at city hall as soon as the school year ended. They'd decided to have their second child shortly after the first so she wouldn't have to interrupt her schooling again later with another pregnancy.

They'd had their issues in the beginning, both too young and headstrong to have any idea how to navigate marriage and parenthood. But in the end, no matter what problems they'd had, raising their sons right had been the one thing they'd always agreed on.

Not everyone believed in the old-fashioned methods, but he wanted his boys to grow up with memories like the ones he had; playing outside with his brothers, eating dinner together as a family each night and having respect for his elders. He intended to raise his kids the same way.

Even if he had to do it alone.

"Are you guys playing in Miss Raina's yard while she's out of town?"

Their newest neighbor, Raina, was a fashion model. She'd walked up one afternoon and introduced herself before inviting the boys to come see her fish. Jackson had been so stunned at first that he hadn't even responded. Most women who looked like Raina weren't overly fond of rambunctious, messy, little boys. This was something that Jackson had learned through experience over and over again in recent years.

Raina, however, actually seemed to enjoy their energy. Once he'd recovered enough to give his consent, she'd answered the boys' million and one questions with aplomb as they walked to her yard. Most impressive of all, she didn't even blink when Jase jumped in the pond fully dressed, splashing them all in the process.

It was no surprise to him that both of his boys had become instantly fascinated with her. They had a new story about "Miss Raina" every other day it seemed.

"Yeah, daddy. She ate the fish. Then she fell down." Jase put his thumb in his mouth and bounced excitedly in his lap.

Matt leaned closer. "Did he say she fell down? Wait, here comes Chris."

They watched as his oldest son, Christopher, came tearing across the yard. He skidded to a stop right in front of them.

"She won't wake up!" He took a deep breath, his chest heaving after his mad dash across the yard. "Miss Raina's hurt! She fell down and she won't wake up!"

Jackson got up and the other guys followed. Raina's yard wasn't directly behind his, rather two yards over and separated by a small creek. As soon as he got to the end of his yard though, he could see the small figure slumped on the ground.

"Look!" He pointed toward Raina's yard.

"There she is." Matt vaulted over the creek and Jackson followed. He could hear the other guys behind him, and the kids shouting. By the time he reached Raina's yard, Matt already had his fingers on her pulse.

"Her heartbeat is strong." He looked over his shoulder at Jackson. "She doesn't look like she's having any trouble breathing, either. But we should definitely call for an ambulance. People don't just pass out for no reason." Matt was a sergeant in the Army and trained in first aid so Jackson was more than willing to trust his judgment.

Trent pulled his phone from his pocket. "I'll call 911."

Jackson knelt down next to Matt. "Look at her arms," he whispered.

Matt lifted her arm and pulled back her long sleeve to expose her skin. Bruises wrapped around her wrist, extending halfway up her arm.

"Is Miss Raina okay?" Chris' voice wobbled.

He turned around. Usually the boys were right underneath him but even they could sense the gravity of the situation and were a few feet back, holding Nick's hands. When he caught his brother's eye, he was surprised to see that Nick looked deeply shaken.

"She's okay. Maybe you should take the boys back to the house."

Nick nodded mutely but didn't move. It was odd to see his usually jovial brother so disturbed. Although, if he was honest, he was disturbed as well.

Violence wasn't something they'd ever had to deal with. Seeing the effects on a woman he knew, even if it was only a casual acquaintance, made his stomach turn.

"Raina isn't even supposed to be in town. She told me just a few days ago that she'd be gone for two weeks straight. She had a bunch of modeling jobs booked in Asia. She seemed really excited about—"

Matt held up a hand and he halted mid-speech. "She's waking up."

They all watched as Raina turned on her side and exhaled a long, slow breath. When her eyes opened, they darted around wildly. When she noticed Matt right next to her, she started scrabbling backward.

"Easy, it's okay." Matt backed away.

She got to her knees and blinked rapidly.

"Raina?"

She held up a hand as if the sunlight was too bright. He wondered if she could even see them.

"It's Jackson. Are you okay?"

Her wide, brown eyes locked on his face. She stared at him for a minute, then glanced away before looking back. Then her lips curled up into a small smile.

His stomach dropped. The sensation was like falling while standing still.

Shock forced him to take a step back. He'd never had this reaction to Raina before, despite the fact that she was an extremely beautiful woman. When she was dressed impeccably and made up like she was going to a photo shoot, he'd only felt the general attraction that most red-blooded men feel around gorgeous women.

But in that moment, as her eyes held him captive, she was more beautiful than he'd ever seen her. With her hair wild and a streak of dirt on her cheek, all he could think was...

Wow.

Chapter Two

RIDLEY HAD ALWAYS been the good twin. The one who followed the rules. Her sister was the one who seduced, cajoled and manipulated to get her way. She'd never understood why her sister did the things she did. Lying seemed like more work than just telling the truth.

So, when she realized the man in front of her thought she was Raina, she knew what she needed to do. Correct him. Tell him who she was.

Then she looked at him and forgot all of it.

Good lord he's gorgeous.

He crouched down and met her gaze. "I'm sorry if we scared you. The kids saw you passed out in the grass. We've already called 911, so don't worry."

"No! You can't call 911." Ridley jumped up, then swayed when another wave of dizziness hit her.

He caught her and lowered her back to the grass. "Don't try to stand yet. Just take it easy."

In that one instant, she understood her sister's dishonesties better than ever. Because she was willing to allow this man to think she was Raina if it meant she got more time with him treating her like this.

Like someone he cared about.

"I traveled overnight to get here and I must have been more tired than I thought. Please don't call for an ambulance. I'm fine."

Her voice failed and heat flooded to her face as she noticed all of the other people standing around watching. There was another man with a buzz cut on the ground near her. A blond man stood off to the side on a cell phone. The two boys she'd seen earlier were there, too. They were holding the hands of another man who looked a lot like the guy in front of her.

Jackson, he'd called himself.

Despite how bad she felt, all she could think was that she needed to stay under the radar. Her name in some sort of incident report was hardly incognito. If someone was looking for her, she wasn't going to make it that easy for them to find her.

"I thought you were supposed to be out of town for two weeks?" Jackson asked. "Did something happen?"

Ridley sighed. That explained why no one had answered at her sister's house. The last time they'd talked had been a month ago and it hadn't ended well. Her sister had always been bossy but she'd been unreasonable lately. They'd both said things they shouldn't have and hadn't spoken since. She'd assumed that Raina was just ignoring her calls. But if she was out of the country, then she'd come all this way for nothing.

There was no one here to help her.

"Are you sure you're okay?" The guy with the buzz cut looked at her arms. She pulled her sleeves down further to cover the bruises on her wrists.

"Yeah, I was in a car accident. But I'm fine. I actually should be going." Something in the back of her mind warned her not to give out too much information. Being too trusting was how she'd gotten in her current situation in the first place.

"I'd really be more comfortable if we took you to the hospital." Jackson gestured toward the one with the buzz cut. "Matt's trained as a medic but he's not a doctor."

"It's really not necessary. I'm slightly anemic and it's worse when I haven't been eating well. This isn't the first time I've fainted after skipping meals. I'm more embarrassed than anything."

He nodded once before turning and walking over to the man on the phone.

"Did I interrupt a party?" she asked.

Matt shrugged. "Not exactly. The actual party isn't until Monday. We just like coming over early to help out. Or to give Jackson a hard time. Both are fun."

Ridley smacked her forehead with her hand. "Oh, right. I forgot it was Memorial Day weekend. You're lucky to have such a big group of friends. I've only got..." She glanced back at the house and sighed.

"So, you just got back from a modeling job?"

She heard the disbelief and wasn't even offended by it. She'd never bothered with straightening her hair or wearing makeup anyway. Considering that she'd been traveling for the better part of the last two days and felt like hell, she was sure she looked nothing like a supermodel.

"Not exactly."

"Well, you're welcome to hang out with us. It's just us guys right now but my sister will probably come over later. Mainly because her new boyfriend is here, the blond guy over there, who happens to be one of my best friends." His face twisted as he said it.

Ridley looked at him and couldn't think of anything to say other than "Oh. Well..."

"Yeah. That pretty much sums it up," Matt deadpanned.

She burst out laughing just as Jackson walked up. He looked between the two of them curiously, which just made them break out into another round of laughter.

"Well, I've canceled the ambulance but we should at least get you inside and cleaned up." He held out a hand.

She hesitated a moment but then allowed him to pull her up. He was even better-looking up close, all golden-skinned and masculine. She was suddenly hyper-aware that she was wearing a ragged, old tee shirt and hadn't showered in the past twenty-four hours. After a few gentle tugs he released her hand, which she immediately tucked in her pocket.

"I can't. I'm locked out."

Jackson took her arm gently. "Well, that settles it. You'll come to my house until a locksmith can come out."

Ridley looked between them awkwardly. "You're going to let me stay at your house?"

"Well, yeah." He looked at her strangely. "We're neighbors. In New Haven that means we're practically family. You can take one of the spare rooms upstairs and relax until a locksmith can come out here."

Ridley watched, open-mouthed, as Matt jogged over to the deck and picked up her backpack. She looked back at Jackson who stood patiently waiting. He didn't rush her or seem pissed that she was holding him up, either. He seemed to understand that she needed a moment.

What had seemed like a simple plan had turned into a tangled mess. Not that she'd thought her plan was perfect. Run and hide was about as far as she'd gotten. But now she was stranded, possibly being stalked and her sister was clearly angrier than she'd suspected if she'd changed the security code. Her plan had taken a huge nosedive, and

Jackson had unwittingly just offered her the perfect solution.

There was no better way to hide than in plain sight.

If she went to Jackson's house, she'd be completely off the grid. It was a much better plan than checking into a hotel, at least until she got in contact with Raina. She'd be on her way before long and no one had to be the wiser. She could travel and leave no trail.

Going off with a stranger probably wasn't ideal but he seemed so sincere, and Raina wouldn't be friends with this guy if he was an axe murderer, right? If she was lucky, Raina would call back tonight and then she'd be on her way. Raina was mad at her but she'd still help her until the police figured things out.

She hoped.

In the end she couldn't see any reason not to trust him.

"Okay," she said at last. "Lead the way." She followed the guys to a section where the creek was narrower and they took turns hopping over it. Then they walked down a few houses to a sprawling, white brick colonial.

Holy cow.

She didn't have to worry about him having bad intentions toward her. Gorgeous men with this kind of money in the bank usually had more women than they could handle. Not that it mattered. This wasn't a social call. She was staying just long enough to get some sleep, charge her phone and get in contact with her sister. Then she was gone.

We're practically family.

She ignored the thrill those words made her feel. The only family she had was a father she'd never met, and a sister who was halfway around the world. These were hardly normal circumstances and, even if they were, the last thing she had time for was a handsome man.

Especially since the last one she'd liked had ended up dead.

～⌐

AFTER SHOWING RAINA to a guest room, Jackson retrieved his cell phone from his office. He'd had his security company on speed dial ever since his youngest son had gotten tall enough to reach the door handle. He'd been locked out plenty of times.

Although he doubted anyone would be willing to come out on a holiday weekend without charging an outrageous amount, it was still worth calling. The Raina Winters he knew probably wouldn't even blink at the price. She no doubt spent thousands a month just on the fancy clothes she usually wore.

You're going to let me stay at your house?

Not that she wasn't usually polite, but she'd seemed stunned and incredibly grateful at the offer. He softened, remembering the look on her face. Why was she having this effect on him now? They'd been neighbors for almost six months. His boys adored her and she was always very friendly, but he'd never felt anything more than passing interest. But she'd seemed different. Approachable even. Which was dangerous, in more ways than one.

He hit the last speed dial on his phone and waited as it rang. As expected, it went to voicemail.

"Hey Len, it's Jackson Alexander. One of my neighbors is locked out. You're probably out of town for the long weekend but if not, let me know. She's staying with me in the meantime. Thanks."

He called a few other companies for good measure, then tucked his phone in his pocket. All they could do now was wait. It was a long shot, hoping that anyone would be able to come out on a holiday, but the alternative was spending the long weekend with a supermodel. Raina Winters was the kind of woman he usually stayed far away from.

After the dark year following Cynthia's death, his friends had pushed him head first into the singles scene, determined to draw him out of his depressive state. He'd gone out with singers, actresses, athletes and socialites. Blondes, brunettes and every shade in between. Curvy and slender, feisty and giggly, he'd been on a mission to feast on all the female delights he'd missed out on by marrying young.

Somehow, he'd thought if he could bury himself in female attention, he could forget that the only woman he wanted was gone forever.

Then he'd met Alana. She'd seemed like everything he could want in a woman: sexy, talented and ambitious. A jazz singer, she'd been someone he could talk to about the business and bounce around his ideas about producing a new kind of album. She'd been excited about the project and even volunteered to sing. When she'd started pressuring him for more of his time and commitment, he'd actually felt guilty that he couldn't give her what she needed.

Until the day he found her ass up over his assistant's desk. In the end, Alana wasn't special. She was just another singer looking for her big break and she'd been willing to do whatever or *whoever* it took to get there. They'd broken up but he'd learned a valuable lesson. He'd been in love with a fantastic woman once and the odds of it happening for him again were somewhere between "not gonna happen" and "a snowball's chance in hell."

Since then he'd only dated women who knew the score and had just as much to lose as he did. Starlets who needed someone on their arm for a film premiere, and models who needed an escort that wasn't prettier than they were.

But in that moment, when he'd seen Raina on the ground with those big wounded eyes aimed at him, he'd experienced an almost startling sensation of *longing*. In the past three years no other woman had tempted him to break his no-strings rule. And none had roused the instinct to comfort and protect. Until now. Until Raina.

Which meant she *really* had to go.

He walked down the hall to his sons' room where Nicholas was helping Chris with one of his toy robots.

"Daddy, look at what Uncle Nick did. He fixed my robot. It lights up and everything!" Chris held up a robot toy that had been broken for weeks.

Jackson looked at his brother, shocked. "I've been trying to fix that one for ages. What did you do?"

Nicholas grinned. "I hit it. Hard."

Chris picked up the toy and flew it around the room making beeping noises.

"Figures."

His phone chirped and he pulled it out to see there was a message. "Hopefully, this is the locksmith."

He hit the button to play his messages.

BEEP

"Um, yes, hello. This is Linda Taylor-Whiting. I'm scheduled to interview for the nanny position this afternoon." She paused and cleared her throat a few times. "I was reading the agency's notes on your children and it mentioned that one of your boys particularly likes insects. I'm not sure I would be the best candidate in this circumstance."

Jackson shook his head as she stumbled through an apology before hanging up. He'd been blessed for years because Cynthia's mother had been able to care for the boys during the day. But she'd recently gotten remarried and moved to Massachusetts.

The boys hadn't made it easy to find a replacement for the grandma they'd adored. He was proud of his children but also completely aware that they weren't choirboys. Between Chris's penchant for playing practical jokes and Jase's current fascination with insects, they definitely didn't make his task any easier. He hadn't met a woman yet who could deal with them for more than a few hours at a time.

"Damn. Another nanny bites the dust."

He just needed someone who could watch the boys during the afternoons while he was working, at least through the summer. Once the school year started, Chris would be in kindergarten and Jase would be in preschool. He'd be able to get by on his own, then. Of course in an ideal world he'd find a caregiver he could retain all year, maybe even one who could also run errands, such as grocery shopping, for him.

Nicholas looked up. "You *still* can't find a nanny?"

"Every time I think I have a candidate there's a catch. The first one was excellent at running a household, but stiff with the boys. She didn't even last a whole day. The one after her was more interested in babysitting *me* than the kids. Her skirt barely covered her ass."

He knew that type and avoided it like the plague. Gold diggers and groupies were a part of life in the music business but he'd learned his lesson about needy women. His ex-girlfriend had made sure of that.

He hadn't realized when he started looking for nannies how difficult it would be or that there were women who'd apply for the job hoping to catch his eye. If he had, he would have asked his mother to handle screening the candidates.

Although, considering how much his mother wanted him to remarry, that might not have been the wisest plan either.

"Then there were the two after that who looked more like convicted felons than Mary Poppins. Now we have the one that I was *sure* was perfect, who was scheduled for this afternoon but just canceled." He hung his head in defeat.

Nicholas shook his head in sympathy. "I don't envy you. Unless you need someone to interview the ones with the short skirts? No? Okay, well just keep me in mind."

Jackson clapped his hands until he had both boys' attention. "Aren't we having fun with Uncle Nick? As a matter of fact, who wants to spend the night at Uncle Nicholas' house?" Jackson asked in a singsong voice.

Jase, who'd been watching his brother from his perch on the bed, took his thumb out of his mouth and yelled, "Me, Me, Me!" while Chris danced in the background in excitement.

Nicholas shot him an evil look. "Seriously? I have a date tonight. And she is..." He cut a glance at the two boys watching them avidly. "Constructed like a solid outdoor restroom facility."

Jackson crinkled his brow in confusion and then almost choked with laughter at his brother's child-friendly version of *built like a brick shithouse*. It took him a few minutes to compose himself before he could answer.

"Well, I'm going to be busy tonight and I'd feel better if the boys were with someone I trust. You can just bring them back when you come on Monday for the cookout."

His brother laughed knowingly and slapped him on the back. "I was starting to get worried about you for a minute there, but I should have known you had plans for later. The player is back!"

Jackson grabbed him by the arm and pulled him into the hallway.

"Nick, I'm not talking about a date. Raina's here, remember?"

"So? You don't think she's trying to hook up with you, do you?"

Jackson narrowed his eyes. "Even if she was, so what? I know *you* aren't going to give me a lecture on morality. What are you always telling me?"

Nick pretended to think for a minute. "That I'm the better-looking brother and you'll never surpass me?"

"Something is wrong with you. Can you take the boys or not?"

"Sure, I'll take the kids. Just stay away from Raina. She was hitting on *me* the last time I saw her. She doesn't care where she gets it from as long as the guy is rich."

"Would you keep your voice down? She'll hear you."

Jackson glanced down the hall at the closed guest room door. He'd shown Raina to the room an hour ago and hadn't heard a peep from her since. She was probably sleeping, but still. They weren't far from her room and his brother wasn't exactly being quiet.

"Whatever. Stacey might not even mind if we just hang out at the arcade or something so the boys can play. Think it'll get me brownie points for being such a good uncle?" He wiggled his eyebrows suggestively.

"Well, it can't hurt."

"Come on, guys. Grab your stuff. We're going to the arcade," Nick called.

Jackson went into the boys' closet and pulled out a small backpack for Jase. He put his favorite pajamas in it, a handful of training pants and three sets of clothes, just in case he had an accident. "Jase, remember to use the potty at Uncle Nick's house, okay little man?"

Jase nodded solemnly at him, without removing his thumb from his mouth.

"Yes, please do. Because Uncle Nick hates changing diapers." Nick sent Jackson a foul look before turning to help Chris put his stuff into a duffel bag.

Jackson hugged Jase and then Chris, running his hands over their tight curls affectionately. All of his brothers and his parents took the boys overnight regularly so he knew they'd have a good time. It gave the boys a fun night out and it gave him a much needed break. It was a luxury that many single parents didn't have. He was so lucky to have his family nearby to help him and he appreciated them more than they knew.

"Okay little guys, let's roll."

Chris raced down the hallway while Jase followed quietly, clutching his Elmo backpack tightly to his chest.

Nicholas gave him a mock salute. "I'll leave you to do your good deed. Just remember what I said about Raina. Don't let her get her hooks into you. That girl is a vulture."

~

"HI."

Ridley watched as Jackson spun around. Her fingers tightened around the bag of laundry she'd taken from her backpack. She'd been about to come ask him if he minded her using his washing machine when she'd overheard his conversation with his brother.

That girl is a vulture.

Asshole.

In a way it was almost a relief to know that her initial assessment had been correct. In her experience, people weren't nice for no reason. Plenty of guys thought nailing a supermodel was something to brag about. But why would his brother be warning him away from her? Unless Jackson and her sister had some sort of history. Maybe they'd dated previously and his brother didn't approve? Well, if Jackson thought he was getting in her pants this weekend he was in for a rude surprise.

Or a swift kick in the balls.

"You said to make myself at home so I thought I could throw a few things in the laundry, if you don't mind." It took everything inside her not to throw the bag at his head.

"Of course. Feel free to use whatever you need. It's not as ritzy as what you're used to, I'm sure. I've been here a year but I haven't really gotten everything organized yet."

"I don't need ritzy. Contrary to what most people think, models don't just show up for a few hours, get paid and then go party. You're holding weird positions for long periods of time and call times are at the butt-crack of dawn to get the best light."

Ridley stopped and took a deep breath. Correcting people's stereotypes about modeling wasn't something she normally bothered with but after hearing his brother call her a vulture, she was already on edge.

You don't have to like this guy. You're just using him for his air conditioning.

Jackson held up his hands in surrender. "Sorry, I didn't mean to imply you don't work hard. I've seen a few of your billboards lately. You're becoming a household name."

Ridley nodded, her hostility meter going down a few notches. "Thanks. It's what I've been working toward for years."

Even though they hadn't been as close lately, nothing could stop her pride at her sister's success. She'd been there in the early years when Raina had done ads for toothpaste and painkillers. She'd been disappointed along with her when she'd been turned down for casting call after casting call because she wasn't the "All-American" girl they were looking for. Code for "not blonde enough."

Women of color had always had a hard time in the modeling industry and Raina had been no exception. However, instead of accepting it, she'd done something unprecedented. While living in Washington, D.C. she'd started a style blog called "Legs" and modeled clothing for small fashion designers for free. Every week she'd featured an outfit by a different designer and then shown photos of herself wearing it on the streets and to trendy restaurants. Before long her blog had a cult following, and everyone wanted to know what she was wearing.

The modeling industry hadn't wanted her initially so she'd gone out and created her own industry. People looked at Raina as just another model but the truth was that she was an entrepreneur. An incredibly savvy one at that.

He leaned against the wall and crossed his arms. "So, you canceled your latest shoot?"

"Yeah, I was in a car accident. I needed a break, anyway." It was as good an explanation as any. Her shoulders slumped. She could hardly tell people she was in town hiding out. "People staring and taking pictures can get old, you know?"

"Really?"

When she raised her eyebrows he backed up a step. "Sorry, I just can't imagine having that kind of opportunity and turning it down. I wish someone would just offer me money for being pretty. I wouldn't have bothered with college!"

"So, I guess I shouldn't have gone to college either, huh? I guess all that time learning was wasted." She glared at him.

"No, of course not. I just meant—" He stopped and ran a hand through his hair. "Wow, can we start over? I've done nothing but put my foot in it today. Let's pretend we're just meeting. Hi, it's nice to meet you. I'm Jackson; my friends call me Jack or J. Or jackass, depending on who you ask." He smiled slowly, the type of grin that probably had women throwing their panties at him usually.

Ridley just sighed. "Nice to meet you, Jackson."

He gestured toward her. "And you are?"

"Seriously?"

"Come on, play along."

Ridley crossed her arms. "Okay. Hi, I'm Raina. You can call me Raina."

His lips twitched at the corners. "Okay, then. You know what? The locksmith is probably not going to call back for a while so we might as well just hang out. We've been neighbors for months now but we've never had a chance to just sit and talk like this. I don't have much to snack on but I'm sure we can find something suitably unhealthy to eat while you tell me your story. The *real* one, not the tabloid version."

Ridley raised her chin. "Who says I have a story?"

"Everyone has a story. I'll tell you mine if you tell me yours," he teased.

"I don't think I need to know yours."

"Okay, suit yourself. I'm going to go get some work done, then. But if you change your mind, I'm ordering takeout around six." He turned and walked away.

Just before he turned the corner she called out. "Fine. I'll eat your takeout. After all, that's what vultures do, right?"

As he turned and stared at her wide-eyed, she grinned and walked back to the guestroom.

The laundry could wait.

Chapter Three

AN HOUR LATER, Jackson had made a sizable dent in his to-do list for the party the next day. The Alexander family had always held a party on Memorial Day weekend but it used to be held at his parent's farm. It wasn't until after his wife died that his mother made the request to have it at Jackson's place.

It was her way of keeping him from withdrawing from the world, something he'd been all too happy to do after Cynthia died. However, it took an iron will to resist his mother when she wanted something so he'd been hosting for the past three years. This would be the first year in his new house.

It was also the first year he was actually looking forward to it.

An image of Raina sitting in her backyard, looking so lost and alone entered his mind. If he ever got locked out he'd have plenty of people to call. His parents, his brothers and a whole slew of cousins. He couldn't imagine not having anyone to help him out. Having a big family wasn't something he'd ever given much thought to but after today... well, he was suddenly really aware of how much easier his life was because of his family.

He groaned thinking of all the ways he'd put his foot in his mouth around her. Not only had she heard Nick call her a vulture but then he'd implied that beautiful women didn't need to be smart.

It was no wonder she'd walked off.

He was so distracted that the shrill ring of his cell phone on the desk next to him set his teeth on edge. He grabbed the phone, cursing as the pile of invoices it was sitting on scattered across the floor.

"Jackson Alexander".

"You are gonna love me for this one. I'm a genius. Tell me I'm a genius!"

"You're a genius, Mac. Now why the hell are you calling me? Aren't you supposed to be finding a group for the song we're working on?"

He stooped to pick up the papers off the floor, sure that his assistant was off task as usual. Some people thought he was crazy for keeping him around after the debacle with Alana. But Jackson believed in loyalty. They'd been friends for years and Mac claimed nothing had happened between him and Alana. Jackson believed him.

The fact that he'd witnessed his friend pushing her away before they knew he was there helped considerably.

"That's why I'm calling. I found a group that's perfect. They're all gorgeous, well most of them and even better, they're local." Leave it to Mac to be more interested in the length of their legs than the quality of their voices.

"Can they at least sing? The last time I heard a group you found, only one member could even carry a tune."

Jackson winced at the memory of the pitiful group trying to sing *a capella*. They had all looked like cover models, which was reason enough for Mac to be interested. Jackson couldn't hold it against him, though. Except for his obsession with beautiful women, Michael MacCrane was the hardest working assistant Jackson had ever had and a good friend.

He'd just learned not to trust his instincts when it came to young female singers.

"I'm telling you Jack, these girls have voices like angels. But hey, you don't have to take my word for it. Girls, sing a few bars for the boss." There was a ruffling sound as if Mac had put the phone down before he heard someone clear a throat.

It was just a simple rendition of the jazz tune "Cry Me a River" but when they were done, Jackson pumped his fist in the air.

This was the break he had been waiting for.

~

RIDLEY ROLLED OVER and yawned. Napping had seemed like a good idea at the time, but she was too anxious to sleep for more than a few minutes here and there, so now she was tired *and* groggy. She reached over to the nightstand where she'd left her cell phone charging.

Still no messages.

"Come on, Raina. I really need you to call back." She blew her hair out of her face and sighed. It was time to consider the possibility that Raina wasn't going to call her back. They'd never been mad at each other this long before.

Their relationship had been strained ever since she'd decided to look for their father. Their mother had been only too glad to tell them as girls what a good-for-nothing their father was, and how getting herself saddled with two kids was the worst mistake of her life. She'd loved their mother but she hadn't been the easiest person to love, even when you were trying. She could understand why Raina didn't want to meet their other parent when the one they'd grown up with had made them so miserable.

But Ridley couldn't help hoping that maybe their father was different. Maybe he *did* want them. Maybe she'd finally find the family she'd been wishing for her whole life. Not that all her wishing had done her any good.

If she had to be locked, out this was a pretty nice place to be, but she still wanted to get to her sister's house. Imposing on family was one thing, imposing on a perfect stranger was an entirely different matter altogether. Especially when the guy in question was sort of a jerk.

Now that he knew she'd overheard him and that his chances of getting her in bed were nonexistent, he was probably more than ready for her to leave. Having her here was sure to cramp his style when one of his girlfriends came over. Although if his brother was to be believed, he must not have many girlfriends, otherwise he wouldn't need to hit on the first girl to land in his backyard.

"There has to be something I can do." The waiting was going to drive her insane. She hated feeling helpless. She sat up and picked up her phone. A few taps later, the contact information for Agent Ian Graham was displayed on her screen. Her thumb hesitated over the number for a moment before she tapped it to initiate the call. It rang three times before she heard his gravelly voice.

"Agent Graham? It's Ridley Wells."

"Good to hear from you, Miss Wells. I've been trying to get in touch with you. Are you out of town?"

"Just for the weekend. Why?"

"I'm finishing up the accident report." He cleared his throat. "We've been trying to get a clearer picture of what your friend was doing in the days leading up to his death. You said he was a private investigator, right?"

"Yes. I hired him to do a search for my father."

"How much did he charge?"

Ridley frowned. "He charged by the hour. Usually about a hundred unless it required surveillance. So far, he hadn't needed to do that. He was mainly looking through paperwork, I think. I know he pulled my mom's credit history. He was trying to figure out exactly where my mother was living and who she had contact with around the time of my conception."

"Did he seem to be having money problems?"

"I didn't think so, but I'm not really sure. Why are you asking all these questions? What does this have to do with his car accident?"

"We're not sure. We noticed some unusual activity in the past month and thought you might be able to help us put the pieces together."

"I wouldn't know anything about his financial situation."

"You didn't wire him fifty thousand last week?"

"Fifty thousand? Uh, no. I don't have that kind of money," Ridley stated.

"Miss Wells, I don't want to alarm you but I'm sure you've figured out by now that the FBI isn't usually involved in cases like these."

"Please tell me what's going on."

"Mr. Finemore was spotted with a person of interest in one of my cases. Alberto Moreno. The FBI has been monitoring Mr. Moreno for years. He's suspected of arms dealing, racketeering, drug trafficking, you name it."

"Moreno? As in the Moreno crime family?" Ridley squeaked.

"Yes. I'm something of an expert on the Morenos, which is why I was asked to assist with Mr. Finemore's case. Mr.

Finemore was spotted by one of our surveillance teams meeting Moreno the day before his death. Do you have any idea why?"

"Maybe he was doing investigative work for them?"

Agent Graham grunted. "If he was doing work for the Morenos it definitely wasn't legal. Miss Wells, I know Mr. Finemore was a friend of yours but whatever he got himself into got him killed. You were the last person to see him alive. Somehow, you were also the first person at the scene of the accident."

He stopped speaking abruptly. Ridley had the distinct feeling that he hadn't meant to say that last part.

"What exactly are you implying, Agent Graham? You don't think I had anything to do with this, do you?"

"I didn't mean that. Miss Wells, we just want to figure out what's going on before anyone else gets hurt. When will you be back in town?"

"I don't know. I'll call you back." Ridley hung up and immediately turned her phone off.

She dragged in a ragged breath, her heart beating so hard she couldn't hear anything else over the sound. It was tempting to pretend she'd never called Agent Graham. To go on ignoring the signs that had been there since the beginning.

Hadn't she thought it odd that an FBI Agent would be involved in something as simple as a car accident? Now she could no longer ignore the obvious—she was in way over her head. Maybe she should have told Agent Graham that David had come to see her right before the accident. Not that she could see how that would make any difference.

Especially since he already suspected her of killing her friend.

If David had found evidence that Moreno was her father, he would have tried to verify it. But it was doubtful that he would have told Moreno directly of his suspicions. So if she could stay off the grid for a while, there was a good chance that Moreno's people would never know what he really suspected. If she was lucky, they would never know that he might have a daughter. *Daughters*, she corrected. After all, this wasn't just about her.

It had been big news in Florida when the Moreno's only son had died. No wonder David had told her to lay low. If he'd suspected her father was a Moreno, then he wasn't just being paranoid when he'd told her he was on to something dangerous. He'd been trying to protect her.

Now he was dead, and if whoever killed him had followed her here, she'd led them right to her sister. If Moreno found her, then it wouldn't be long before he found Raina, too.

She and her sister might be his only surviving children.

I have to get out of here.

After pulling her cell charger from the wall, she stuffed it in her backpack and made sure it was zipped securely. The thought of someone following her here, possibly hurting her sister or Jackson, made her sick to her stomach. It was a stupid idea to come here. All she'd done was bring trouble to her sister's doorstep. She was the one who'd wanted to find their father. This was her mess.

No one else deserved to be dragged into the maelstrom of her life.

The day hadn't been a total waste because at least she'd been able to rest for a bit and charge her phone. It seemed petty to leave without saying goodbye to Jackson but it was probably easier this way. No explanations. No goodbyes.

Business as usual.

**One More Day is available now

TEASING TRENT - the PREQUEL

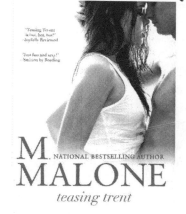

~ *The Alexanders, prequel* ~

One girl. One guy. One *unforgettable* night.

Trent's supposed to keep his best friend's sister company on her birthday. He just has to remember the promise he made to himself in college to keep his hands off her. He's not worried until he finds out she wants to stay in. Just the two of them.

Ever since Mara walked into her brother's dorm room freshman year and came face to face with a shirtless Trent, she's known he was *The One*. She finally has a plan to get him exactly where she wants him. *In her bed.*

If Mara has her way, she'll get a lot more for her birthday than a Hallmark card...

WARNING
This book contains yoga as an erotic torture device and the unexpected appearance of a vibrator. I'm just saying...

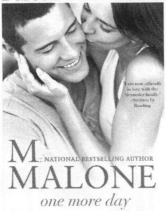

M. NATIONAL BESTSELLING AUTHOR

MALONE
one more day

- The Alexanders, Book 1 -

Ridley Wells has no idea what to do with her life now that she's graduated from college. But when a friend is murdered and her apartment is trashed, she runs to the only person she trusts, her twin sister. No one will think to look for her in the rinky dink Virginia town of New Haven.

Of course, her luck lands her passed out in the grass in front of resident badboy, music producer Jackson Alexander. *Strike 1!* Then she realizes Raina's out of the country and she has nowhere else to go. *Strike 2!*

So when the handsome producer with the platinum smile mistakes her for her sister, she gets an idea.

Where better to hide than in plain sight?

WARNING

This book contains cloak and dagger intrigue, family drama, brothers fighting, supermodels with attitude and hot sex between people who can't keep their hands off each other. Just saying...

HE'S THE MAN - BOOK 3

M. NATIONAL BESTSELLING AUTHOR

MALONE

he's the man

~ *The Alexanders, Book 3* ~

Matt Simmons is over Army doctors poking him. But when his sister won't stop nagging him to see their old babysitter, now a sought after physical therapist, he gives in just to get some peace.

Penny is finally putting down roots after a lifetime of moving around. She's got everything she wants, except the settled suburban life she longs for. All she needs is the perfect guy, which means NO military men.

When Matt realizes that his old babysitter is h-o-t, he's suddenly seeing the benefits of therapy. But Penny still sees him as the bratty kid she used to babysit.

Suddenly he has a new mission in life...

WARNING
The book contains sweaty muscles, a heroine who's not afraid to get in your face, an elderly lothario and the kind of sex therapy that med school doesn't teach.

Look for Book 3 in late summer!
Sign up to be notified at
www.MMaloneBooks.com

ALL I NEED IS YOU - BOOK 4

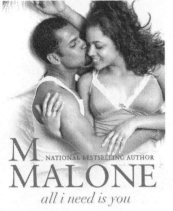

Elliott Alexander & Kaylee Wilhelm
Coming in 2014

ABOUT THE AUTHOR

National Bestselling author M. Malone lives in the Washington, D.C. metro area with her three favorite guys: her husband and their two sons. She likes dramatic opera music, staid old men wearing suspenders, claw-foot bathtubs and unexpected surprises.

The thing she likes best is getting to make up stuff for a living.

www.MMaloneBooks.com

26435347R00176

Made in the USA
Lexington, KY
01 October 2013